MW01230830

Also by Steve Brown

Black Fire
Fallen Stars
Radio Secrets
Of Love and War
America Strikes Back

The Susan Chase™ Series
Color Her Dead
Stripped To Kill
Dead Kids Tell No Tales
When Dead Is Not Enough

Read the first chapter of any of
Steve Brown's novels at
www.chicksprings.com.

At this web site you can also
download a free novella.

Woman
AGAINST
Herself

Woman
AGAINST
Herself

Steve Brown

Chick Springs Publishing
Taylors, SC

First published in the USA in 2001 by
Chick Springs Publishing
PO Box 1130, Taylors, SC 29687
e-mail: ChickSprgs@aol.com
web site: www.chicksprings.com

Library of Congress Control Number:
2001130845
Library of Congress Data Available

ISBN: 0-9670273-5-7

10   9   8   7   6   5   4   3   2   1

For Elmore Leonard

Acknowledgements

For their assistance with this book,
I would like to thank Missy Johnson, Ellen Smith,
Susannah Farley, Kate Lehman, Phil Bunch, Mark Brown,
Dwight Watt, Bill Jenkins, and, of course, Mary Ella.
Additional expertise was furnished by Capt. Jackie Kellett
of the Greenville County Forensics Unit.

Author's Note

This is a work of fiction.
Names, characters, places, and incidents are
products of the author's imagination or are used
fictitiously. Any resemblance to actual events, locales,
organizations, or persons, living or dead,
is entirely coincidental and beyond the intent
of either the author or the publisher.

All men kill the thing they hate,
unless, of course, it kills them first.

–James Thurber

Once upon a time, drug smuggling was
a much simpler business.
This story takes place during that time.

One

"**M**iss Johnson!" called the little girl, hurrying around the corner of the sixth grade wing. "Please hurry!"

Katherine Johnson was already hurrying back to her classroom. A week from now spring break would begin and it wasn't smart to leave the children alone too long. This time of year you could lose them and never get their heads back into their books. And with all the paperwork the school board assigned, you couldn't afford to fall too far behind.

"What is it, Dorothy?" Katherine let the brown-haired girl with the ponytail pull her around the corner and down the hallway in the direction of their classroom. The eleven-year-old was genuinely frightened.

"It's Timmie! He's gone crazy."

Across the hall Mr. Inman stuck his head out the door of his classroom. There was a frown on his face. Inman had never approved of Katherine's methods of class control and he was probably thinking her relaxed attitude toward discipline was the cause of all the crying and whining coming from her classroom.

Crying and whining? Coming from her classroom? What was going on? Timmie Beck crazy! The very idea was absurd. Timmie was one of her better students, even though he came from a broken home.

Roger Olsen peered around the corner of her doorway. The boy appeared afraid. No. Make that scared, which made little sense. Roger was the class monitor, a position that normally caused a child to strut, not stand trembling in a doorway.

Katherine Johnson could see this was no trick. Smirks and snickers, not fear, invariably gave tricks away, and both children were truly alarmed. This wasn't like the grease fire in the cafeteria, when the children had appeared to enjoy the excitement of filing out of the school and watching the firefighters put out flames.

This was something entirely different.

"Roger was scared to come find you," said Dorothy. She still clutched Katherine's hand.

Roger Olsen said nothing, only grabbed Katherine's other hand as she came through the door. Katherine never felt it. She was staring at the boy lying in the middle of the floor, arms and legs jerking spasmodically, kicking and shoving desks away, scattering books, pencils, and notebooks in all directions. Face white, Timmie Beck drooled from both corners of his mouth.

Oh, my God! Timmie's having a seizure!

Katherine scanned the room. Her students cowered against the walls, most huddling in corners, some crying, a few whining, many holding hands and not minding if the hand belonged to the opposite sex. All stole glances at the boy flopping around in the middle of their room.

Katherine pulled her hands away—she had to peel Roger Olsen off her—then stooped down in front of Dorothy to make sure the girl could see her. The sight of her schoolmate thrashing around on the floor transfixed the girl. "Get the nurse, Dorothy."

Instead, the child peered over Katherine's shoulder as Roger Olsen lay his head on her other shoulder and started crying.

Katherine grabbed the girl's hands. "Dorothy!"

She blinked and looked at her teacher.

"Get the school nurse!"

When Dorothy didn't reply but only stared at her, Katherine shook the girl's hands again. As she did, Roger Olsen wrapped an arm around Katherine and sobbed into the nape of her neck.

"Understand, Dorothy? Get the nurse for Timmie. He's sick."

The girl nodded but didn't speak. With another glance at the boy on the floor, and a small shove by her teacher, she stumbled out the door.

Only when Katherine heard Dorothy's footsteps running down the hall did she face Timmie. That was when she saw the blood bubbling from Timmie's mouth, dribbling down his chin.

He's biting his tongue! He'll chew it up if I don't stop him. And I need to protect his head, the way he's flopping around.

Woman Against Herself

Katherine peeled Roger Olsen off her once again, then moved in a circle around Timmie Beck, pushing and shoving desks out of the way. As she did, she picked up a notebook and smashed it across the back of a chair. After a couple of licks the notebook fell apart. Katherine ripped the binder in half, took the half without the rings, and knelt beside the boy.

She ignored Timmie's arm slapping against her thigh and forced the binder between his teeth. Pencils and pens lay around her, but if she placed one of those in the boy's mouth, it might snap in half and fall down his throat, choking him.

Immediately, Timmie's teeth bit into the vinyl-covered binder. Katherine held the binder in place and pulled a book bag over with her foot. She maneuvered the bag under the boy's head and held it there—almost impossible the way he was flopping around—and held on tight. This couldn't be happening! Timmie Beck was never sick. He never missed a day of school.

Katherine looked around. Her students cringed against the wall, huddling in corners. "Bring something to cover him. He could go into shock . . . someone . . . who wore a coat . . . today."

No one moved. It was as if she'd spoken in a foreign language. Katherine began calling children by name, trying to remember who had worn jackets.

The children only stared at the floor or turned away. If they hadn't been crying, they started now. Even Roger Olsen stood in a group in a corner of the room. Roger's parents had warned him to stay away from danger, and right now, Timmie Beck, friend and fellow student, looked terribly dangerous.

Katherine fought back panic. Where was the school nurse? What was taking so long? With Timmie jerking around, it was a struggle just to keep the pack under his head, the notebook between his teeth, and a shoulder across his chest holding him in place. Katherine had an overwhelming urge to straddle the boy, but how would that look to her students?

God, but he was strong! Timmie played all those sports, and he wasn't a small child. All she could do was wait for the nurse. And the teacher across the hall? Did Leslie Inman actually think all this crying and whining was nothing more than a classroom out of control? Why didn't he step across the hall and investigate? She would under similar circumstances.

Why didn't anyone pass her door! But this was an elementary school and the children were usually found inside their classrooms. What was she going to do?

Beneath her, the notebook binder slipped from Timmie's teeth and he sprayed his teacher with blood. That's when Katherine screamed.

*   *   *

Across town, John Peake opened the door to IINTELL's computer center, nodded to the secretary behind the desk, and inclined his head toward the office behind her.

"May I go in?"

"Sure, Mr. Peake. Sallie's just on the phone."

John Peake masked his concern over a secretary

calling her boss by her first name. He crossed the room and opened the door to Sallie Beck's office. Sallie saw her boss, flashed a big smile, and waved him inside, pointing at a chair in front of her desk. Peake took a seat and waited for the woman to finish on the phone. John Peake was a silver-haired gentleman who never shed the jacket of his suit during business hours.

Behind Sallie stood a credenza covered by bound printouts, and on the floor at each end, plants in baskets reached for the ceiling. At Peake's feet, in a golden pot, was some plant he wouldn't attempt to identify. He did, however, recognize the African violets on the corner of Beck's desk. His wife had similar plants near the sink at home that she fussed and clucked over.

The wall behind Sallie was made of glass and you could see the twenty-two girls in there, hunched over their computers and ringing up one hundred to one hundred six percent of quota just like clockwork. The computer center hadn't always functioned in such a manner.

After being under fire for more than a year, Sallie's predecessor had quit, and without giving notice. Worse, he quit during the Christmas rush—a busy time for anyone in the credit business—and at a time when the home office couldn't supply another man. Peake had to put Sallie in charge, but only temporarily, and he made that perfectly clear from the start.

Then the impossible happened. The numbers jumped, and during Christmas rush, too, when no supervisor had been able to keep up with the demand. Ninety days later, the computer center stood at a hundred percent of quota. It was the first time that had happened since the plant had been relocated to this rural area of the Midwest.

Peake shook his head. It never ceased to amaze him what women could accomplish when given the opportunity. With the exception of Robert Whittle, the computer center was all female and seemed perfectly happy with their boss. Well, maybe not the girl on the other end of the phone.

"I'm sorry, Charlene," Sallie was saying, "but you've been out for four days, and there's nothing wrong with you but your love life. You can be off until Monday, but if you miss another day you go on probation."

Peake stifled a laugh into a cough. Charlene was pleading for leniency? He'd fire her and find someone who wanted the job. Someone who would attend the local tech school, a primary reason for the intelligence-gathering business to locate their credit check operation here.

But Peake wouldn't say anything, couldn't say anything. Sallie had argued long and hard for the right to run the computer center her own way. Finally, he had given in, saying he'd stay out of her hair as long as she met her quota. Sallie hadn't missed one yet.

"Sorry, Charlene, but that's my last word on the subject. I've got to go. Someone's in my office. See you Monday." Sallie hung up and smiled across the desk again. "Good morning, Mr. Peake. What brings you to our corner of the building?"

Sallie was an attractive woman with graying black hair cut short in a no-nonsense fashion. Today she wore a navy blue jacket over a white blouse but with a scarf that was a bit too loud. Still, despite the occasional bit of flashy clothing, Sallie conducted herself in a businesslike manner. John Peake had never heard the males on his staff make the comments they usually made about other female employees. Instead, the men called her "Balls Beck" because Sallie never backed down in staff meetings. In that way Sallie reminded John Peake of his youngest child, a daughter he'd been glad to see go off to college.

"This isn't what I came for, but I ran into Robert Whittle. He asked about his transfer again."

"And what did you tell him, sir?"

"That he would have to work his way out of your department, not merely transfer."

"Thank you, sir. I appreciate your support."

"I support my department heads or I remove them."

Sallie smiled broadly. "Yes, sir. I'm well aware of your policy."

Peake glanced through the glass wall and saw several girls staring at him. When they saw Peake looking at them, they returned to their computers.

"Sallie, why is your department all female? Out of twenty-two employees, you have only one man: Whittle."

"Was Robert complaining about that, too?"

"When he originally asked for the transfer, yes, reverse discrimination did come up."

"I disagree, Mr. Peake. What do you think?"

Boy, did this woman deserve her nickname. She had an uncanny way of putting the ball back in your court. "I've never seen any discrimination. But I can see how working in an all-female environment might make a man nervous. Personally, I would've gotten rid of him long ago. I'm not much for whiners."

Peake glanced into the computer room again. None of the women were looking at him now. "But it does surprise me how you get this kind of production from ladies. Females are notorious for their days off with . . . all their responsibilities." Peake gestured at the telephone. "Charlene's been out four days, but for some reason those ladies in there take up her slack."

"All those women know what Charlene's going through. They've been through it before."

"Charlene's getting a divorce?"

"She's already divorced, but her ex is insisting they get back together. He's making it pretty rough on her."

Peake stared through the glass. "All those women are divorced? I never thought about it before . . . ." He looked at the woman behind the desk.

Sallie smiled sheepishly. "I think word got around that—"

"That there was a supervisor at IINTELL, a fellow divorcee, and women could practically name their hours as long as the department maintained its quota."

Sallie said nothing.

"Other department heads have one or two women working for them who've asked to transfer into your department. Probably divorcees."

"But I won't take them. I wouldn't like someone proselytizing my people." Sallie leaned back in her chair. "It's not something I'd want to get around, but my best workers are the sole supports of their families." Sallie shrugged. "You know the feeling, after putting four children through college."

Peake cleared his throat. "Which is why I'm here. You run the largest department in our company for someone who's not a vice-president. I suppose you've heard the talk: If you want something done, drop it on Beck's girls."

Sallie couldn't help but grin.

"The people at the home office are concerned you might think IINTELL discriminates against you because you're a woman." Peake shifted around in his chair. "They're offering you a vice-presidency, with all the perks accompanying it."

Sallie opened her mouth but closed it when Peake continued. "I want you to know I gave the home office hell. Being a woman's no reason to make you vice-president. People should earn their promotions. But you've earned yours."

"Thank you, sir."

"I would've done the same for any man. I almost turned down the offer, but I wanted to check with you. I told the home office you'd probably prefer to have an increase in your departmental budget to hire an assistant so you would be able to spend more time with your son."

"But I *am* interested, Mr. Peake, and let the home office know I accept their offer."

"You . . . do?"

"Absolutely. Will you tell them for me? Sir?"

"Well, yes, I will. Then, in a few weeks, if you haven't done anything to embarrass the company—"

The phone rang.

"Mr. Peake, I'd like to thank you more profusely, but

let me take this call." Sallie picked up the phone. "Don't you know Mr. Peake's in here?" It took only a few seconds for the color to drain from Sallie's face. "Timmie's where? *He's what?*"

Two

L ieutenant Jeff Ellis stared at the woman across the desk from him. Only thirty-six years old and already gone to seed. Sallie Beck was overweight, her short black hair was graying, and her face had little color from too many hours behind a computer at IINTELL.

Truth be known, IINTELL probably had more information about the people in this town than the cops. Was there a file on Jeff Ellis? Had to be. Everybody bought stuff on credit. It was weird to talk to someone who might know as much as you did. Sort of took away your edge.

Beck wore one of those ladies' business suits with a cut and a color that always looked better on a man than any woman. Her eyes were dark green. A hard green. One look at Beck and you knew this woman was all business.

His partner, a rumpled-looking man, sat next to

Ellis's desk. "Cocaine killed your son, Mrs. Beck. He overdosed."

"My son never took drugs, Sergeant Clancy."

"Then how do you explain over twenty milligrams of cocaine in his body?"

"I can't. I just know my son never took drugs."

Clancy slid back in his chair, forefinger and thumb rubbing together, a sure sign that he needed a cigarette. Both men had seen more than one Sallie Beck: Parents who wouldn't, couldn't admit their little darlings bought drugs on the way to school and got high in the rest room between classes. Not their child. Not *their* little darling.

"We hear what you're saying," said the lieutenant, "but, Mrs. Beck, we'd still like you to consider *how* something like this could've happened."

"Since it did happen," added Clancy, his thumb and finger rubbing together.

"I don't know. Maybe you could tell me?"

"Probably made the buy at the junior high. He'd have to pass it every day on the way to the elementary school."

"No, no, Timmie would never buy drugs from some pusher."

"No needle marks on his extremities and his nasal membrane wasn't inflamed," said Clancy. "Your son had to have ingested the coke, Mrs. Beck."

"I dropped Timmie off at school each morning. A car pool picked him up every afternoon."

"What are you saying, Mrs. Beck? Not only did someone *not* sell the coke to your son, but somebody also *made* him take it?"

Though sitting down, the woman stamped her foot. "You aren't listening, Sergeant. I told you Timmie never took drugs. It's up to you, and Lieutenant Ellis, to find out who . . . who killed him."

"Mrs. Beck—"

"Now listen to me. Timmie was an honor role student who played baseball and basketball. He was on the Little League tournament team. Timmie's dream was to pitch in the majors. That's why he didn't play football or soccer. He didn't want to hurt his knees. Why would a child who understood that take drugs?"

"Lots of major leaguers use drugs."

"They started taking drugs at eleven and still made it to the big leagues?" Beck looked from one man to the other. "Why are you interrogating me as if I had something to do with this when you should be out looking for my son's killer?"

Sergeant Clancy let out a sigh and leaned back in his chair, thumb and forefinger hard at work.

Jeff Ellis could see this woman was beyond his partner. Most women were. "If I'm hearing you correctly, Mrs. Beck, you're not denying your son took cocaine?"

"I can't deny the autopsy report."

"You've seen the autopsy report?" Clancy's fingers stopped moving.

"It was my son who was killed." She quickly added, "But what I don't understand is where the drugs came from. The only drugs Timmie ever took were for his allergies."

"You want me to check with your pharmacy to make sure they didn't accidentally fill your boy's prescription with cocaine?"

"No, you fool, I was just trying to explain—"

Clancy slid forward to the edge of his chair. "Mrs. Beck, I'm not going to sit here and be called a fool by some woman who didn't stay home and raise her kid but went charging off to have a career, leaving her son to be raised by the neighborhood pusher."

"Sergeant, you can't lay any more guilt on me than I already have. It's my son who's dead. Forget that I love my work and I'm damn good at it. Even if that were not the case, I'd still have to go to work every day."

"Who're you trying to kid, Mrs. Beck? You were once married to Alstair Beck. The Becks own half of this county."

"I don't take child support from Timmie's father."

"Mrs. Beck," Ellis said, "I don't think—"

"No! Your *partner* wasn't thinking! I want him to know not all working mothers leave home by choice, but for other reasons."

"And what did you leave home for?" asked Clancy with a smile.

"Sergeant, I think this interview would proceed much quicker, and you'd have me out of your hair much faster, if you kept your mouth shut."

"I'm all for that!" Clancy slid back in his chair and shoved his hands into his pockets.

To Ellis, Sallie said, "In regard to Timmie's medication, I was to have the prescription refilled next week, so if a mistake had been made, I would've known about it weeks ago."

"I thought hay fever medication could be bought over the counter," said Ellis.

"This was something special. Something long-lasting. It never makes Timmie . . . ." Her voice cracked and she stared at the floor to finish. "It never made Timmie sleepy or sluggish." When the woman looked up they saw tears in her eyes. She made no move to wipe them away.

"But the remaining capsules were full of cocaine," insisted Ellis.

"I know, I know. They shouldn't have been, but somehow they were."

Clancy's hands came out of his pockets. He sat up. "You *know* the other capsules were full of coke?"

The woman nodded numbly.

"You've seen the autopsy report, and now I think you've gotten your hands on a police report. How do you know these things? Where'd you get your information?"

"I just know. Can't we leave it at that?"

"No. I want the name of your contact inside this department and I want it now."

"The autopsy report came from the hospital."

Clancy leaned forward, pressing his advantage. "You're stalling, Beck. I want the name of the policeman feeding you your information."

Sallie swallowed. "I read your file."

"Yes, yes, I know you read the file. Now what I want to know, and what I'm going to find out, is who gave that information to you."

"It's in your computer!"

"Beck! The name!"

"All you have to do is call it up!"

Clancy sat there for a moment. When it clicked what the woman meant, he came out of the chair. "What the hell are you saying, Beck, that you went through our files? Last time I checked that was against the law."

Sallie set her jaw. "He was my son, Sergeant."

"And those are *our* files. I can put you in jail."

"If you can prove it."

"You all but admitted it."

"To policemen who never read me my rights, and who are so anxious to clear this case that they're willing to close it as a drug overdose."

"It *was* a drug overdose!"

Sallie scooted back in her chair and crossed her arms. "I think my attorney would like to know why you prefer treating me like the guilty party instead of finding whoever killed my son."

"Lady, I don't need someone telling me how to do my job."

"It appears someone should."

Clancy's fists clenched at his sides. "You . . . . ."

"Bitch. Why don't you say it, Sergeant?"

"I don't have to. You did."

Sallie turned to Ellis. "Lieutenant, I'm not going to sit here and be harassed by a man who's been divorced three times, and one of those times had charges preferred against him for wife beating."

Clancy's mouth fell open. Ellis felt his do the same. Sweet Jesus! Was there nothing this woman didn't know? When his partner stepped forward, Beck came out of her chair and met him.

"Go ahead. Hit me, Sergeant. I'm not your wife, and

if you're not going to help me, you sure as hell aren't going to intimidate me."

Ellis hurried around his desk and pushed his sputtering partner into his chair. Once he was sure Clancy would stay there, he turned back to the woman.

"Now, Mrs. Beck, I consider myself a professional so I'd like to put all this behind us. But I'm still going to ask you why you're so adamant your son couldn't have been taking drugs."

Sallie's breath came hard and fast. Her eyes flashed. She tried to see through Ellis to Clancy. "Because Timmie hated drugs! Absolutely hated them. And this went beyond any eleven-year-old's tendency to moralize about people who do drugs. Timmie didn't even like taking hay fever medication if he was having a test or pitching. He said it took his edge away.

"No," she added, shaking her head, "my son taking drugs doesn't fit and I can't accept it." She looked around Ellis at Clancy. "I won't accept it, and I won't let you accept it either."

With a sneer, Clancy said, "Then *you* tell us who killed your boy."

"Did you ever consider that the other boys might've been jealous of Timmie's talent?"

Clancy laughed. "Are you telling us someone killed your boy because he made the honor roll and they didn't? That just won't wash."

Sallie looked from him to Ellis and found the lieutenant's face blank. Neither man had anything to offer. She whirled around, turning her back on them. When she did, she saw a short, dark-complected man staring at her through the half-glass wall dividing Ellis's office from the squad room. He turned away, quickly crossed the squad room, and started a conversation with another cop. The voyeur's slicked-back black hair and dark suit made him look like a Mafia hit man.

"Little League practice starts next week," Sallie heard herself say.

"So?"

"The league Timmie's in requires a physical, and a urine sample is a part of any physical. Timmie's doctor didn't mention anything abnormal about his urine."

"Anyone can clean out their system for a scheduled drug test."

Sallie faced the two men again. "Really, Sergeant, we're talking about an eleven-year-old." She paused. "The school district requires children entering the second, fourth, and sixth grades to have a physical. Timmie had one before going into the sixth grade. He wasn't on drugs then, either."

Clancy shrugged.

Sallie looked from the sergeant to the lieutenant. Both men thought she was crazy. Or worse: that she couldn't face her son's having been a drug addict. But she knew her baby was no addict.

She turned and headed for the door. "Check my son's academic record. Interview the neighbors to see if Timmie was a troublemaker. Find out whether he came home to a baby-sitter or was merely a latchkey kid. Talk with his doctor. Phelps in Whitehall Plaza. See if he thought Timmie took drugs."

"Your son could have been another Len Bias."

At the door, Sallie faced them. "Then bring me his pusher. That should be easy enough for cops to do. But you can't, because Timmie's pusher doesn't exist." She opened the door. "I want Timmie's killer found and I want him found soon. My son's not going to be remembered as the kid who overdosed in sixth grade." She went out the door, shutting it firmly.

"Bitch!" muttered Clancy.

"But a sharp one," said his partner. "And no one we've talked to thinks Timmie Beck was on drugs. No teacher, no coach, or his doctor."

Clancy didn't answer. He was staring through the glass wall at Beck, who had stopped in the squad room.

"And all of us wish we had a son like Timmie Beck."

"Not if I had to be married to a bitch like that. No wonder Alstair Beck divorced her. No amount of money would make me live with her."

"She didn't take alimony or child support."

"Yeah, and with her divorce sealed under a court order we'll never know why."

"Or why Alstair Beck didn't put up much of a fight."

Clancy watched the woman as she began talking to an officer at one of the desks in the bullpen.

"Rumor has it that Alstair's suing her in civil court for being an unfit mother."

Clancy looked at his partner. "After his kid is already dead?"

"I don't think Alstair is after money either."

"Yes, Mrs. Beck, what can I do for you?" The patrolman looked up from his paperwork.

Sallie inclined her head in the direction of the lookalike for a Mafia hit man. He was still talking to the detective, but Sallie had seen him glance at her when she left Ellis's office.

"Where've I seen that man before? The one with the deep tan? I can't place him."

The officer looked across the room. "I doubt you know him. He's from Miami. One of those guys who busts major drug dealers. D-Wars is what it's called, but between you and me, it's a waste of taxpayers' money. We bust more dealers on a Saturday night than they do in a whole year."

Sallie glanced at the hit man again. "I guess I don't know him. Thanks anyway." She turned to go.

"Mrs. Beck?"

Sallie faced the patrolman again.

"I just wanted to say . . . ." The policeman cleared his throat. "I wanted to say I'm sorry about what happened to your boy."

Sallie's head canted to one side. "I'm sorry, but I'm not tracking all that well. Do I know you?"

"My whole family knows your son. Timmie struck out my boy three times to advance to Divisionals in Little League. My boy was so mad that he made me take him to the batting cage every night the following week even though he wasn't going to play until next season."

Sallie's legs weakened. She had to put a hand on the desk to remain on her feet.

"What I'm trying to say is . . . ." The policeman cleared his throat. "My boy was crying about what happened to your son. He was looking forward to facing him this spring. He's been taking extra batting practice just for the occasion."

Sallie willed back the tears, then pushed off the desk. "Thank you. I . . . I appreciate your telling me . . . so many people . . . have special memories of my son . . . and they've been kind enough to share them with me."

Sallie rushed out of the room and ducked into a rest room. After composing herself, she started downstairs.

"Sallie! Sallie Beck. Wait up!"

She looked up to see a beefy, red-faced man hurrying down the stairs toward her.

"I almost missed you." Phil Rainey wore a short-sleeved shirt and slacks, tie knotted loosely around his neck. In one of his rather large hands was a thick folder.

"Hello, Phil." Sallie didn't want to talk to this man. She didn't want to talk to anybody. There had been so many people . . . so many messages of condolence.

"Sorry to hear about Timmie. I should've called or come by . . . ." The heavyset man gestured at the building. "This isn't much of an excuse, but it's all I've got. We don't see much of each other since we both got kicked out of the country club set."

"We only fit in while we were married to the right people."

A uniformed patrolman came upstairs, nodded to them, and continued to the next floor.

"Jeez, Sallie, I don't know what to say."

"Just come to the funeral. It's at Wingate's. Tomorrow at two. Timmie really missed you when we had to

22

move. You'd take time to throw the ball with him."

The heavy man's face lit up. "But remember who taught him how to make the ball curve."

Sallie heard herself chuckle. A sound she hadn't heard in quite a while. Two days to be exact. "That wasn't skill on my part, and I had the blisters to prove it. Timmie wanted to play ball when he grew up. Probably to make his father notice him."

"And he would've. He was a natural." After a pause, Rainey asked, "How's your dad? I miss those arguments we had over the backyard fence when he'd come to visit."

"Living like a hermit up in Minnesota. After Mama died he bought a whole island. Now he can hunt and fish year-round, if they don't catch him. I have to use a plane to fly in to see him."

"You still flying?"

"I was . . . I should've spent that time with Timmie. He should've been enough to make me forget IINTELL . . . for a few hours."

The policeman took her arm. "Sallie, don't do this to yourself. It wasn't your fault. I don't know a better mother a boy could've had. Sure, you worked—these days who doesn't? But you were there when Timmie needed you."

Sallie stared at the floor of the landing. "I should've taken the child support."

Rainey let go of her arm. "You're being too hard on yourself, as usual. Have anyone to stay with?"

Sallie looked up. "No. Why?"

"You should. A girlfriend. Your dad. Anybody."

"Daddy doesn't have a phone. He won't know about Timmie's . . . he won't know about Timmie until I fly in and tell him." Sallie leaned against the railing behind her. "Some of the girls at the office have offered to stay with me, but I'm holding up pretty well."

"You think so, but you aren't as tough as you think. You weren't all that tough when Timmie fell out of that tree and broke his arm."

Sallie straightened her back. "Divorce toughens you up, Phil. You ought to know about that."

"Nobody's tough enough to handle this. You've lost your only child. You aren't going to make it without help. You need someone to talk to or you'll break down. I see it all the time. It'll slip up on you when you least expect it. Now you're on guard, but how can you be on guard every time you walk past his room or find one of his toys around the house? Or when someone calls his name? Anything could trigger it. You can't keep this inside. Let it out or it'll eat at you."

Sallie forced a grim little smile. "I just survived one hell of an interrogation by Ellis and Clancy. They think Timmie overdosed."

"Well, he did, didn't he? I mean we can't raise perfect children, can we?"

Sallie recoiled from this man she'd thought was her friend. "Of course he didn't. He was murdered."

"Murdered? What in the world are you talking about?"

She told him.

"You don't really believe—"

"I don't want Timmie remembered as a drug overdose. He wasn't that kind of child." Sallie turned on her heel and finished the steps to the ground floor.

Rainey shook his head, then returned upstairs. He opened the door to Jeff Ellis's office and stuck his head inside. The two detectives looked up.

"Got anything proves the Beck kid didn't OD?"

"What the hell's it to you, Rainey?" asked Clancy. "It's not even your case."

Rainey held up his hands in surrender. "Okay, okay, but you'd better cover your ass. That woman who just left here? She's one of those superwomen, and if you don't find what she wants, and she has to do it for you, I wouldn't want to be the cops assigned to her case."

Three

"**O**kay, Phil, what have you got for me?"

"Why don't you sit down, Sallie?"

Sallie stared at the heavy policeman for a long moment, then pulled a metal chair from under the table in the interrogation room and sat down. Rainey stood on the other side of the table, a VCR and TV at the far end of the table and a two-way mirror on the wall behind him. Behind her, heads had marked a greasy line around the wall. The edge of the table was burned by cigarettes.

As usual, Rainey had his tie loose. "Since you were here, Clancy and Ellis have spent quite a bit of time questioning people about where Timmie might've gotten the cocaine."

Sallie shook her head. "Clancy didn't help."

"Sallie, please . . . ."

"I thought you wanted to help me get to the bottom of this."

"I do."

"Then lies, big ones, little ones, from friend or foe, aren't going to make a believer out of me."

Rainey stared at his former neighbor. This woman was so hard to reach. She hadn't been this way before the divorce. Had Sallie Beck made herself into what she was today or had she had some help along the way?

"Okay," said Rainey with a shrug, "it was Jeff Ellis and myself. There were some loose ends that needed to be tied up."

"Like the fact Timmie didn't use drugs."

"We felt we owed it to you."

"Owed it to Timmie."

"Sallie, if you'll just give me a chance—"

"Phil, let me make one thing clear. I'm not doing this for me. I'm doing it for Timmie, and the way he'll be remembered." She stared at the scarred tabletop. "It's the only thing left I *can* do for him."

"Well, you won't have to worry about Timmie's reputation any longer."

Sallie looked up. "What did you learn?"

"A boy came forward."

"Who?" Sallie's voice was a breathless whisper.

"Davy McBride. Know the name?"

Sallie shook her head.

"Since Timmie's death, Davy hasn't been sleeping all that well, and when he did he had the worst nightmares. After a few nights of this, his parents took him to the family doctor who recommended the boy see a psychiatrist. The family doctor was aware of what had happened at school. You may not know this, because you're out of the school loop, but since Timmie's death more than one child has had to enter counseling. It's no wonder, the way a fear of drugs is drummed into kids—"

"What did the shrink say?"

"That Davy would have to tell someone what was bothering him. That he would have to confess to an authority figure before there could be any chance for the healing process to begin."

"Confess to a policeman?"

"Or a priest. A priest is what Mrs. McBride wanted—that's Davy's mother—but Davy's father is a corporate attorney and he understands this could come back to haunt his kid. McBride and the shrink convinced the Missus to let her son talk with Ellis." Rainey pointed at the electronic equipment on the far end of the table. "It's on tape."

"Good—because I want to see it."

Rainey stared at his former neighbor for a long moment before turning on one machine, then the other. The TV screen filled with snow and the sound roared until the tape engaged the head of the VCR.

In black and white, Sallie saw a child she faintly remembered from her son's school activities. The boy sat in the very same interrogation room flanked by his mother and father. Jeff Ellis was there. He faced the two-way mirror and introduced everyone, including himself.

"Davy McBride is eleven years old and attended Eisenhower Elementary with Timmie Beck, was even in the same home room with him."

While Ellis spoke, Davy's eyes flickered around, always returning to his mother, an attractive woman wearing a tastefully tailored suit, blouse open at the neck, and very little jewelry. Mrs. McBride sat close to her son, holding his arm and chewing her lip. Her husband, wearing a pin-striped suit with a vest, lounged in his chair and occasionally rubbed his son's back.

"Yesterday," continued Ellis, "Mr. McBride called and said his son might be able to shed some light on the death of Timmie Beck." The detective faced Davy. "Now, son, what is it you wanted to tell me?"

Sitting in the same interrogation room where the scene had been taped, Sallie leaned into the table and held her breath. On the screen Davy glanced at his mother.

"I—I just know what happened to Timmie, that's all."

"What happened?" asked Ellis in an inoffensive manner.

Another shrug by the boy. "Someone put coke in his medicine, that's all."

Sallie gasped. It was one thing to suspect it, another to have it confirmed. She looked at Phil, but the policeman merely continued to stare at the television.

"Oh, they did, did they?" asked Ellis as if what he had been told was an everyday occurrence. "And why did they do that?"

Davy looked at his mother, and his father rubbed his son's back. "Go ahead, son, tell the policeman what you told us . . . and the doctor."

"It was supposed to be a joke," blurted out the boy. "We—they were playing a trick on him."

"And how was the trick supposed to work?" asked Ellis from the other side of the table.

The boy's eyes widened. "Oh, we—they were going to make fun of Timmie." He looked at the table. "Nobody was supposed to get hurt."

"But something went wrong, didn't it?"

Davy didn't look up. "Yes."

"What I don't understand is why these boys wanted to make fun of Timmie Beck in the first place."

Davy's head shot up. "Oh, that's easy. He's the teacher's pet."

Mrs. McBride gripped her son's arm. "Now, Davy—"

"It's true," said the boy, turning her way. "All the teachers like him the best. Timmie is always put in charge of the bulletin board."

"And how did Timmie get to be the teacher's pet?" asked Jeff Ellis.

The boy looked at the policeman. "By getting hundreds on all his tests. He knew all the answers and he did it . . ." Davy glanced at the tabletop again ". . . just to make the rest of us look bad. I couldn't see that at first, but Keith knew. Keith knew all along, and he figured out how we could get even."

Sallie stared at the small figure on the screen. If that little punk knew all the hours Timmie had studied . . . all the hours she had drilled him. Find a boyfriend, her friends said. Lighten up. But how did you do that when your only son needed you?

"But, Davy," continued Ellis on the TV screen, "what I don't understand is how these boys, the ones who played the trick on Timmie, could be sure he would have a hay fever attack. No hay fever attack and Timmie wouldn't take a pill. Then nobody has a chance to laugh at him. If you see what I mean."

Davy leaned back in his chair, more relaxed. "That's easy. Timmie always sneezes when he comes in the bathroom and we—where those boys are smoking. When he came in, they blew smoke in his face and wouldn't let him go. It was funny—Timmie thought that was the trick."

"And you're the one who put the cocaine in the hay fever capsules that killed Timmie Beck, aren't you?"

Shocked at the suddenness of the accusation, Sallie's mouth fell open.

On the screen Davy's eyes blazed with fear. He sat up. "No, no! Not me!"

"Yes, you did," Ellis said very quietly.

"Keith did it! I didn't! I couldn't. I didn't know where to get the coke. Keith got it from his brother. Keith's brother said people do funny things when they take coke." Davy realized his mother was there and grabbed her arm. Looking up at her, he pleaded, "It wasn't me. It wasn't me!"

The boy's father remained calm as he rubbed his son's back. "Watch yourself, Lieutenant."

The blond woman looked across her son at her husband. "I think we should leave."

Her husband shook his head. "This has to be done. We need some leverage."

Clutching his mother's arm, Davy cried out, "I want to go home! I don't like this policeman. You told me he'd be a nice policeman, but he's scary. Let's go home. Please!"

McBride took his son's shoulders and turned the boy to face him. Still, Davy would not look him in the eye. "Remember what I told you, son. All you have to do is tell this story once and you won't ever have to talk to another policeman. That's right, isn't it, Lieutenant?" McBride gestured with his head at the camera filming from the other side of the mirror.

On the videotape the detective nodded.

Sallie whirled around. "You made a deal with them! Damn you, Phil! You made a deal with the McBrides."

"Of course. We make deals all the time. Police departments all over the country do it, or rather the prosecutor does. It's how the system works or it would break down under the case load. Now Clancy and Ellis are free to pursue other cases."

The images on the TV screen continued to speak, but Sallie didn't hear them. "It's not fair."

Rainey put his hands palm down on the table and leaned toward her. "And what would you've done?"

"I would've put them in prison for murder!"

"You would've put three eleven-year-olds and a thirteen-year-old in prison? Have you forgotten how old Timmie was?"

"But they—"

"Accidentally killed your son. Let me say it again so you can hear the word. *Accidentally* killed your son."

When Sallie tried to protest, he waved her off. "You don't have to tell me about your son. I'm the guy who threw the ball with Timmie when Alstair was too busy."

"But—"

"For crissake, Sallie, they didn't mean for Timmie to

die and they're sick to death about it. I told you some of the kids at Eisenhower had to go for counseling. Three of the four involved in Timmie's death were those children."

Sallie fell back in her chair, gulping for air. She was drowning. Drowning in her own helplessness. "What—what's going to happen . . . to them?"

"Probation at the most."

"But that's not fair," she said again, sitting up. "My son will still be dead."

"Life's not fair, and I wish to God I wasn't the one to have to tell you that after what that louse Alstair put you through."

A voice on the videotape identified the other boys involved in the misadventure. Two of the boys were simple accomplices, but Keith Kelly was different.

"Keith Kelly differs from the others in that he has a history of bullying smaller children and taking things that don't belong to him," said Rainey.

"Stealing."

Rainey nodded. "He failed fifth grade and has a December birth date. That makes him almost two years older than the other boys and their natural leader. And he comes from a broken home."

"So did Timmie!"

"Not that broken." Rainey reached over and turned down the sound on the TV. "Keith's a minor, and as far as we know, not into drugs. His lawyer says we can't prove he's a pusher—maybe a user, but not a pusher—and I'm afraid that's true. We don't even know where the drugs came from."

"What do you mean?"

"Keith's brother buys drugs from more than one source, and we're pretty sure his brother didn't know Keith had taken cocaine from his stash."

Putting her head in her hands, Sallie stared at the floor. "My son is dead and no one's going to be punished for it." Glancing at the image of Davy McBride cringing between his parents, she added, "I don't want to ruin those boys' lives, but I want satisfaction. Is that so wrong?"

Rainey cleared his throat. "No."

Sallie thought for a moment. Her hands came away from her head. "Where do they come from, Phil—the drugs, I mean?"

"What? Oh, the Florida pipeline, and before that, Colombia."

"This drug thing, it's been going on for years. Why haven't you people done something about that?"

Rainey sighed. "I've been asked that so many times it's not fun going to parties. Everyone's either doing drugs or asking what we're doing about them. Sometimes both. The truth is, drugs are going to keep coming into this country until the law's changed."

"Make drugs legal?"

Rainey shook his head. "I'm not for that. Alcohol already gives us enough headaches. What I'd like to see is all pushers, not just the kingpins, executed. We execute murderers, so why not dealers? Ultimately they're the ones who killed Timmie. And we should declare war on Colombia. Why should we care what any third-rate country thinks of us? They don't care about our children. They actually get off humbling a country as mighty as ours. Let's show them the real price for dealing drugs. Stop all foreign aid to the bastards. Politicians say that would only create chaos, but to tell you the truth, I can't find a cop who gives a damn what happens in any banana republic. It's the streets of our city they're concerned about." Rainey glanced at the mirror behind him. "Some people don't understand, but I live with what politicians don't see or don't want to see."

"What can I do to help?"

"Not much—unless you want to raise hell about Timmie's death. The newspapers would love that. It sells lots of papers."

As she considered what Rainey had just said, Sallie noticed the mirror for the first time. She glanced at the TV. Was someone taping her agony as they'd done the McBrides'? She shook her head at the thought. She was becoming paranoid. "You really think raising hell would accomplish anything?"

Rainey took a seat on the edge of the table. "Who knows? With the fear of drugs . . . ?"

"And that's why you asked me to view the videotape, isn't it? To put me in the position of knowing that I would ruin those boys' lives if I chose to go public about what happened."

"Sallie, please—"

"And no one can muzzle me, can they?"

Rainey shook his head.

"And it wouldn't be slander because everything I'd say would be true."

"No," said the policeman, his voice gone hoarse. "There's nothing anyone could do."

Sallie pushed back her chair and stood up. She snatched her purse off the table and headed for the door.

Rainey came off the table. "Where you going?"

Sallie whirled around, hands coming up, one with the purse in it. "Stay away from me! Don't come near me!"

"But we used to be friends—"

"Used to be. You couldn't tell me straight, could you? You didn't trust me to make the right decision, whatever that decision was. But you and your fellow policemen might be wrong. I might not play fair. What seems to be lost in all this is that my son is dead. Did you hear me? My son is dead!"

"Sallie, I insisted on showing you the tape. I didn't want you to think—"

"I'm finished talking. You can't help me, so I'll have to help myself."

"What are you saying? What are you going to do?"

"I don't know—yet. One thing for sure is I won't need your help. I'm finished with you policemen. You're supposed to help me. You can't, so I'll have to do it myself." She went out the door, slamming it behind her.

But in the hallway Sallie found she couldn't let go of the knob. She had to hold on to stay on her feet. As she leaned into the door, she looked up and down the hallway. Besides some cops at the water cooler, she was alone.

Oh, Timmie, they've killed you and there's nothing I

can do about it . . . without making things worse. We— we were such a team. Not even your father's expensive gifts could come between us.

But someone found a way.

Tears formed in her eyes. *No! I'm not going to cry. Phil Rainey believes I'll break down, but I'm not going to.* She brushed away a rebellious tear.

I don't have time to cry. I have to fly to Minnesota and tell Daddy that Timmie . . . his only grandchild is dead. She let out a sick little laugh. *That his only grandchild is dead and IINTELL's about to make his daughter a vice-president. A vice-presidency not worth having without my son.*

Sallie took a deep breath and let it out. *Maybe I'll have a good cry during the flight up. Maybe I'll make a mistake. A pilot's error. Something I've never believed in, but something I'm looking forward to.*

Sallie stumbled past the adjoining room and glanced at the door. *Is someone in there? It can't hurt to look.*

Humor yourself . . . oh, God, why didn't I have more children? Because I was married to a control freak.

Sallie looked through the small window and saw a well-dressed, dark-skinned man. Still looking like a Mafia hit man, he was talking to a balding man with rounded shoulders who stood with his back to her. Through the two-way mirror, revealing the room she had just left, she could see Phil Rainey pop the cassette out of the VCR. Her old friend was shaking his head.

The hit man saw Sallie staring through the small window and stopped talking. The balding man turned around, and Sallie recognized him from his visits to IINTELL. He was the chief of police.

More voyeurs!

Sallie slammed her hand against the door and stumbled in the direction of the stairs. Even the chief of police was worried about some mother running around telling everyone her son had been killed by drugs—trafficking the police were helpless to stop.

I should scream my head off! Then they'd have to do something. But that wouldn't bring Timmie back. And is that how I'd want him remembered?

I told Phil Rainey I'd take care of what the police couldn't do, but what am I to do? What can I do? I've got to do something. Someone should pay for my baby's death.

Oh, God, please take care of my baby. I never believed in you. Now I have to. There has to be someone who can take care of him. I thought it was me, but I can't even take care of his memory.

Teardrops filled her eyes, clouding her vision as she started down the stairs. Sallie was wiping the tears away when she tripped and fell. She grabbed the railing and dropped her purse, ending up stretched over the stairs, feet hung up several steps behind her.

A uniformed patrolman took the last few stairs in a bound. "I've got you, lady!" He grabbed Sallie and helped her to her feet. At the landing, he retrieved her purse.

Sallie shrugged him off. "No! I don't want your help." She wiped away more tears, took her purse, and staggered across the landing.

"I don't want your help," she said to no one in particular. "You can't help me. Nobody can." She continued to the ground floor, using the railing. "You can't do anything. I have to do everything. And I'm going to do it. I'm going to do something for my baby."

Four

Ned Clanton had no clue as to what would happen next. But he wouldn't let on. He was out of prison and that was all that counted. Sure, he was chained to a nigger and on his way to the courthouse in this California town for a hearing, but he had no idea why. All that mattered was he was on the outside, and when you were outside, you had a chance to escape. Escape. The only thought on his mind since that guy had given him the news.

The guy appeared on the other side of the bulletproof glass of the wall down the middle of the visitation room. He was of average build, wearing a navy blue suit with a yellow shirt, shades, and a red—no, a maroon tie. Ned had had a fucking bike that color once, and everyone had made fun of it. One of his mother's many boyfriends had bought it because the asshole needed a place to lie low. The bike was supposed to keep Ned quiet.

Ned tried to wreck that frigging bike, and along the way learned how to make the other boys eat dirt. Now here was another asshole, on the other side of the glass, lounging back in his chair and looking like he didn't have a care in the world. Who was this guy anyway?

The guy picked up the phone on his own side of the glass and motioned for Ned to do the same. Why not? It broke the monotony of a sixteen-year stretch. Only eight years if he kept his nose clean and if the State of California needed room for repeat offenders. Ned was a repeat offender. It was just that the State didn't know about all his offenses.

The man took off his sunglasses as he sat down, revealing a pair of pale blue eyes. "Don't expect you'd remember me," said the man into the telephone. Both men had to lean forward because of the shortness of the cords. "I'm your cousin's brother-in-law."

Ned said nothing. One thing you learned inside this place was to keep your fucking trap shut. He didn't even remember the cousin this asshole was talking about. Evidently the asshole didn't know either because he never mentioned anyone's name. But that only occurred to Ned after he had been returned to the cell block. By then it wasn't important who had sent this guy. All that mattered was he was being given a chance to blow this joint.

The brother-in-law of the cousin Ned had never heard of added, "Your cousin's a little bit under the weather so I brought you the news."

Ned didn't have any family to speak of, let alone anyone who gave a damn about him, except for the shyster lawyer who was doing diddly to get him an early release, so Ned merely sat there and listened.

"Ned, there's a problem with your conviction. Your attorney will be in touch. He'll probably see you when you're brought before the judge." A thin smile crossed the face of the man across the glass from Ned. "Looks like there's an appeal in your future."

Ned scanned the room with its row of booths, telephones, and the glass separating prisoners from their visitors. A guard was posted at the door, another in a small room overlooking the visitation room. That guard watched and listened, and every once in a while his voice came over the telephone line to remind the cons of some Mickey Mouse rule. Probably listening in on their conversation right now. A problem with his conviction? Shit, that bitch Jackie and that bastard Shorty had ratted out the whole frigging operation.

"I suppose the only thing important to a man who's been in three years and fifteen days is getting out."

Now that got Ned's attention. That was exactly the number of years and days he'd spent behind these frigging walls. Not the number of days since that bitch had finked on him and agents from D-Wars had picked him up. Now Ned was all ears and leaned closer to the glass.

"Your cousin's worried you might try something before your appointment with the judge." The man who was absolutely no relation to him glanced at the guard looking down from the glass window. "Your cousin knows being behind bars can make people crazy, but she says when you get on that bus, don't make an attempt to escape. If something's going to happen, let it happen in the courtroom. Go with the flow."

Ned nodded that he understood.

The man straightened up. "Anything you want me to tell your cousin, you know, about how you're doing inside?"

For the first time Ned spoke. "Just tell her I hope she's feeling better."

Now Ned sat on this bus, hands and feet chained together, shackled to this damn nigger. Well, he'd done his part. He was sitting here, not even talking to the nigger, not making the least ruckus. The two of them were the only cons on the bus. A guard sat in the rear; another peered down the road at the traffic slowing down ahead of them.

Two guards to make sure two cons didn't escape. And chained together to boot. Damn! What'd they expect? He was going nowhere, and neither was the frigging bus. Traffic was backed up. If these assholes fucked up his opportunity to be released . . . well, he just might have to try something after all.

It was all Ned could do to sit there as they poked along. Sure, he made nasty remarks about traffic, and the nigger had some of his own, especially with traffic moving at a snail's pace. The air conditioning on this bus really sucked!

Through the window Ned surveyed the countryside. Nothing but fields of melons stretching for miles and miles along a two-lane blacktop. Maybe if . . . .

Then he remembered his promise to the so-called

cousin-in-law. He had promised to sit tight. Shit! Jackie and Shorty hadn't kept their word and both of them had gone free as birds.

Security on this bus was nothing compared to what they'd have at the courthouse. Now would be his best chance to escape. Anyway, what'd he owe that bastard who'd come to see him?

As a kid he'd been kicked around, and finally kicked out by one of his mother's boyfriends. On the street everyone was picking on everyone else and taking things: money, dope, a piece of ass. Everything was there for the taking, if you knew who to pick on. When you picked on whores, dopers, and small-time crooks, even the cops left you alone. Cops thought you were doing them a favor, keeping the assholes in line. And once he learned that, Ned did the fucking cops one hell of a lot of favors.

But penny-ante results can wear on a man. There were just so many asses you could kick—before you kicked the wrong one. He had done just that and someone had cured Ned of his bullying. So Ned was ready when he met Jackie Mustard flying grass in from Mexico. Once again, he fell into a line of work the cops winked at. Grass wasn't as bad as dealing the hard stuff. Shit, this was Cali-fucking-fornia. Everybody was on something.

Sure, you could make more money dealing coke, but selling grass, said Jackie Mustard, was like having a "get out of jail" card. Several times Ned was picked up for dealing, but more often than not, more pressing matters kept the cops, courts, and prosecutors busy, such as murders, rapes, burglaries, or guys dealing the hard stuff.

There weren't enough jails for everyone selling grass until that asshole Wes Taylor stuck his nose in where it didn't belong. Fucking D-Wars had been determined to show up the locals. No wonder the cops hated the Feds, and now one of those cops was walking down the middle of the frigging highway toward them. Walking between cars on this side and the empty lane returning from town.

What did this asshole want—sauntering toward them, wearing a neat pair of shades—best he stayed with the wreck or whatever it was and get traffic moving. Ned had a judge to see!

The uniformed patrolman was on the other side of the bus now, motioning for the driver to open the door. As he did, the guard in the rear got to his feet and strolled up the aisle with his shotgun. The patrolman used one hand to pull himself aboard, the other to shoot the driver where he sat. The driver fell back and collapsed against the window.

Before the guard from the rear could bring up his shotgun, the cop wearing the shades put two bullets into him. The guard followed the shotgun to the floor, collapsing on top of it. No expended shells hit the floor. The gun was inside a plastic bag that collected the shells as they ejected from the chamber. The cop pulled the baggie off and stuffed it, the clip, and the spent shells into a pocket of his uniform. Then he pulled out another clip, jammed it into the base of the handle, and stuck the pistol inside another plastic bag. Never once did his shades leave Ned or the nigger.

As the killer fished around in the driver's pockets, Ned realized he wore latex gloves. "Shot a few who turned out to be HIV-positive," said the man. "Wouldn't want their blood on my hands."

The cop came out of the driver's pocket with the key, and Ned was so dumbfounded by what was happening that he had to be told to raise his hands so he could be unshackled. Ned did and the chains came off.

Then the killer relooped them around the metal bar making up the seat in front of him!

"What the hell's going on?" demanded the nigger, rising up beside him.

The cop dropped the key into his pocket and shot the nigger, throwing him up against the side of the bus and spraying the window with blood. Ned scooted up and away as the bullet passed through the man, then the window. He thought he might pee in his pants.

"Sit down," said the cop, taking off his sunglasses and revealing a pair of pale blue eyes.

Ned nodded and slid down in his seat. The man with the pale blue eyes returned to the front of the bus, where he pulled the door shut and threw the driver out of his seat, tossing the dead man into the stairwell.

Horns blew behind them. Might've been blowing forever as far as Ned knew. He glanced out the rear window and saw a single line of traffic backed up. In front of the bus was nothing but the occasional car approaching from the opposite direction, and on each side of the road, miles and miles of melons.

When the last car passed that was leaving town, the killer turned the bus into the empty lane . . . slamming into a Nissan Sedan that thought it might slip around the bus. For its trouble, the Nissan was knocked into a ditch running along the fields. Workers raised their heads and stared as the bus made a U-turn and headed in the direction it had come from.

"Where—where we headed?"

"Florida," said the man behind the wheel, "and if you haven't noticed, I'm serious about getting there."

0722X0808

TOP SECRET

FR: AGENT LILIANA ALVAREZ

TO: DIRECTOR FRAZIER

SUBJECT: ALLEN ROGER NELSON, AKA
*   AL NELSON, AKA "THE HAWK"*

A. Early Life:

Allen Roger Nelson was born in Minneapolis-St. Paul, August 15, 1947. His family owns and operates a gasket company that has been in the family since the birth of the automobile. Nelson graduated near the top of his class at the Academy of Science and Math. This school is for the brightest minds in the state, and this fact is important because there Nelson organized a high school football team.

His father, along with several other prominent families, put up the money for the uniforms and equipment. They also

hired a coach. The Academy of Science and Math has a class of approximately 150 (grades 9-12) with a heavy dose of nerds. Many students are female (Nelson's field goal kicker, and a quite accurate one from the available records, was a member of the women's soccer team). Nelson appears to have been a decent athlete but a much better tactician, and with his education and father's influence, he had no trouble securing an appointment to the US Military Academy at West Point. There he was just another player, but, in the classroom and on the field, he excelled at small unit tactics. Nelson earned a Rhodes scholarship for additional study in England but volunteered for service in South Vietnam.
B. Career in Vietnam:

Nelson served only one tour because the war was winding down, but he was there long enough to distinguish himself and then be court-martialed. At a time when the Army was trying to disengage itself, Nelson led his company on a renegade mission against a North Vietnamese position across the border in Cambodia. (At that point in the war, lieutenants were commanding companies so higher ranking officers might be engaged in safer duties in the rear.)

The renegade company's operation was

successful and the enemy's position wiped out, but its leader, Allen Nelson, was brought up on charges. (For more information, see Alvarez Memo: The Court-Martial of Allen Nelson.) It was during his time in the stockade that Nelson and Robert Spano first met. Sergeant Spano was in charge of interrogation. More information about Staff Sergeant Spano can be found in Alvarez Memo: The life of Robert Wayne Spano. Nelson was acquitted of all charges, but required to tender his resignation. Nelson spent the next six years employed as a mercenary.

C. African Adventures:

Working with small units, Nelson, once again, was successful, and in Africa his masters did not question his tactics. It was also during this time that Nelson learned of the banking system in the Caymans. After suffering a chest wound in Angola, he returned home to the United States.

D. Drug Career:

As a civilian, Nelson experimented with drugs, or perhaps this was an extension of a habit picked up in Africa or Southeast Asia. Interviews with his known associates about this period of Nelson's life indicate a young man bored with life. When Nelson was arrested for possession a third time, he was told by his father to leave *the Minneapolis-St. Paul area. By then, a younger brother had taken over the gasket business.*

Nelson headed for Miami where he began smuggling, first grass, and then the harder stuff. There he ran into Robert Spano, and the ex-staff sergeant set about securing Nelson's operation with expertise gained while serving in the military. Sergeant Spano had been known as one of the army's most fierce interrogators. This became especially useful to Allen Nelson in his new line of work.

Five

Wes Taylor looked around the gymnasium. Its child-sized chairs had been arranged auditorium-style in front of a stage built into the far end. Moments before, the chairs had been filled with adults, but now the audience was on its feet, moving toward the stage. The dedication of the new community center in one of the worst ghettos in Miami was over. Taylor stood up. Adults sure looked silly sitting in chairs built for children.

And don't you wish you could still look silly sitting in child-sized chairs at PTA meetings for *your* children?

But that would never happen. Jenny had talked the judge into forbidding him from seeing the kids until he quit D-Wars. What kind of choice was that? A man can't have his work, can't have his kids? Appeared he couldn't have his wife, either. Or talk any sense into her. Jenny never understood that nobody in their right mind went after the children of government agents. It would bring every government agent down on them—and had.

Well, he wouldn't be a government agent long if he didn't nail The Hawk. And if he failed would Jenny take him back? Not hardly. Not the way she looked at the lug she'd just married. Big, goofy guy—caught Jenny on the rebound, he did, but Jenny wouldn't admit it. And the lug had plenty of time to spend with the kids. *His* kids, not the lug's. And damn if the son of a bitch wasn't likable, at least the one time he'd met him, except for the fact the guy was raising *his* kids.

By the time Taylor reached the end of his aisle, The Hawk stood center stage, beaming. True, it was only a neighborhood community stage, but The Hawk was receiving the adoration he thought he deserved. Today the bastard had taken a giant step toward respectability and the irony wasn't lost on Taylor.

Damn! Now all the son of a bitch needed was a woman to give him a set of kids to play at this community center. Would The Hawk be a better father than he had been to his children?

A congressman, the mayor, and even a cardinal huddled around The Hawk, shaking hands with the bastard before taking their places in the receiving line. Two large men, their buffed-up physiques hardly hidden by business suits, hovered around their boss, eyes flickering over the crowd as people formed lines at the side of the stage or at tables laid with refreshments.

Taylor wondered if he should have some punch and cake—paid for out of profits from The Hawk's illegal drug trade. A drug trade it appeared Wes Taylor was helpless to stop.

What am I doing here? The Hawk is as much out of reach on that stage as if I was back at my office. This is as close as you'll ever come, and Julius has told you that on more than one occasion.

Turning to go, Taylor saw a face he recognized. He stared at the chunky woman with the graying black hair as she pressed forward, trying to be one of the first to reach The Hawk.

Where did he know her from?

As he watched, the woman slipped around a young black man to become the third or fourth person up on stage. The woman was intent on reaching The Hawk.

But who was she?

Taylor didn't realize it when he started for the stage, but as he did, he was sorting and discarding faces from drug busts, mug books, and lineups.

I know that woman! I know her!

When the name came, it didn't come from any drug bust, mug shot, or lineup. Sallie Beck. The mother of the kid killed by the cocaine trick. He had seen her back in the Midwest, and Beck had a son about the same age as his own. Taylor couldn't help wondering what Jenny and her lug of a husband were telling his kids about the dangers of drugs. A more relevant question would be: What was Beck doing in Miami?

Taylor pushed past an elderly couple, and when he did, the woman commented on his manners. Now Beck was leaning forward, anxious to take her first step up on stage. In her hand was a red purse, and the purse contrasted sharply with the black cocktail dress.

Woman Against Herself

Beck's got a pistol in that purse!

Taylor glanced at the bodyguards. The shorter of the two, Fuentes, scanned over the woman, watching the crowd and speaking into a microphone in the lapel of his jacket. Beck just might reach her target. Fuentes didn't see any danger from some dumpy, middle-aged broad.

Damn it, Beck. You can't shoot my drug dealer.

Taylor shoved his way through the crowd, then looked up to see he'd goofed. Fuentes was staring at him instead of noticing the threat from Sallie Beck.

You've screwed up. Any woman waiting patiently in line isn't the threat a man hurrying to the stage is. Now what are you going to do? Fuentes will never allow you on stage. If he's doing his job, people are already on their way to throw you out of here. Oh, you can fight your way up there, and while doing so, watch Beck shoot The Hawk. And she'll be able to reach the drug dealer because you'll have distracted his bodyguards.

You can shout why you think she's here. Do that and the bodyguards will shoot Beck—no questions asked—and probably waste several bystanders in the process. For the dedication of the community center, The Hawk seemed to have talked his men into giving him some space, but you can't coach reactions. If a bodyguard stopped to think, the opposition would already be killing the person the bodyguard was supposed to protect.

Taylor took the arm of the first person within reach: a senior citizen in a purple dress and long, white gloves.

Someone had just handed her a glass of punch. Taylor almost knocked the glass out of the woman's hand.

"And how do you like our new community center?"

The woman frowned at the hand on her arm. "I'd like it much better if you took your hand off me, young man. You almost spilled punch all over my gloves."

Taylor was counting to himself. *One thousand one, one thousand two, one thousand three.* Where would Beck be now? Was she up on stage? Was she maneuvering now to shoot The Hawk as Taylor talked with this woman? How much time did he have to save the life of a man about to run him out of the drug enforcement business?

One thousand seven, one thousand eight.

Too many people to watch, and only two bodyguards. Fuentes can't watch me all day. But he can stall me long enough for his boss to be assassinated.

"Young man?" asked the old lady. "Would you please turn loose of my arm?"

"Aren't you Julius's wife?" asked Taylor.

"I am not," said the woman, pulling her arm away.

"Really?" Taylor expressed astonishment.

"My husband passed away several years ago and I don't appreciate—"

"I'm sorry to hear that. Really, I thought you were Julius's wife."

"Well, I'm not, and furthermore . . . ."

The rest was lost on Taylor. Fuentes had moved to the stairs, inspecting the line. And Beck was practically at the head of that line! Only a few people stood between her and The Hawk.

Taylor boosted himself up on stage, right behind Fuentes, and before the bodyguard turned around, Taylor was crossing the stage behind him.

The fat congressman turned out of the line to introduce a Latin couple to The Hawk, and, as he did, threw up a huge wall of flesh between Beck and The Hawk. Beck shifted to one side of the fat man, trying to point her purse around him.

Beck does have a gun!

When she shifted to the right, trying to reach around the congressman, a young black man behind her moved up in the line. This blocked Taylor from Beck.

Can't have that! Got to have that gun!

Taylor stumbled into the black man, putting his shoulder into him and pushing the man away. "Excuse me." He reached over and grabbed Beck's wrist, digging in with his fingers on the woman's gun arm.

Pain flashed across her face and she let out an "Oh!" She looked from her wrist to Taylor. "You!"

"Come with me, Mrs. Beck," said Taylor in a low voice.

"I will not." Her voice became shrill.

The government agent took the purse from her hand and pulled the woman out of line. Beck resisted. Out of the corner of his eye, The Hawk had seen Taylor stumble into the line. Now he was openly staring at the two of them.

"Don't do this!" begged Beck in a hoarse whisper.

The congressman shifted his bulk around. "Is there a problem here?"

In the moment it took the huge man to turn around, Taylor let go of Beck's hand. After all, he had the purse.

"No problem, Congressman. My wife thought we had time to thank Al for the new community center and still make it to a Cuban-American meeting across town." Taylor took Beck's hand again. "But I don't think so." He pulled Beck toward the front of the stage and she pulled back.

The congressman gave the once-over to the dark-complected man in the business suit and his female companion in the black cocktail dress. The woman's hair was graying, but she was still a good-looking woman for middle age. Cuban-Americans? The husband for sure, but the woman . . . should he know them?

The bodyguards strolled over. "Is there some assistance I can provide?" Fuentes eyed Taylor.

"Oh, no," said the congressman. "These good people are in a rush to speak to Al and make it across town to another meeting." He smiled all around as if everyone had assembled there to see him. "I certainly know how that is." To The Hawk he said, "Al, these people are in the same kind of predicament in which I occasionally find myself. Would you take a moment to speak to them so they can scoot across town?"

The fat man took Taylor's arm and pulled him, and indirectly Sallie, over until she was face-to-face with the man she suspected had smuggled into the country the cocaine that had killed her son. And the drug enforcement agent had her pistol. What could she do?

The D-Wars agent was saying, " . . . thank you for what you've done. I grew up in this neighborhood, and it's good to see something positive happening for a change."

The Hawk's quizzical look became a smile. "Thank you, Mister . . . ."

The government agent turned to Sallie and shoved her purse up under her arm, snug into her armpit. "Honey, you were in such a hurry to get up on stage and thank Al that you left your purse on your chair."

Sallie felt the hardness of the pistol through her purse and knew it would be impossible to pull the weapon out and kill this man, especially with all these people watching. It was okay if she died killing this monster—she halfway expected to do so—but to be trotted off to jail while The Hawk continued his deadly work was too much to bear.

The D-Wars agent was talking. "Tell Al how much we appreciate what he's done. Then we can get across town."

Sallie turned to The Hawk: tanned, narrow face, slicked-back hair, and coal black eyes. Dammit! She'd worked so hard to get here and now this government agent had spoiled everything. Was this agent on The Hawk's payroll, or was it like cynics said, without pushers many a drug enforcement agent would be out of a job?

"Er—actually, Al, I'm not from around here, but my husband's sincere in his compliment. He's fussed about how run-down the old neighborhood has become."

"I was happy to do something." The Hawk smiled and extended a hand. "Mrs. . . . ?"

"And the after-school care is a nice touch," ran on Taylor. "We've got a couple of kids and the after-school care is eating us alive."

The Hawk looked at the government agent, and as he did, Sallie pulled her hand away. She resisted the urge to wipe it off. Her hand wasn't all she wanted to wipe off either. She wanted to wipe every drug dealer off the face of the earth, and she'd been prepared to start with The Hawk. Instead, here she was, treating the bastard as if he were a guest in her home. It was absurd. It was sickening.

Taylor thanked The Hawk again, and Sallie smiled as she was pulled between the two bodyguards. She said, "Al, I just hope one day I can pay you back for what you have done for me."

Taylor almost choked on his smile. He had to force himself to wave good-bye as he pulled Sallie to the edge of the stage and helped her to the floor.

The Hawk watched them leave as he shook hands with a Latin couple who had waited for their chance to speak with the guest of honor. As The Hawk watched, Taylor dragged Sallie toward the rear of the gymnasium.

"You bastard!" she whispered hoarsely. "I had him and you ruined it. I should shoot you. You know how hard it is to get that close? Usually he has more bodyguards or stays in his compound. I was face-to-face with the son of a bitch and you ruined it. Ruined it, you bastard!"

Sallie tried to pull away, but Taylor wouldn't turn loose. "If I hadn't, they would've killed you."

"After losing my son, do you really think I care?"

As Taylor pulled the woman down the aisle, he glanced at her. "Okay, if I hadn't stopped you, you would've queered the deal for D-Wars. The Hawk's our target, too."

Near the rear of the room, Taylor leaned down to an elderly woman sitting in one of the children's chairs. This woman had a slice of cake on a plate on her lap and a cup of punch in her hand. She was talking with a young man in a business suit.

"Are you Julius's wife?" As the government agent asked the question, he reached inside his coat and opened a line to his people outside. That was followed by a quick glance behind him, and Taylor didn't like what he saw.

"No, I'm not," said the woman with a smile.

"I'm sorry." Taylor straightened up. "Julius said he would meet us here." Taylor began pulling Sallie down the aisle again.

"Let go of me! I don't want to go with you."

"You'd better, Mrs. Beck. Your double-entendre just got a tail set on us."

Sallie looked over her shoulder and saw Fuentes following them and speaking into the lapel of his jacket.

Six

Outside the community center, Taylor made his way to the street with Sallie in tow. As he did, another bodyguard blocked their way and slipped his hand inside his jacket. Instead of Taylor's bringing out a weapon, he raised his heel and brought it down on the man's instep. The bodyguard yelped and his hand came from under the jacket. He stumbled back.

"Sorry," mumbled the government agent, continuing toward the street, "but we're in a hurry."

A cab pulled up while the bodyguard righted himself. Taylor opened the rear door and shoved Sallie inside. The bodyguard came after them, only to have the cab door slammed in his face.

"Try the next one," Taylor said through the lowered window. "We have a plane to catch."

The cab leaped forward. Tires screeched and horns blared as the cab forced its way into traffic. The driver, a skinny black man wearing an orange shirt and a

Miami Heat baseball cap, glanced at Sallie, then Taylor, via the rearview mirror.

"I've got to tell you, man, you're lucky I wasn't still
hung up behind that funeral."

"We've got a tail, Julius. Take us across the river
and make it quick but make it look normal."

"For a cab in this town that could be anything."

Sallie looked out the rear window and saw the bodyguard standing in the street. A sedan pulled up beside
him—the door was already open—and the bodyguard
leaped inside.

"They're coming after us!"

"No kidding, lady."

A hard right turn threw Sallie into the corner, and
when she sat up, the cab was taking the next light on
red, then switching to the wrong side of the road to
pass a truck. A pedestrian stepped into the street, then
quickly stepped back. A kid on a bike wobbled, then
threw himself and his bike out of the way of the approaching cab.

"Good God!"

"He can't help you in this town, lady."

Onlookers gaped as the cab passed the truck, and
then returned to the proper lane. Ahead of them the
road split. The cab veered left, and Julius leaned on his
horn. A vendor selling hot dogs made the mistake of
thinking he could reach the other side of the street. Both
he and his cart ended up on their sides. The last Sallie
saw, the hot dog vendor was lying on his back and shooting them the bird. Three blocks later, the cab swung out
on a four-lane, weaving in and out of traffic.

Sallie gripped the front seat, saw a white-knuckled hand in front of her—*hers!*—and a bridge coming up fast.

"Right-hand lane!" shouted Taylor.

"Oh, man!" moaned Julius.

The cabbie had maneuvered into the open lane, the left-hand lane. Now he floored the accelerator, racing ahead of a minivan filled with children, then whipped over to the right-hand lane. When Sallie looked out the rear window for the trailing sedan, Taylor snatched her purse away.

"Give that back!"

Taylor swung his shoulders around, blocking Sallie from the purse, and pulled out the pistol. As the cab raced across the bridge, he tossed the weapon out the window. They were across the canal before the pistol hit the water. Moments later, the cab turned into an industrial park.

Sallie whirled around after watching the pistol disappear. "I'll buy another one! There are plenty of places in Miami that'll sell me one!"

Inside the industrial park, the cab turned left among a row of warehouses. People unloading a truck scattered at the sound of the horn and the sight of a cab bearing down on them.

"Mrs. Beck, I know you can buy another, but now that The Hawk's seen you, you won't be able to get within a hundred yards of him."

The cab took a hard right into an alley, and the turn threw Sallie against the door again. It also surprised a workman pushing a hand truck stacked with boxes. The workman leaped out of the way, and one of the boxes bounced off the cab's bumper. Glancing in his mirror, Julius saw the workman shaking a fist at him.

Sallie righted herself by grabbing the window and a piece of the front seat. "You jerk! That's why you came on stage, isn't it?"

The cabbie laughed. "Socializing with The Hawk? That your latest plan, Wes?"

"Take us to the airport, Julius. Mrs. Beck is going home."

"I'm not going anywhere."

"You're going home, whether you like it or not."

"You can't tell me what to do!"

"Just watch me, lady."

Sallie swung at Taylor at the same time Julius wheeled out of the alley and hard to the left. Instead of slapping the government agent, she slid across the seat and ended up against him, arm around Taylor's neck.

"Watch it back there! This is a high-class cab."

Sallie fought her way to her side of the cab and grabbed the door handle. "Let me out of here!"

"Julius!" shouted Taylor.

All four doors locked with an audible "thump."

"You get out at the airport, Mrs. Beck."

"You have no right doing this to me."

"I do. I will."

"What about my things at the hotel?"

"Julius will see that they're put on the next flight."

Sallie glared at Taylor. "You've got this all figured out, haven't you?"

Taylor didn't answer. He was staring out his side of the cab.

"If you're so smart, why isn't The Hawk in jail? That's D-Wars' job, isn't it? Putting drug smugglers in jail?"

Taylor didn't answer.

"Well?"

"I'm working on it. I'm working on it."

"You're working on it! Well, buster, I wasn't just working on it. I was doing something, and if you hadn't stopped me, I would've shot him dead."

Julius moved the cab around a car and glanced at Taylor in the rearview mirror. "This lady got close enough to ice The Hawk?"

"You're damn right!"

Julius slipped up on a car by using the breakdown lane. Road litter rattled and clattered against the side of the taxi as they blew by.

Again Sallie grabbed the seat. "Good God, Julius! Do you always drive like this? You make me wish they *had* caught us."

The cab slowed at a sign directing them to the airport, then turned up a ramp and remained at that speed once they were on a palm-lined parkway.

"That's better," said Sallie, sitting back and patting down her dress. She brushed back her hair and picked up her pocketbook, placing it in her lap.

"I say again, Wes, did she get close enough to ice The Hawk?"

Taylor gave a quick nod.

In the mirror the cabbie's eyes flickered over Sallie. "That's pretty good, lady. Nobody usually gets that close."

"It was a public place," explained Taylor. "There

wasn't anything The Hawk could do without having his men hanging all over him. And that's just what he doesn't want. He only had Fuentes and Payne with him. I didn't see Spano. Come to think of it, I haven't seen Spano *or* Richey in the last few weeks." He returned to staring out his side of the car. "Damn tight-lipped organization!"

"There wouldn't be any organization if you'd let me kill him."

"This is no job for cowboys. I'm after bigger game than The Hawk."

"Bigger game? For that you'd have to go to Colombia."

Taylor glanced at the woman, and then went back to staring out the window.

"Ten minutes to the airport."

"I'm not going to the airport, Julius. I'm not finished here."

Now Taylor faced her. "Mrs. Beck, you're going home if I have to put you on that plane myself. Having you in Miami jeopardizes my whole investigation."

From the front of the cab, the driver snickered.

"Put a cork in it, Julius. Mrs. Beck, if you return to Miami, I'll have the police arrest you. You return to Miami and *I'll* arrest you."

"Just whose side are you on anyway? His or mine?"

"I'm on the side of the taxpayer. D-Wars wants The Hawk *and* his organization."

Sallie gestured over her shoulder. "He was right there. All you had to do was reach out and grab him."

When Taylor said nothing, Julius spoke up, "It's not that easy, Mrs. Beck."

"Yes, it is." Sallie met the black man's eyes in the rearview mirror. "Ask Taylor. I was on stage with him."

Taylor only shook his head.

Sallie looked from the cabbie to Taylor and back at Julius again. "What's bothering you? That I did it? That I'm an amateur? What is it?"

The cabbie checked the parkway, then Sallie through the mirror. "Listen, Mrs. Beck, as a way to eliminate The Hawk, yours was as good as any, but as to wiping out the organization, it left a lot to be desired. You can't cut off the head and expect the organization to shrivel up and die. That's been done in the past. It's what Eliot Ness did to Al Capone, but Capone's organization survived."

Sallie sat back in her seat. "Then how do you get rid of him—I mean, all of them?"

"Tell her how it's done, Wes."

"Oh, you're doing such a good job, Julius, why don't you do it?"

"You'll have to forgive him, Mrs. Beck. Wes is having a bad week, a bad month, a bad career."

"Shut up, Julius."

"Give her a break, Wes. This is the woman whose son was killed by the cocaine trick, right?"

Taylor turned back to his window.

"Yes," Sallie said quietly.

"Then tell her what we're up to. Give her some peace of mind. What can it hurt?"

Taylor continued to stare at the roadside: palm trees, rows of flowers, water shimmering off in the distance. Nothing he could enjoy.

Sallie reached for Taylor's shoulder but saw Julius shake his head. She returned to her side of the car and stared at the dark-haired and dark-complected man in the navy blue suit. Taylor still looked to her like a Mafia hit man.

It was a few minutes, but finally he faced her. "Okay, Mrs. Beck, but I'm still putting you on that plane."

"Why? I want The Hawk, too. In jail or dead. I don't really care. You tell me what to do and I'll do it."

Taylor stared at the woman. Beck was absolutely sincere. She meant every word. She was also a damned fool.

Julius gaped at Sallie. Then he remembered the parkway wasn't a controlled-access highway. He looked ahead, shouted a warning, and jammed on the brakes. Tires screeched. Taylor and Beck flew forward, catching themselves on the front seat.

"What the hell!" Taylor saw the red light and the cars stacked up ahead of them. "Watch your driving, hot shot." He glanced at Beck. The woman was all right, just shaken.

"You okay, Mrs. Beck?"

Sallie nodded to the black man but continued to tremble as she sank back in her seat.

"Sorry 'bout that. Airport in five minutes."

This time Sallie didn't object, and that wasn't lost on Taylor. Beck might be smart enough to find a way to get to The Hawk but never could've iced him. The woman didn't have the nerve.

"Look, Mrs. Beck, I'm sorry about what happened to your son, but if you really want to help, you'll go home."

Steve Brown

"Then tell me . . . ." Sallie gulped for air. "Tell me that you're doing something about that man, that he's going to jail. My son is dead. I need to know something's being done." She finally regained control of her breathing. "How long have you been trying to catch him?"

"A little over two years."

"What!" Sallie's trembling stopped. "Over two years and you still haven't put him in jail?"

"Mrs. Beck, do you want to hear this or not?"

"I'm listening, aren't I?"

"The reason it takes so long to put someone away is we use the conspiracy law to dismantle the whole organization, not just send the boss to prison, as Julius said. And we do put them away, but it takes time."

"That's obvious." Seeing the look on Taylor's face, she quickly added, "Okay, okay. How does this conspiracy law work?"

Taylor glanced at the driver. "Let's say you and Julius decide to rob a bank but don't have a getaway car, so Julius goes out and steals one. While stealing the car, Julius kills the owner. Whether or not you rob the bank, you can be brought up on charges of conspiracy to commit murder."

"I could?"

Taylor nodded.

"But that hardly seems fair. I didn't do anything, if we didn't rob the bank."

"That's the way RICO works. It was the only way the government could think of to stop organized crime and bring down whole organizations, so the RICO act was passed."

"So, under that law, everyone in the organization is guilty of the least little crime?"

"Yes, and what I need is some higher-up to squeal on the whole group. I had one, but he disappeared in your neck of the woods."

"That's why you were there?"

Taylor nodded.

"Then why not put someone else inside? Like me?"

Julius rolled his eyes. Sallie didn't see this. What she did see was Taylor staring out his window again.

"Don't shut me out, Taylor. I had a husband who did that. Why can't I work for D-Wars? You seem to forget it was my son who was killed. I'm motivated to chance it. I don't have much left with my son gone."

Again he faced her. "But *I'm* not willing to take the chance."

"I'll sign a paper to that effect, if that's what it takes. Something to absolve D-Wars of all responsibility . . . if anything happens to me. I'll have my attorney draw it up. Better yet, your attorney. You could train me to be a smuggler. Teach me what I need to know to work undercover."

"Mrs. Beck, you've been watching too much television."

"I can do it! I want to do it."

"No, you can't and I can name several reasons why not."

"Name them!"

Taylor used his fingers to tick them off. "First, The Hawk won't let you work for him unless you pass a polygraph test. He'd learn you're working for us and have you killed. Second, you're an amateur, and even though you're pretty sharp, the drug world is a jungle. Killing someone they're only suspicious of is nothing to them. That's why it's so hard to penetrate an organization. And third, you're a woman."

"What are you saying," asked Sallie with a chuckle, "that The Hawk is a chauvinist?"

"The whole drug scene is. In the drug business all women are whores. You go to work for him, Mrs. Beck, and you go to work on your back. I don't think you'd like that."

"And they're into girls," Julius added from the front. "Pardon me for saying, Mrs. Beck, but you're a little old for . . . ."

"Is there anything else?" asked Sallie, ice hanging from every word.

"Yes," Taylor said, "as a matter of a fact there is. You're too independent. I don't think you'd follow my orders or The Hawk's. In my case that's easy to remedy: I won't hire you. But if you don't do what The Hawk says, he'd have you taken out and killed."

"I'd do anything you told me if it meant that man would go to prison."

"Would you? Think about it. Didn't your friend, Phil Rainey, tell you to stay out of this?"

Sallie was taken aback. "Phil talked to you?"

"I talked to him. About you."

Sallie stared into her lap. When she looked up she saw Julius watching her through the mirror. There was sadness on the black man's face, the first sign of compassion she'd seen since beginning her quest.

"So I could do it if I were a man. Right?"

The cabbie nodded from the front. "I'd take a chance on you, Mrs. Beck. You showed me something trying to waste The Hawk in front of that crowd."

Taylor shook his head and looked out the window again. A sign said the airport was up ahead.

"Nothing personal, Mrs. Beck, you being a woman and all that. Man like The Hawk would take a woman like you to bed to see how good you were. If you didn't measure up, you'd be gone. Most likely dead. If you were what he liked, you'd never get out of bed until he was finished with you. When he was tired of you, he'd hand you over to his men, and after they were through, they'd kill you."

Julius saw the look of disbelief on the woman's face. "What I'm saying, Mrs. Beck, is I've never found any of The Hawk's ex-girlfriends, and it's not for lack of trying. And The Hawk wouldn't let anyone wander around his operation. That wouldn't be good security, and believe me, he's got security out the ass, if you'll pardon my French. Forget about this, Mrs. Beck. Go home and make a new life for yourself. Let the men work in this sewer. It's not something ladies should do."

"There are no ladies in the drug trade," Taylor said.

Sallie looked at him. "Well then, what are you men doing about him?"

"That's our business."

"Good God, but you are in trouble, aren't you?"

Taylor returned to staring out the window. Beck was his wife all over again, trying to tell him how to run his business. Run his life.

"Is your name 'Wes' or is it 'Wesley'?"

"It's Wesley," Taylor said, facing her. "Want my badge number or something?"

Sallie only smiled.

Taylor studied the chunky woman and remembered all the computers she had sat behind to gain that extra weight. "I get it. You're going to use your computers at IINTELL to see if you can find a point of leverage. My explaining the facts of life to you wasn't enough to make you leave well enough alone."

"Got a middle initial?"

Taylor looked out the window again.

From the front of the cab, Julius laughed. "It's 'L,' like in Lawrence. Pure white bread despite the tan."

Taylor's head snapped around. "Oh, shut up, Julius! Why aren't we at the airport yet?"

"The lady asked me to slow down."

"You're slowing down your career, too."

"No more than The Hawk."

Taylor turned to Sallie. "You used your computers to find The Hawk, didn't you?"

"Wrong. I used *your* computer."

Julius chuckled as he wheeled into the airport. Taylor also smiled. The woman would be more attractive if she'd lose those extra pounds and tone down her attitude. But career women were like that. Pushing and shoving their way through life—without a man. Or a real one. Well, Ms. Independent Sallie Beck had finally run into something she couldn't do because she *was* a woman. Maybe it'd take her down a peg or two. She could definitely use it.

He said, "I hardly think you accessed our files."

"Who cares what you think." It was Sallie's turn to stare out the window. A wasted trip, that's what this had become, screwed up by this jerk beside her. Why hadn't she considered someone coming out of the crowd? Why hadn't she thought of that?

Sallie sighed. There were so many variables to be considered . . . but if she had to bring The Hawk in to stand trial, so be it. Someone was going to pay for Timmie's death, and if the police weren't going to make it happen and the government couldn't, she would. By whatever rules she was made to play by.

Offhandedly, she said, "I'll send down your personnel file."

"What you're suggesting is against the law, Mrs. Beck."

Sallie whirled around, nostrils flaring. "Letting people kill children is illegal, too, and if you think I'm going to let you forget it, you're dead wrong."

Seven

The men had finished with the girl by the time Carlos walked out of the warehouse to stretch his legs. Carlos was under doctor's orders to get up and move around every hour on the hour whether he wanted to or not. Walk to the end of the room, the other side of the building, just get up and move.

Mother Mary and Joseph! Not yet forty and already falling apart. His doctor said human beings were built for moving around, not being stuck behind a desk all day counting money. The Miami warehouse was just that: filled with money waiting to be counted. Now the last truck had left, and the security detail was bored and restless and taunting a girl they would plainly have to kill, after what they had done to her. Besides having scratches on her arms and face, the young woman dribbled blood from between her legs.

"What's going on here?" demanded Carlos.

The head of the security detail faced Carlos. All three

members of the security detail wore light blue T-shirts, blue jeans, and running shoes, and had stubby-nosed pistols strapped to their belts along with walkie-talkies. All illuminated by floodlights.

"Just breaking the monotony," said the senior man, tucking in his shirt.

Carlos looked at the thin, black-haired girl. Spread legs, skirt hiked over her knees, and wearing no panties, she sat in the middle of the loading dock with her hair in her face. She held her crotch, rocked back and forth, and moaned.

"You've been having your way with this girl."

"Shit!" said a red-headed member of the security detail. "It weren't that much fun. She were screaming most of the time." Red gestured at a younger man. "Turned old Danny off, she did. The boy couldn't even get it up."

The face of the third member of the security detail reddened. He stared at the concrete surface of the dock.

"But she won't be no bother. We'll toss her down the hole."

What were these idiots thinking? That hole was only used for disciplinary purposes. He scanned the empty parking lot. Everyone in the adjoining warehouses had left hours ago. As he stood there, surveying the area, he noticed that the area illuminated by floodlights didn't seem to offer much protection. What did it matter if security patrols moved through the darkness on the other side of those powerful lights? How many of those men had heard the girl's screams and would insist on their turn with her. If she hadn't drawn the attention of anyone so far, her screams certainly would when the remainder of the security detail demanded their turn. "Take her away. I don't want her here."

"Take her yourself," said the senior man, heading toward the warehouse. "I just came outside for a smoke."

"Yeah," said Red. "It ain't our fault she picked our place to camp out. There's plenty of room under the interstate."

At the door the senior man faced Carlos. "We're tired of doing all the work while you sit on your ass and never get your hands dirty." He glanced at the girl. "Now's as good a time as any to get started."

The other members of the security detail grinned, then followed their boss through the door, sliding it shut behind them. As an additional act of defiance, the leader of the three-man detail locked the door so Carlos would have to ring for admittance.

Carlos wanted to tell these cretins it wasn't his job to move the occasional drifter along, but whenever Spano wasn't around, security always became lax. Carlos returned his attention to the girl. She still sat there, moaning, hands between her legs, blood oozing from her privates.

"You must leave here at once. And you had best not return," he said to the girl, putting some force into his voice, as if it mattered. Another patrol would catch her and have their way with her. Was that the way to secure a building containing so much money? Carlos didn't think so.

The teenager brushed back her hair, revealing a

rather attractive face, in spite of all the scratches and bruises. She nodded, got to all fours, and then used the side of the building to help herself stand. On trembling legs, she staggered across the dock. At the edge of the concrete pad, she teetered.

"The steps are to your left," said Carlos.

The girl nodded and staggered in their direction. The steps were of little help. With no railing, when her legs gave way, she fell down the steps, the only sound being that of flesh slapping concrete.

✳   ✳   ✳

"Fed Ex for you," said Liliana Alvarez over the intercom on Wes Taylor's desk. "Want me to bring it in?"

"Who's it from?" asked Taylor.

"Whoever mailed this thing did it in the rain. Can't read the sender's address, but the bomb people assure me it's no bomb."

"Bring it in. Probably more paperwork from Washington."

The young man on the other side of the desk snorted and pushed his thick horn-rimmed glasses up on his pimply face. "More paperwork won't put The Hawk away. What we need is someone to tie all that paperwork together." After sounding off about the package, he picked at one of the eruptions on his face.

"We still have to be prepared, Mark. That gives us leverage. A snitch won't know what we know and what we're guessing at."

The Chicana limped into the room and handed the

Fed Ex to her boss. Taylor's office was on the upper level of a building that had been confiscated by the DEA and assigned to D-Wars. Taylor's desk and chair were from the downsizing of the army. A metal hat rack purchased from K-Mart held jackets and baseball caps. The hat rack and a file cabinet, found in storage downstairs, were both within reach of Taylor's desk in the small room.

Surrounding the building, in any direction, lay a half mile of concrete, dirt fields, and railroad tracks. The parking lot was always empty; the fields had nothing in them, not even weeds, and the railroad tracks led nowhere. In an adjoining room, a wall of monitors was fed from cameras sweeping the area twenty-four hours a day. The screens were monitored, in eight-hour shifts, by three master sergeants who wanted to put in their thirty and retire with full pension and commissary privileges.

Inside the building, the air was crisp and cool, not for the comfort of those working inside but for the pimply-faced youth's machinery. His computers were fed from dishes mounted on top of the building and hidden by a retaining wall, which not only concealed the dishes but protected a heavy-duty air conditioner. Because of the temperature, Wes Taylor's secretary wore a lightweight sweater to ward off the chill.

Liliana Alvarez was forty-two, childless, and husbandless, and walked with a limp from the time a bomb exploded in a regional office of the DEA. Pensioned off and practically told to get lost, Liliana was a reminder of a day when the DEA's security had broken down. Liliana didn't care to return to government work—that is, not until the director of D-Wars called. Frazier said all her experience and multilingual talents shouldn't go to waste.

"More coffee?" Liliana asked with a smile.

Taylor ripped open the envelope. "No, thank you."

"Mark?"

"Not now, but since you make the best cup of coffee in the building, I'll take one along when I go downstairs."

Liliana nodded and dragged her leg out of the room, closing the door behind her.

Taylor slid a stack of papers out of the envelope and leafed through them. "Damn!"

"More bad news?" Mark uttered a nervous laugh. "I don't think I can stand much more."

Taylor clenched the paperwork, crushing it in his hand. "Mark, do you remember me telling you . . . ." Taylor stopped. "Is there any way anyone could break into our computer?"

The young man shrugged. "Officially or unofficially?"

"I think your question answers mine."

"Wes, there's not a system in the world that can't be accessed. But to access ours, the hacker would have to be top-notch and have the right equipment, not to mention the time to break in."

Taylor tossed the papers across the desk where they slid off the edge, landing in the young man's hands. "Meet a top-notch hacker. Do you remember me telling you to change the access codes after Sallie Beck tried to kill The Hawk?"

"Wes, you don't think—"

"Read it!"

In a moment, a low "goddamn" was uttered, followed by a louder "shit." Taylor was leaning back in his chair and tapping out a rhythm on the armrest when Mark asked, "Is this true about your ex not allowing you to see your kids and the judge going along with it?"

"Yes," Wes said bitterly, his fingers thumping away.

"I didn't know they could keep a father from seeing his own kids. I mean, for keeps."

"They can if the wife reminds the judge it was the husband's job that caused some scumbag to kidnap their son and drop him across town without any way home."

"Er—this one of the guys found on the beach in San Diego?"

"One of his associates." Taylor's fingers stopped thumping. He sat up. "Mark, you lied to me. You didn't change the codes."

"Look, Wes—"

"Next time I find out you haven't done what I've told you, you're out of here. Understand?"

The young man straightened up. "I understand."

"You didn't think she was that good, did you?"

"No." The young man picked at one of his pimples. "I didn't."

"So there was no reason to go to all the trouble of changing the codes." Taylor pointed at the papers in Mark's hands. "Not only did Beck break in, but she accessed the personnel files. They're supposed to be ultra-confidential. I don't like you reading my file. I don't think the director would either. Maybe she's accessed Frazier's file and it's on the way to *him.*"

The young man gulped. "She won't get in again. You can count on that, Wes."

"Guaranteed?"

Mark nodded rapidly. "I have this special code I worked out. It's never been used. I was just waiting for the right opportunity—"

"But you just told me any system could be accessed with the right amount of equipment and time."

"It's one thing to slip in when I don't know you're coming, quite another when I do."

"Uh-huh. Well, put it in writing. Her name is Beck. Sallie Beck."

Mark glanced at the file. "I don't think the paperwork's necessary."

"That's not how we're going to play it." Taylor leaned forward. "Mark, you're supposed to be one of the best, just like Julius behind the wheel of any car. That's why you were chosen, and Frazier let me pick my own people so I wouldn't have any bitch. In an operation like this, you don't get many chances to nail someone as big as The Hawk. I expect my people to be on their toes and ready for that opportunity, when and if it comes along."

Mark placed the file on the desk. "Then I'll put it in writing. Beck's not getting in again and you can take that to the bank."

*   *   *

Phil Rainey leaned against the doorway of the indoor firing range and stared at the woman behind the yellow line. Sallie Beck was hunched over, aiming at a silhouette twenty-five feet downrange. The owner stood alongside Rainey, an unlit cigar between his teeth, staring at Sallie as she squeezed off a couple more rounds. He pulled the cigar out of his mouth.

"We get more and more of them in here every day. They don't think you people are doing your job."

Rainey turned on the owner and the shorter man raised his hands. "Hey, no offense. I'm telling you what they say." He chuckled as he walked in the direction of the sales area at the front of the building. "But Beck won't kill anyone. That broad can't hit the broad side of a barn."

"I thought she was in here every night?"

The owner turned around and pulled the cigar out of his mouth. "Yeah, she's here. Fires off a full box of fifty just as religious as Jesus." He jabbed the cigar in the woman's direction. "But she can't hit shit. Beck insists on using a Magnum. Hell, she's not strong enough to hold up the thing without using both hands and she can't hit the target after the first round's fired. Her hands are shaking too much. She should use a Lady's Smith & Wesson instead of that cannon, but you know how these liberated broads are. They won't listen to anyone, especially a man."

Sallie fired off her last round and started reloading from a small, cardboard box on a table behind the firing line. Rainey walked over, a slight ringing in his ears.

"Improving any?"

Sallie glanced at the target. The only holes were in the white, not the black, and there were only a few of them. Thirty or forty shells lay at her feet. She shook her head, took out an earplug, and adjusted it.

"Then why not use the Smith & Wesson?"

Sallie shot a look in the direction of the sales area. She glanced at the policeman before completing her reloading.

"He's nothing to worry about, Sallie. You want something to worry about? I got a call from Wes Taylor, the D-Wars agent in Miami."

Sallie faced the target and raised her hands. "Leave me alone. I have work to do."

Rainey walked around the loading table and planted himself between her and the target. Now he stood in the sand making up the firing range's floor—with the barrel of Sallie's weapon pointed squarely at his chest.

"Now if I hadn't gotten that call, would I have picked up on your choice of words? That you have 'work to do'? Or would I have thought with all the hours you're putting in at IINTELL, and at this firing range, you'd found a way to stay busy since your son's death? A rather compulsive way, but it does fill the void."

Sallie lowered the pistol and stepped into the sand. "You've been spying on me."

"After hearing about that fool stunt you pulled in Miami—what did you think you were doing?"

"Trying to cut off the drug supply that killed my son. You people couldn't, so—"

"You could've been killed!"

"I would've killed The Hawk if Taylor hadn't intervened."

Rainey stepped toward her. "You little fool, he saved your life. If you'd gunned down The Hawk, his men would've killed you."

Sallie shook her head. "It doesn't matter."

The detective gaped at her. "Because Timmie's dead?"

She nodded, staring at the sand floor, pistol limp at her side.

"D-Wars should've put you away for rifling through their files. We should've put you away. You need help."

Sallie's head came up. "I know how to use the information in your computers, even if you won't."

"You hack into their computer again and they'll put you away for a long time."

"Sorry, Phil, but I'm preparing my own private war against The Hawk and I need all the information I can get."

Rainey stared at his former neighbor, squinting at her as if looking into the sun. "You're serious?"

Sallie nodded and her finger slipped inside the trigger guard. She never noticed.

"You could foul up whatever Taylor has going for him."

"Taylor doesn't have anything. He told me as much when I was there. His only contact was killed weeks ago. Up here. You know about that."

The detective opened his mouth to say something. Instead he shut it and stomped off downrange. Moments later, he returned. "Now you listen to me. You have no idea what Taylor has to go through to put a collar on The Hawk. He can have the best agents, get all the breaks—which never happens—and if he does get lucky and some snitch squeals, Taylor doesn't know if the DA will prosecute."

"He'd have to!" Her finger brushed the trigger.

"Contrary to what you think, no DA has to prosecute any case he doesn't want to prosecute. District attorneys prosecute cases they think they can win so they'll be reelected. A case Taylor puts together against The Hawk might be too complicated for a jury to understand. You have no idea the paperwork involved in pinning a conspiracy rap on someone. That's one hell of an organization he's trying to bring down. There'll be mountains of telephone records, ledgers, and correspondence, enough to choke a horse, not to mention confusing the average citizen on any jury. What good old Joe Citizen wants the DA to say is 'this is what we caught them doing and this is what we caught them with.' Show and tell, just like in kindergarten."

Sallie got in his face. "And you listen to me, Phil Rainey! I've told you I'm not messing up anything. Taylor's investigation is going nowhere!"

"Uh-huh, and Sallie Beck's just the one to save the world from The Hawk."

"I can try, dammit, I can try! If you'll get out of my way!"

The pistol discharged and the bullet slammed into the sand floor. Jumping back, Sallie dropped the weapon.

Rainey went into a half crouch, gun in his hand. He saw the Magnum lying in the sand. "Goddammit, Sallie, you could've shot one of us." Rainey stood up, holstering his pistol and bringing hers with him.

Sallie's hand was at her mouth. "I'm—I'm sorry."

The owner of the firing range stuck his head through the door. "Everybody okay back here?"

"Everything's fine," said Rainey, turning over Sallie's pistol in his hand. "Mrs. Beck was just showing me how to fire her pistol."

"Yeah," said the short man, "she's one hell of a shot. Use whatever she can teach you, Phil."

After the owner returned to the sales area, Rainey asked, "Sallie, what's gotten into you? You're learning to fire this weapon with every intention of killing someone. Not to mention using language you'd never let Alstair use around Timmie."

Sallie hung her head. "They . . . they killed my son."

"And you think you can even things up?"

She looked at him. "I—I can try."

Rainey shook his head. "Not only is Timmie gone, but those boys will have to see a shrink the rest of their lives. The guilt, the scar, runs that deep. How'll you set that right?"

Sallie slapped her hands to her ears. "I don't want to hear about those boys! You said put all that behind me and move on with my life. Well, I'm moving on."

Rainey waited until Sallie removed her hands from her ears. "You call killing someone in cold blood moving on?"

"Whatever it takes." Sallie set her jaw.

"Sweet Jesus, Sallie, you need a shrink as much as those boys do."

"They tell me to move on. Everyone tells me to move on and forget that my son's dead. Forget that nobody can do anything about it. That nobody *will* do anything about it! I won't! Now it's my turn!"

Rainey didn't know what else to say. As he stood

looking at her, he realized Sallie's black hair was longer, no longer gray, and she'd lost the extra weight. If he didn't know better, he'd think she'd adjusted to life without her son and was getting on with her life. Perhaps even thinking of having another child before her biological clock ran out.

Rainey whirled around so fast Sallie flinched. The policeman bent his knees, bracing his right hand with his left, and fired two shots, one right after the other.

Sallie opened her eyes and peered downrange. Both bullets had hit the target. In the chest.

Rainey turned, ears ringing, weapon in hand. "That's how good you have to be to kill someone and you can't even hit the damn target. You probably think The Hawk will stand still while you're shooting him." The detective opened the cylinder. "Damn. You didn't leave an empty chamber for the hammer to rest on." He shook his head. "That's why the gun went off." He emptied the remaining rounds onto the sand.

"I'll learn," Sallie said firmly.

"And where'll you learn how to kill someone? I've been on the force over sixteen years and I've never taken my gun out of its holster. I don't know if I could kill someone. What makes you so sure you can?"

"They killed my son!"

Rainey shook his head. "You'd better think about what you're getting into. The Hawk's surrounded by men who kill for a living. Stone killers, they're called. You've never met anyone like them, and they can't show that kind of perversion on television. The Hawk's men will be raping you repeatedly, and you'll be wondering how they can continue to get it up, if you can even think at that point. The reason is because the last time they stick something inside you, it'll be a gun barrel." Rainey turned and threw the Magnum downrange, where it ripped through the silhouette target.

Rainey didn't see the gun hit the target. He was already stalking out of the firing range, through the sales area, heading for the front door.

Sallie looked from the target to Rainey and back to the target again. That was the second pistol thrown away by some man. Dammit! They can't help me, but they don't want me to help myself.

She nodded to herself as she walked downrange to fetch the pistol. The taxi driver—what was his name? Julius, yes, Julius. He was right. If I were a man, they wouldn't be making such a fuss.

The owner of the firing range was waiting for her when she returned to the loading table. "If it's all right with you, Mrs. Beck, I'd like to close early, and you have to fly in the morning, don't you?"

Sallie stared at the man. "Yes, I do."

"You sure keep a busy calendar." He chuckled. "I guess it makes it hard for men to keep up with you."

Sallie dropped the pistol, her earplugs, and the small cardboard box of ammo into her bag. "I haven't seen many trying."

As she headed for the door, the owner of the firing range pulled another cigar from his pocket and ran it under his nose. "Maybe you're running too fast for them to catch you."

Eight

0652X0908
TOP SECRET
FR: AGENT LILIANA ALVAREZ
TO: DIRECTOR FRAZIER
SUBJECT: RICHEY MILLER

To be honest, we don't know if this person even exists, aside from the fact we have photos of him: always with a ponytail, granny sunglasses, T-shirt, jeans with sandals or high-top tennis shoes, and a jacket from time to time. (See accompanying photos.) We have pictures, we have prints, and we have his voice on tape, but there is no record of a Richey Miller having been born or currently being alive, as the man shown in the photographs. Miller owns no credit cards, no memberships in any clubs, any property or real estate. He has no record or outstanding warrants in the NCIC. He appears to be approximately thirty years of age, a white male with a thin frame.

We suspect the mysterious Mr. Miller was born in California and became a beach bum at an early age; hence the lack of a social security number, fingerprints, or registration for the Selective Service. When picked up for speeding, however, Miller can produce any number of licenses for any state in which he resides. And a permanent address.

Sometime in the past he left the West Coast and drifted east, then down to Florida where he met Allen Nelson. Today, he is an important member of Nelson's organizational staff, used as an expediter. Whenever anything needs to be done, outside of security and planning, Miller does the job. He wasn't at the dedication of the new community center, but Miller contacted the church and handled the details, down to the choice of food and drink.

If Nelson needs a new car, Mr. Miller picks it out and has it delivered, and whenever furniture or electronic equipment is delivered to Allen Nelson's compound, Miller is always there. Security may inspect deliveries for listening devices or explosives, but Miller is there with his clip-

board, going over each item, making sure nothing is damaged or missing. It is rumored Miller is the point man for Allen Nelson's drug operation. If so, Mr. Miller is a very smooth operator. We can find no record of him leaving or reentering this country, and efforts by the Colombian authorities to establish that a person matching Miller's description entered their country turned up nothing.

Our information is based on bits and pieces of conversations overheard by listening devices when Miller was outside the compound, eating, dating, or shopping. His female companions seem to know little about their date, as Miller appears to take perverse pleasure in lying to women about his current occupation. To one he is a record promoter, to another an advertising executive, and to some, a spy for the Central Intelligence Agency.

Like Nelson and Spano, not once has Miller offered anyone drugs or been seen using them. Unlike the other two men, he seems to have no fear of traveling alone and has killed several people who tried to kidnap him or steal his sports car. (See the Taylor memo: Jamaicans blow snatch of Richey Miller.)

Surveillance will continue.

*   *   *

"How long before I get out of here?"

Ned Clanton sat on the edge of the bed, shackled, but wearing new clothes and new cowboy boots—new shackles, too. The two of them had been together a week, having followed an overland route from California to Florida, and Ned was sick and tired of wearing these damn shackles, sick and tired of lying on this damn bed, and sick and tired of being with this man with the pale blue eyes.

The killer, who had never given Ned his name, looked up from his work at the table in the adjoining room. An avid fly fisherman, he was making a new lure. He had tried to interest Ned in the sport, but Ned was too anxious to get out of this cabin to give a shit about fishing.

"Like I said, Ned, that's up to you."

Clanton came off the bed, dragging his chains with him. Sure, he'd been unshackled to bathe every other day, but at those times the killer held a pistol on him, and there was little doubt, from what Ned had seen in the bus, that if he dared make a move the asshole would use that gun. Fucking embarrassing to have to strip in front of another man with a pistol pointed at you. Made the ole weenie frizzle.

"I'm sick and tired of your fucking riddles."

"And I'm sick and tired of your being so dense."

The killer returned to his lure in a miniature vise mounted on the edge of the table. He was referring to what he called the Hundred Thousand Dollar Question.

Woman Against Herself

Ned had no idea what the answer to the Hundred Thousand Dollar Question was or where this guy came up with all the vehicles they used. First there had been the police car, ditched for the bus Ned had been riding in; then a truck, later dumped for the Lincoln Town Car, which had been stored in the truck and was now parked outside this frigging cabin located somewhere in the Florida Everglades.

The killer told Ned he'd be dropped off at a jai alai court where he could mingle and get lost, but only after answering the Hundred Thousand Dollar Question.

"So we're in Florida. Why?"

That time, too, the man had been working on a lure, and on the other side of a tackle box lay an automatic pistol. Ned had been at the table, too, shackled, and listening to some new CDs. Ned loved country music, and the sound seemed to bother the killer, making Ned love it even more. The killer allowed him anything he wanted. All he had to do was ask, and suffer through being shackled to a monstrous outboard motor in the sweltering heat of a shed behind the cabin while the killer rode into town in his fucking air-conditioned Lincoln Town Car. A couple of waits in that shed convinced Ned that he didn't need much from town. Wherever the hell town was. Both times the killer left, Ned worried that the son of a bitch might be in an accident and leave Ned at the end of this road, somewhere in the middle of the fucking Everglades. So Ned stopped asking for stuff from town and the killer stopped going. Hell, all the asshole wanted to do was work on his fucking lures.

The first time Ned asked the Hundred Thousand Dollar Question, the killer returned the favor, without looking up from his work. "Why do you think?"

"Why'm I here? Why'd you go to all the trouble of busting me out? Not that I mind being out, but I don't have a clue what's going on."

The killer glanced at him. "It costs a great deal of money to hire me. You're important to someone."

"Aren't you going to tell me who I'm important to?"

"I never met those people. It was all handled through a post office box. You have to figure it out or they'll think you're too stupid to do the job."

"Job? What job? I'm sick and tired of all these fucking riddles."

The killer put down his equipment and leaned back against the wooden chair. "And I'm sick and tired of being stuck here with someone who can't complete a sentence without being vulgar. But you don't see me whining."

Clanton got to his feet. "If I didn't have these damn chains on . . . ."

"If it were me, I'd spend more time trying to figure out why someone would pay a hundred grand to have me busted out of prison and delivered to Florida, instead of doing so much fussing and cussing."

"A hundred grand to bust me out . . . ?"

"And transport you to this side of the country, then turn you loose with ten thousand dollars."

"Ten thousand dollars!" Ned had to sit down. "You're going to give me ten thousand dollars . . . ?" All this was happening too fast. What the hell was going on?

The killer returned to his lure. "It's in a false bottom of my ditty bag."

"Can I see it?"

Without looking at him, the man asked, "Don't you have any patience?"

"What for?"

The fisherman pulled the thread through the lure. He was working on a steelhead lure, and it wasn't for Florida but for use elsewhere. The lure wasn't to tempt the fish but startle them. That would make the steelhead strike, and the killer would catch a mess of them.

"Why *you* think I'm here?"

"Like anyone else: to do a job."

"What's the job? You haven't told me."

"I don't have to tell you if you're the man they think you are."

"Now what the fuck's that supposed to mean?"

The killer put down the small pliers used to draw the thread through the lure. "Ned, why don't you go back to your room and try to figure why you'd be important to anyone. A hundred grand is a lot of money to bust some marijuana dealer out of prison. And three men dead. Did you ever think of that? Do you ever think at all?"

Ned clenched his fists. He was so pissed . . . .

The fly fisherman watched those hands. He didn't want to kill this fool, but he would. Actually, he found it fascinating to figure out how someone as infantile as Ned Clanton could be of use to anyone. But he'd never know the answer. He'd be fishing in Montana when Clanton was doing his business, whatever that was.

"Ned, you can't think if you're angry."

"I have the right to know—"

"People don't care about you. They're only interested in what you can do for them."

"But what do they want of me?"

"That's the Hundred Thousand Dollar Question: What could you possibly do for anyone? Don't get fanciful. It has to be something you're capable of accomplishing."

Ned held out his hands in a gesture of helplessness and the motion rattled the chains. "I have no idea."

"Then, like I said, get back in there and figure it out. I can't tell you because I don't know myself, but I am allowed to kill you if you get on my nerves."

"Kill me? Then you won't get your money."

"I already got the money."

"In advance?"

"In advance."

"I don't believe it."

"Believe it."

Ned shook his head. "I'll bet they gave you half. You get the other half if I do the job."

"I get the other half after turning you loose."

"After I'm gone?"

"After you're gone."

"Then how will you know whether I did whatever I'm supposed to do?"

"I'm not supposed to know what you're doing."

"I'm supposed to kill somebody?"

"You tell me."

"Me tell you! I don't even know what the fuck's going on."

"Could you cut down on the profanity? It's becoming rather tiresome."

"Fuck you! I don't give a shit what you think."

The fisherman got to his feet and took a pistol from the tackle box. It was a Glock nine millimeter and could fire rounds fast enough to empty the clip before its victim hit the floor.

The killer motioned at the door with the Glock. "Get out there."

"Outside? Why?"

"Because I'm going to kill you, Ned. I've decided you're not worth another fifty grand."

"You're bluffing."

The killer took the safety off. "So the bet is: I can't kill you and convince those who hired me to take care of the business they busted you out of prison for. Is that a bet you want to make: that I can't replace a fool like you?"

Ned's hands came up. "No, no, I believe you."

The killer clicked on the safety and gestured with the pistol again, toward the door leading to Ned's bedroom.

Ned nodded, but at the doorway of the bedroom he stopped. "There's one thing I don't understand."

"I'm sure there is," said the fisherman, removing the safety on the pistol once again.

"If these people want someone killed, why didn't they hire you? Why go to all the trouble of busting me out of prison?"

"That's the Hundred Thousand Dollar Question, Ned."

So Ned returned to the bedroom, lay down, and tried to figure out what he could do that would be worth a hundred grand, plus the ten thousand dollars in the false bottom of a ditty bag. Plus two dead guards in California. And a nigger. Once he cleared his mind of all hostility—actually Ned dozed off—it didn't take long for a name to come to mind, which, at this point, surprised even the fisherman.

Ned sat up and swung his legs over the side of the bed, bringing his chains with him. "Taylor. Wes Taylor. Taylor's fucking with your organization."

"I'm not part of any organization," said the man in the other room.

Ned sat there, thinking. Well, it couldn't be the Mafia. They could take care of their own. There had to be another group Taylor was hassling. But who? The Gold Rings Gang had enough firepower to eliminate anyone who crossed them; the Cripes would shoot first and think later; and Big Dan had overdosed—by accident, people said—not been poisoned like the rumors said. Poisoned by some skirt. Shit! Ned could relate to that.

"But why bring me all the way to Florida?"

The man in the other room said nothing.

"I don't know anybody in Florida."

Still no sound from the other room.

"Taylor's in Florida?"

"I don't know who you're talking about." The killer had been told to ask Ned a question if he ever said the correct word. The killer thought his instructions had to do with tailoring, though what the dope in the other room could do with a needle and thread was beyond him. "Tailor" could be "Taylor."

"How you like your hot dogs, Ned?"

"Why, I like them with chili."

That got only a blank stare from the killer.

He was returning to his lure when Ned blurted out, "I like them with mustard!"

The fisherman laid down his pliers and started putting away his gear. "We leave for Miami tonight."

＊　　＊　　＊

A doctor in a white jacket, a stethoscope around his neck, stepped out of the emergency room. He called to a policeman talking with a nurse who sat behind the admitting counter. When the uniformed patrolman joined him, the young doctor said, "Someone brought in a girl. She was torn up rather badly."

"Beaten?" asked the policeman as he was ushered into the emergency room.

"Raped."

"And you think the guy who dropped her off was one of the perps?"

The doctor shook his head. "He didn't have the look."

"What was his story?"

"That he almost ran into the girl when she stumbled into the street."

The teenager lay on a table behind a curtained-off area. A nurse was gently swabbing her between the legs.

Outside the curtained-off area, the cop asked, "Where is this guy?"

"Gave his name and address to security, and they let him go after checking his driver's license."

The doctor glanced at the doors of the emergency room as they were knocked open. Through the doors came a stretcher on which lay a man with a bandaged head. The bandage was bloody and an EMS tech called out his vitals to a nurse looking in his direction.

Turning back to the officer, the doctor said, "Guy was a tubby Chicano. My height. Wearing a business suit. Had a bad back."

"Bad back?"

The doctor touched his lower back and smiled. "I know the look."

*   *   *

When the door to the computer center opened, Sallie Beck leaned back from one of the many computers. A man wearing the brown uniform of an IINTELL security guard looked in on her.

"Oh, Mrs. Beck. I didn't know you were still here." He glanced at the clock. "Do you know it's past one?"

"Yes, Clyde, but I'm almost finished."

"Oh, stay as long as you want." The guard paused. "I'm just worried about the hours you've been keeping. This makes four nights in a row and all past midnight."

Sallie felt the upward turn of her mouth. "Thanks for looking in on me." She touched her lips and the smile they made. "I won't be much longer." She pulled down her hand.

Clyde looked around the computer center. The other

machines were quiet, screens dark. "I'll have to admit sometimes it's better to work than go home. It's not the same now that all the kids are gone. I've been trying to convince the missus to sell the house like you did, but she says she can't bring herself to do it. Too many memories running around in that old barn."

Sallie was silent, poised over the machine. From where the guard stood, he couldn't see the screen scrolling in front of her.

"Anything I can get for you? A cup of coffee? Soft drink? I don't think George will miss me. He's watching that double feature of M*A*S*H on Channel Seven."

"I appreciate you asking." Sallie held up a cup of coffee that had gone cold hours ago. "But I have something."

In front of her, the computer stopped at a picture of a long-haired blonde with a smile on her face. Sallie glanced at the screen. She did a double take.

Clyde said he'd see Sallie out to her car when she was ready to leave. When the woman didn't respond, he left the computer center, closing the door behind him. It wasn't the first time Mrs. Beck had faded on him while operating one of those machines, and for the life of him, Clyde couldn't understand what was so fascinating about those screens. Sure, you could call up all sorts of information, but the one or two times he'd stood behind the ladies who operated the machines, it hadn't been long before he ended up with a headache. Just like watching George's little black-and-white TV. He'd rather make rounds than watch that teeny screen.

Inside the computer center, the woman's face on the screen was shoved to the side while lines of information filled the space. Sallie leaned forward reading the material.

Disappeared while working at a Wal-Mart in Southern California. Hot damn! This could be it.

While the computer compiled its information, Sallie pulled a photograph of another blonde from her briefcase. Her action uncovered a summons to appear in court. A note from Sallie's attorney was paper-clipped to the summons. The note encouraged her not to miss this new court date. Sallie held the picture alongside the blonde on the screen.

"Yes! Yes! This is it!"

She looked up to see if anyone had heard her. The computer center was empty and the lights in her office were off. Clyde was gone. She hadn't noticed him leaving. She looked at the screen, then the photograph, comparing one to the other.

They'll never notice the difference unless they dig and dig. And Spano's been known to do that for his master.

You're being silly. If you're worried about that, you might as well forget this whole damn scam.

It was then that Sallie noticed the difference between the two pictures. The blonde on the screen was smiling. In the photograph the blonde was frowning. The one who's missing, and presumed dead, was smiling. Sallie studied the blonde in the photograph.

Why are you so angry? Did your anger make it pos-

sible for you to survive in a business where you had no business?

Sallie touched her lips again. Is that why I don't smile? Does my subconscious know something I can't even suspect? Is it preparing me for my descent into the sewer?

She pulled her fingers away and sat up. Get a hold of yourself. You've planned everything down to the last little detail, readied yourself for every contingency, even for men coming out of the crowd.

The blonde stared at her from the CRT.

I'm sorry you're dead, but I appreciate your showing up. You were the last bit of cover I needed. Now I'm going to get that son of a bitch for Timmie. Yes, baby, Mama's going to take care of that bastard. All the others in the organization are merely icing on the cake. I'm going to get The Hawk just for you.

Nine

"**A**re you serious, Hawk? You're going to over-throw a foreign government and run our operation from there?" The dark-skinned man on the sofa mopped his forehead with a handkerchief. Carlos was a squatty fellow with a ring of fat around the middle. In contrast, the man at the other end of the sofa had the look of a bodybuilder.

"Do you realize how much money that'll cost?" asked Carlos.

The Hawk sat behind his hand-carved desk. It was late, and he had slipped into a silk dressing gown and was drinking brandy from a finely blown glass from the Virgin Islands. The glass brought back memories of three girls in a hot tub, none of whom had been a virgin. The Hawk leaned back in his chair, the one with the extended legs. With the additional height, he lorded it over anyone on the soft cushions of the sofa. Once again, Carlos was concerned with the bottom line.

Woman Against Herself

At one time The Hawk had found all this amusing, but Carlos had become a bore. The money arrived stacked in boxes, packed in suitcases, jammed into coffee cans. He only wished it was as easy to launder, and since it wasn't, the money piled up in the warehouse along the river. All that money made The Hawk consider what a person might accomplish with a river of money. It was time to clean out that warehouse. Time to invest in real estate. In a somewhat different manner: no more shopping malls, high-rises, or syndicates. He was going to buy his own . . . country. Certainly not something the mob was capable of, and they'd play hell trying to harass him once he was established overseas, as would American drug enforcement agencies.

Ironic that his meeting with the Mafia representative—at a Chinese restaurant, of all places—was where the concept had germinated.

Sonny the Hatchet had been sent to move him along. The Hawk knew what sort of images the name was supposed to conjure up, but he would not be intimidated. Sonny recommended meal number six and Hawk ordered number seven without looking at the menu, explaining, with a smile, that seven had always been lucky for him.

The surrounding tables were empty. A couple of heavyset men with five o'clock shadows stood near the door, and the remaining customers had hastily finished their meals. At the register sat a young Chinese girl, and behind her, a TV that The Hawk could see from where he sat.

"Six good years, Mr. Nelson. That's what you've had."

The Mafia representative wore a pin-striped suit, white shirt, and club tie. The Hawk didn't have to look under the table to know Mr. Mafia Representative wore wing tips. All part of the corporate image.

"It's simple business evolution," said the hatchet man with a smile, "the strong driving out the weak. You won't be around to celebrate your lucky year. Matter of fact, you could say that six has just become your new lucky number."

The Hawk said nothing.

Sonny drank from his wine glass. "Like any profitable sector of the economy, sooner or later it goes through a period of consolidation. Retirement will take the day-to-day pressures of running a business off your shoulders."

"I thought it was your people's policy to let a few small fish live in the same pond so the DEA would bust them instead of you. Are you closing down McNally and Garcia?"

"We're closing down everyone."

"Even the Jamaican gangs?"

"Everyone."

"That'll be a trick."

"We've sent people to Jamaica to explain what their loved ones are up against."

"You can't believe you'll control everything."

Sonny shrugged. "There will always be cowboys."

"Are you going to give me the real reason why you're doing this, besides cornering the market?"

The representative considered the question. "With

you, Mr. Nelson, I'll make an exception. My people can control the number of smugglers, but we cannot control the number of government agencies attempting to police the drug trade. Besides Metro Dade, there's the DEA, the FBI, the President's Task Force on Drugs, and now D-Wars reporting to a congressional oversight committee. And every one of those agencies needs headlines."

The Hawk said nothing.

"You're right, we left you and other small fish alone so there would be people for these agencies to bust. We didn't know the government wouldn't respond in kind. Instead of respecting our abilities, they created more agencies to catch fewer smugglers. Not a sound economic policy, but when did Washington ever do anything that made sense? It may take time, but sooner or later South Florida will calm down."

"What if I've become so attached to my business that I don't want to leave?"

"You're a bright fellow, Mr. Nelson. My organization doesn't know of one dumb move you've made since arriving from the Twin Cities."

"Maybe my partners aren't as smart as I am."

"We're perfectly aware of that possibility and willing to tie up any loose ends for you."

Over the Mafia representative's shoulder, on TV, The Hawk could see helicopters and gunships flying into an airport. As the camera drew back, it revealed a middle-aged, slender woman speaking into a microphone. Wind blew the woman's short blond hair around, and the information at the bottom of the screen told the viewers that Casey Blackburn was reporting from Port-au-Prince for CNN.

Without looking at the man across the table, The Hawk asked, "How long did you say I had to wind up my affairs?"

"Thirty days."

"It may take a bit longer than that," said The Hawk, still watching the screen.

The woman pointeu with her hand and the camera followed to show soldiers leaping from helicopters and going about the business of securing the airstrip.

"Thirty days, Mr. Nelson."

Now The Hawk looked at him. "I thought you were sent here to negotiate. If so, negotiate."

"Sixty days and that is my last offer."

The Hawk stood up and reached across the table. He moved so quickly that bodyguards instantly surrounded him. Ignoring them, The Hawk shook the hand stuck reluctantly across the table. "It's a deal."

So it was over. He was finished. There was no other choice but to get out. He would move along like the mob wanted but not as they expected. He would move his business overseas, just as many other American businesses had done.

Carlos opened his mouth to protest, but his boss silenced him with a raised hand. "Enough!" The Hawk liked simple gestures and short sentences when making a point. Something in which all great leaders excelled. "You sound more like a banker every day." Which was true. It was also true The Hawk couldn't find anyone with Carlos's dedication to account for every single damn dollar that came into their hands. Or was owed them. Without robbing them blind.

Carlos had no social life. He had no life but the totals spit out by his electronic counting machines. A wimp in every manner, Carlos defended the organization's money against all comers. Including The Hawk. Sometimes it became rather tiresome, and sometimes The Hawk got the impression Carlos thought all that money belonged to him.

"It'll ruin our bottom line."

"And cut the Colombians out of the pipeline," said the man with the look of a bodybuilder. Spano, The Hawk's security chief, kept his distance on the sofa. He wore a pair of slacks and a pullover. On his feet were a pair of running shoes and holstered on his belt a snub-nose .38. His eyes were dark and his hair receded from his forehead. To compensate, the security chief grew a small, tight mustache under his nose.

"Really?" There was hope in Carlos's eyes.

"Once my overseas base is established," said The Hawk, "what use would we have for middlemen?"

Carlos rubbed his hands together. "That would take a serious bite out of the overhead. What country?"

"Suriname."

"Suriname? Where's that?"

"On the coast of South America, north of Brazil. It's the smallest country on the continent in both area and population. Half the people live in Paramaribo, the capital, the country's largest city and chief port; the other half live in the bush. The Dutch ruled Suriname before the country became independent."

"Never heard of it."

"Ever heard of Dutch Guiana?"

"I think so . . . ."

"Jonestown Massacre?"

"You mean the religious nut who talked all those people into killing themselves?"

"It's one of the Guianas, and its population of less than half a million is roughly divided into two groups: one in the bush, working as near slaves on multinational plantations." The Hawk went on, "They're lorded over by the second group, those in the city, Creoles, people of European and African ancestry and fairly well-educated. That group elects the National Assembly and a president who appoints a council of ministers. That's all ancient history. The military staged a coup. Suriname still has the assembly and president, but the military runs the show."

"What little military there is," contributed Spano.

"But why would you want such a country?"

"Because no one else does. Not even the Dutch. I'm about to give those Surinamese foreign aid beyond their wildest dreams." The Hawk raised a finger from the arm of the elevated chair. "Then, when I have my own country, nobody'll be able to touch me."

"But how can you take over an entire country?"

"With money, a couple of hundred commandos, and a load of bullshit—with the accent on bullshit."

"With the accent on commandos," said Spano.

Carlos and The Hawk looked at the security chief. Spano's shirt barely contained his chest and he didn't think it odd that the other two men stared at him.

"Spano's been training commandos for the last month. It's only natural he would think they were more important than any public relations effort."

"You'll see . . ." Spano said.

"Where did you find these people?" asked Carlos. Although a breeze blew in through the double doors of the patio, it didn't cool Carlos. His handkerchief appeared and he mopped his brow.

"In the Surinamese community."

"There's a Surinamese community in Miami?"

"There's a community of everything in Miami," said The Hawk. "It's the breeding ground for people of every political persuasion. If you loot your country and want to retire, you move to the Riviera. If you fail, you move to Miami and open a public relations campaign to regain control of your country and its treasury."

"Yeah," Spano said, "you give those niggers a gun and tell them they're going back to run their country and they'll kill for the chance."

"Which is just what we want," said The Hawk. "And the few lording it over the many isn't something Surinamese are uncomfortable with. The Dutch told them what to do for centuries, and they loved it. There were riots when the Dutch pulled out."

"But how do you go about something like this?" asked the man mopping his brow.

"Spano's commandos are going to seize Suriname in the name of Lucas Tasman."

"Lucas Tasman?" Carlos stopped mopping his face. "That witch doctor?" he asked. "I've seen him on TV, cutting up chickens and forecasting the future."

The Hawk nodded. "I've had polls commissioned in the Surinamese community in Miami and in Amsterdam. He overwhelms all other rivals. But Tasman isn't only strong overseas. The junta's scared to death of him. It's against the law to talk or write about him. Those who do, tend to disappear."

"That's credentials enough for me," added Spano.

"I don't know," said Carlos, shaking his head. "You're going to spend millions on this project, then turn it over to some madman . . . we could lose our whole investment, not to mention this Tasman tying us to the drug trade."

"Goddamn it, Carlos!" said Spano, sitting up. "There's two cut-outs between us and that damn nigger."

The accountant shook his head. "I didn't mean—"

"I know exactly what you meant!" He looked at The Hawk. "Why does this twerp have to know anything? Why can't he stick to counting money?"

"It's time." The Hawk glanced at the door. "And time Richey was here." He looked at Carlos. "That's why I had you ship all that money to the Caymans."

"All that money . . . ." The accountant gulped. "But there's thirty-two million, five hundred and seventy-six thousand dollars in that account. That money was set aside for buying politicians in South America. You're going to spend it all on Suri—on that country?"

"Suriname. Learn how to pronounce it. That's where you're going to live, up in the mountains where the air is fresh and cool. Servants waiting on you hand and foot, a world-class chef on call twenty-four hours a day, and a private jet waiting to take you anywhere you want to go in South America."

"But, Hawk . . . ." Carlos stopped when he saw the look on his boss's face. He turned to the security chief. "Your commandos—have they all been polygraphed?"

"Not only them, but Tasman's asshole buddies. Turned out one was working for the CIA. I haven't seen much of him lately."

"But how are you going to control these people once you've put them in power? What if they decide to throw us out? What if the United States decides to intervene like they did in Haiti or Panama? We could lose everything."

Spano looked to his boss for relief.

From his position overlooking the two men, The Hawk said, "The United States has never invaded a South American country, some unwritten rule about one major country respecting another, not a banana republic. Our invasion would be a South American problem, and those countries have a history of staying out of each others' affairs, dating back to when most Latin American countries were run by juntas or strong men."

"What's . . . what's the plan?"

The Hawk took a sip of brandy. "Day One, Spano's commandos will be airlifted into Suriname where they will seize all four radio stations and its lone TV station, which will broadcast a message from Lucas Tasman. In this message Tasman will say he's compelled to take over the country to improve the living conditions of his fellow Surinamese."

"What—what if they don't believe him?"

"I doubt they will, but there's a short-wave service

operating off-shore, feeding this bullshit to the natives. Richey set it up. It's our responsibility to sell Lucas Tasman to the world, most of which has never heard of him. That's why I established a PR center, staffed by some of the most well-intentioned and highly motivated graduates of the University of Miami."

"And none over the age of twenty-five," injected Spano from his end of the couch.

The Hawk glanced at his security chief. "Day Two of the invasion, the Democratic Party of Suriname, Lucas Tasman's party, will announce a referendum for thirty days hence. That referendum will determine whether Tasman should stay in power or not. Washington loves elections, rigged or otherwise. After all, what could possibly happen in thirty days?"

"One hell of a lot," Spano said flatly.

"Day Two is also when American construction crews begin arriving to rebuild the Surinamese infrastructure. Hurricane Gloria leveled everything, scoring an almost direct hit on Paramaribo, and the Dutch people are complaining about pouring even more money down some Latin American rat hole. After World War Two, the Netherlands was devastated. The people who grew up at that time want to enjoy their retirement and they don't want to worry about inflation threatening their lifestyle."

After another drink of brandy, The Hawk said, "Every Surinamese knows the importance of their rivers, and that's why we're going in with construction crews. They need to get those hardwoods out of the jungle, downriver, and overseas. Bauxite and aluminum production have fallen below fifty percent since Hurricane Gloria. Those two items account for seventy-five percent of Suriname's exports. Until they're up and running again, the country will continue its downhill slide. The fact that Dutch companies own them and nothing has been done to repair the infrastructure means Dutch interests are waning. Not to mention that the high incidence of AIDS-related illness gives them pause for thought. Dutch companies are having a hard time talking single men into moving there, much less families."

"Hawk, I don't know how comfortable I'd be living in a country suffering from AIDS."

"I don't see why that would be any concern of yours," Spano said with a sneer.

The accountant was glaring at the security chief when The Hawk said, "Day Three, Tasman will invite his countrymen into Paramaribo to see the improvements being made. While they're in town, each male will receive a new pair of shorts and each female a new dress. They'll also be given a bar of soap, a toothbrush, and access to inoculations against every disease known to man. In other words, Lucas Tasman will be doing what everyone knows needs to be done in the Third World: repairing the infrastructure, healing the sick, and counseling safe sex."

"Counseling safe sex?"

"The media love AIDS. They haven't had a disaster like this since Vietnam."

"Okay, okay," said Carlos. "You're going to hide our operation behind Lucas Tasman. But the junta won't be sitting on their hands."

"No," said Spano. "They'll be scrambling to get the hell out. I have several warehouses full of weapons to throw at them, including a couple of helicopter gunships and enough Stinger missiles to down every Surinamese aircraft twice."

"And during the fighting," added The Hawk, "Lucas Tasman will appear simultaneously around the country, appealing to soldiers to throw down their weapons and join him in rebuilding their country."

"There's going to be more than one Lucas Tasman?"

The Hawk smiled. "Bush Negroes are descendants of slaves who ran off and lived in the jungle to avoid slavery—where they continued their practice of voodoo and a strong belief in a spirit world." The Hawk stood and crossed the room to stand in front of a bookcase filled with first editions. "Day Four of the invasion, Lucas Tasman announces anyone can run for Congress with the exception of the former junta, and while the country is buzzing with hope and the rest of the world is scratching its head, we'll be ferrying in television crews to film the rebuilding of Paramaribo."

"You think the junta will have folded by then?"

"Certainly by Day Four."

"Shit!" spit out Spano. "By the time the construction crews arrive. Day Two."

Carlos looked from one man to the other. "But if Lucas Tasman meets the press they'll ask where all his money came from. What's he going to tell them?"

"Come on, Carlos, you've seen him on television. What do you think he'll tell them?"

"You mean he's going to tell them the spirits of your

ancestors will make you contribute to driving the evil spirits out of his country?"

"Of course. Where else could all that money have come from?"

There was a knock, and the door to the study opened. Dancing through the door came a young man sporting a ponytail, tinted glasses, faded blue jeans, and a sport coat over a T-shirt. In each ear was a tiny earring.

"Oh, the places I've been and the things I've seen." The young man closed the door behind him. On his feet were a pair of purple high-top tennis shoes.

From where The Hawk stood in front of the bookcase, he said, "I was just explaining the Surinamese Operation to Carlos, Richey."

"Ah, yes, Operation Cut-Out." The young man sang a few bars of "Don't cry for me, Colombia" as he shuffled to the couch.

"Tell him where you've been."

"To such exotic places as Missoula, Montana, and Greenwood, South Carolina, and points in between. Matter of fact, I've been to Greenwood, South Carolina; Greenwood, Mississippi; and Greenwood, Arkansas; and I would rather be shot than go back to any of them."

"That can be arranged," said Spano without a smile.

To the accountant, Richey said, "I've been traveling the country, mailing envelopes of hundred-dollar bills to the Surinamese Liberation account in Miami. You probably didn't notice, but I've been gone over two weeks. The Hawk bought a list of the most politically conservative contributors—"

"Who always send cash," said The Hawk, "and for the most part live in small towns in the South and the Midwest."

"They send cash . . . through the mail?"

"Of course. They wouldn't want their enemies to know what they're up to."

The accountant fell back into the couch. Out came his handkerchief again. He mopped his forehead. "I can't believe . . . sending cash through the mail . . . it's insane."

"What does it matter if these people aren't playing with a full deck?" asked The Hawk, returning to stand behind his desk. "They're useful to us, fools enough to support anyone who calls themselves freedom fighters, and known for having a good bit of cash around the house."

"Yes," Carlos said, nodding. "Probably stuffed under their mattress."

"Probably."

"I was making a joke, Hawk."

"I wasn't. The point is there's a paper trail to the Surinamese Liberation account in Miami. Now all that money, and plenty of mine, resides in a Cayman account by way of one of the Miami banks. That's how Lucas Tasman is financing his revolution."

"Yes," said Richey, taking a seat on the arm of the sofa next to Carlos. "It seems this voodoo priest, or freedom fighter, has grassroots support in this country."

"Thanks to the spirit world," said The Hawk. "And if *60 Minutes* did a follow-up piece on Lucas Tasman, they'd discover the Movement received its largest donations following their interview."

"More money will be sent in when the show's re-run," said Richey with a grin.

Carlos gaped at the young man who looked like a hippie. "You sent all that money, all those millions I signed out to you—you sent it through the mail, didn't you? We filled up the trunk of your car with money . . . over three million dollars."

"Amateur hour," muttered Spano from his end of the couch.

"I don't believe it," mumbled Carlos. "All those millions . . . sent through the mail."

"Then you don't care to hear any more?"

"No, no, Hawk," said Carlos, using the handkerchief to wipe his brow again. "I—I want to know the whole plan."

"Very well. Tasman will win the referendum because the people in the bush will come into town and vote."

"How can you be sure?"

"Because the night before the referendum Tasman will perform a complete voodoo ritual on television, the first time the Surinamese will have seen voodoo on TV. It'll legitimize what half the population practices, and it'll be for the express purpose of calling up the spirits of the dead so the old ways of the junta won't return."

Richey smiled. "Who knows, Carlos, Suriname might be the first country to recognize voodoo as their state religion."

"The Pope will shit in his cassock," said Spano.

"But what if Tasman doesn't win," whined Carlos.

"There's always the possibility something will go wrong."

"Nothing will go wrong," said The Hawk, taking a seat at his desk again. This was becoming tiresome.

"Well," said Richey, patting the accountant on the shoulder, "Lucas Tasman did warn the old ways might return, didn't he—if people didn't vote correctly?"

"I like that," said Carlos, visibly brightening, "and it'd be a lot less expensive than a bunch of soap and toothpaste."

The Hawk leaned forward on his desk. "Forget about the start-up cost and concentrate on the bottom line. Bypassing the Colombians will make me the low-cost producer of coke in this part of the world. I'll be dealing direct with the Shining Path, the source of all cocaine in the hemisphere, especially now that their leaders have been killed. It's a vacuum waiting to be filled, and I'll do the filling. I'll undercut everyone. When the mob wants to deal in coke they'll come to me. It'll be cheaper and will contribute to their profit margins. The first year I should hit over a billion dollars in sales."

"Any chance Tasman might cut a deal with Washington and turn us over to the DEA?"

"Really, Carlos, and give up what no Latin American leader, and damn few in the world, can do: Thumb his nose at Washington? I'd rather think Lucas Tasman would kill to—"

Through the doors of the study came the sound of a splash as something landed in the swimming pool. Everyone looked toward the doors leading to the compound behind the house, but it was Spano who was out of his seat and across the room, pistol in hand.

"Kill the lights!" he ordered.

The Hawk turned off the desk lamp while Richey followed Spano to the doors and turned off the room's lights. Richey had a gun, too, and joined Spano. The Hawk moved to the other side of the doors and took up a position across from them. Behind them, Carlos slid off the sofa, crouched behind The Hawk's desk, and peered around the corner.

"Stay away from the doors," ordered Spano. "We don't know what they've got out there. It could be a starlight on a scoped rifle." Spano raised his voice to those outside the house. "Anytime you want to give us a situation report."

A chorus of shouts came from outside.

"What—what are they saying?" Carlos' voice quivered from behind the desk.

"Something about an airplane," Spano said.

Richey knelt at the edge of the door and looked into the night sky. "I don't see anything."

"Listen!"

The Hawk dashed onto the patio. He scanned the night sky.

"I don't think you should be out here," said Spano as he and Richey followed him.

The brick walls were still intact; lights illuminated a stepping stone walkway, and men with machine pistols hurried toward the swimming pool. From around them came the hubbub of voices.

"Have everyone shut up!" ordered The Hawk.

Spano did.

To the south and over the bay, an engine sputtered.

"Airplane!" shouted Richey, looking to the sky.

The men inside the compound looked up and resumed their chattering. This time The Hawk told them to shut up. They did and everyone heard the plane fly away.

"But—but what did the plane have to do with what we heard?" asked Carlos, slipping onto the patio.

"That!" shouted The Hawk, pointing at the pool.

A dark bulk floated near the diving board.

The Hawk started down the footpath with Richey and Spano behind him.

"Watch it," warned his security chief. "Remember the stunt Black Tuna pulled."

At the mention of Black Tuna, Carlos retreated to the study. Then he remembered that Black Tuna had firebombed their enemies' homes—from the air. He hurried onto the patio and watched the men at the pool.

"It's a bale of grass," said The Hawk, standing poolside. "Get the pool hook, Richey."

The hippie ran to the cabana and returned with a long pole. After a couple of tries, he finally managed to hook the bale and tug it over to where his boss stood.

"Waste of good grass if you ask me."

Spano scanned the compound. "It could be a set-up. The Feds have tried everything else."

The Hawk ripped off a piece of the bale and stuck it to his nose. "It's not even grass. It's only hay." He looked into the sky. The sound of the plane was no longer there.

Richey and Spano pulled off strands, sniffed them, and then joined The Hawk in staring into the starlit night.

"Get that thing out of there," ordered The Hawk. "And have the pool cleaned."

"I don't understand," asked Carlos, finally making his way to the pool. "Why would anyone want to drop a bale of hay in your swimming pool?"

"It's not hay. It's someone's calling card."

Ten

"Miss Mustard, you really gave us a scare when you lost power over the Pointe."

"Did I follow the proper procedures?" came the woman's anxious voice over the radio.

The air traffic controller smiled at his fellow controller. Just like a woman. If it'd been a man, the guy would be screaming about how the damn plane had almost gotten him killed and how he was going to sue hell out of the manufacturer, the rental company, and anyone else his attorney could think of.

"Yes, ma'am," said the controller. "You followed all the proper procedures. We'll have that plane checked out before it goes up again."

"Then I'm returning to your location," said the woman.

The controller closed the circuit. "That's one cool lady."

"And damned good-looking."

Woman Against Herself

"Aren't all blondes?"

The two men watched an airstrip outlined by lights on the water and waited anxiously for the woman's return. There were no further complications, and fifteen minutes later her plane was tied up at the dock, where a fire engine stood by.

The controller pulled off his headset. "I have to have a break." He watched the blonde climb down from the plane. One of the firemen gave her a hand ashore, and she thanked him. "I don't care how many certificates that woman has—they'd have our pensions, not to mention our asses, if that plane had gone down. Do you know how many important people live on that point?" The controller shook his head as he left the room. "Why didn't I take my father's advice and go into the insurance business?"

As he stumbled off to the break room, his partner spoke to another pilot practicing "touch and goes" on the watery airstrip. Out of the corner of his eye, the controller watched the blonde talking to the fireman. She pointed at the plane, then the sky.

The controller picked up his binoculars and trained them on the blonde. She had taken out a cigarette but was having trouble lighting it. Her hands shook.

The fireman said something. The blonde nodded and tossed away the cigarette, slipping the lighter into a pocket of her red jumpsuit.

Shook you up, didn't it, babe? Having engine trouble in daytime's bad enough, but at night you can't see where you're going to land.

The woman walked away from the pier but without

the purposeful stride she had taken going to the plane earlier in the day. Still, she was a looker. Filled out that red jumpsuit real good. Nice ass.

Mechanically, the controller warned the pilot practicing "touch and goes" of a water hazard, then cleared him to land. By then the blonde was through the gate and in her car.

Nice-looking Z-car. Red. The woman definitely had a thing about red. The blonde lit a cigarette and took long drags off it.

Will you be going up again, babe? I doubt it. Next time you might not be so lucky. It'd be a pity to lose such a fine-looking woman. Maybe you should find a boyfriend to do your flying for you. And how long would such a line of volunteers be?

*   *   *

"I'm kind of busy, Rainey. What you got?"

The D-Wars agent was in his office, sifting through printouts, trying to make heads or tails of the calls The Hawk had made from his house. Even calls coming in didn't make sense, if you were trying to make a case for drug smuggling. None of the calls appeared to have anything to do with the drug trade.

"Well, Taylor," came Rainey's voice, "maybe you ought to talk to me. I just might know something that could upset your apple cart."

Taylor pushed the paperwork away and gripped the phone. Last week he'd coaxed one of The Hawk's operatives into working for D-Wars—dammit, the ass-kissing you had to do to cultivate the right person—and now Phil Rainey was calling with more bad news.

"Beck again?"

"Been gone about a week."

"Dammit, Rainey, I thought you were keeping an eye on her."

"For her sake, Taylor, not D-Wars'. Anyway, she took a leave of absence from IINTELL, paid up her bills a month in advance, and closed up her apartment."

"Hopefully she's on vacation."

"Sallie gave away her houseplants. That's a sure sign she's headed your way."

"I hope not. The Hawk's men will kill her if she tries anything. I'll kill her if she tries anything."

"You think she really cares?"

"Dammit, Phil! I thought you were going to talk with her."

"Sallie can't hear me. These days, I don't think she can hear anyone."

"She's nuts. Anyone's nuts who thinks they can bring down The Hawk. I'm beginning to think I'm nuts for taking this assignment."

"Sounds like The Hawk is getting to you like he has Sallie. Listen, Taylor, I've got a judge who'd like to talk to her."

"He won't get the chance. When I find her, I'm tossing her in jail and throwing away the key. I'm through playing games with that woman."

"He's a *she* and knows everything Sallie's done."

"Everything?"

"More than even you know."

Wes sighed. "Give it to me."

"For starters, Sallie missed a session in court. Her husband's suing her for being an unfit mother."

"After the kid's already dead—what kind of man does that?"

"Alstair Beck, and you have to meet the bastard to understand. Too much money and time on his hands, and no one to tell him what he can and can't do."

"Hasn't Beck suffered enough?"

"Not according to Alstair Beck."

"Anything else?" asked Taylor, shaking his head.

"Drugs. Sallie's carrying a ton of tranquilizers."

"Why? Is the thought of killing someone in cold blood getting to her?"

"She told the doctors—three of them I've been able to locate—that she can't sleep at night."

"No kidding. She lays awake thinking up ways to screw up my investigation."

"You want me to tell you this or what?"

When Taylor didn't reply, Rainey went on, "Sallie used her son's death to play on the doctor's sympathies. She's also seeing a doctor who counsels auto-suggestion and self-hypnosis. Sallie's started smoking again and can't break the habit. You catch her and I can have her committed for psychiatric observation, especially after what she tried with The Hawk."

"Then wish me luck. If I hadn't recognized her . . . sweet Jesus! I hate to think about it. The Hawk dead, and Richey and Spano, and even that wimp Carlos fighting over how to cut up The Hawk's business. I'd have a hydra on my hands, not to mention a bloodbath. That doesn't go over well with the locals—my boss, either."

Rainey didn't respond immediately.

"You still there?" asked Taylor.

"Just waiting until you finish venting."

Taylor sighed again. "I shouldn't be dumping on you. Evidently you have some plan." He picked up a pencil. "What is it you want me to do?"

"When you put out the APB, say Sallie's a mental case. Tell the arresting officers not to believe anything she says, just hold her. My judge will talk with a judge she knows in Miami. Sallie will be given a choice of returning home and undergoing psychiatric evaluation or being jailed for attempted murder. You'll have to see my judge's colleague there in Miami and swear to what Sallie pulled at the community center."

"I'll do it. I'll do anything to get that woman out of my hair." Taylor paused. "I've got a private detective in my pocket. I'll put him on her."

"Put him on the firing ranges. Sallie still can't shoot worth a damn but keeps trying."

"That should keep him busy. Miami's like the Old West: citizens arming themselves against the muggers, thugs arming themselves to mug the citizens, and drug peddlers buying whatever it takes to keep rivals off their turf. No wonder tourists don't come any farther south than Disney World. What's Beck carrying?"

Rainey told him what he had seen at the firing range.

"She'll never kill The Hawk unless he holds up the barrel for her. Anything else?"

"Sallie's not overweight anymore. She's slimmed down and wears her hair longer."

"What's she planning on doing, seducing him or killing him?" Taylor bore down so hard on his pad the point on his pencil broke. "This is nuts! This isn't woman's work. Hell, I've got an ex-wife who doesn't think this is the kind of work a man should be doing."

"Yeah, but with what Sallie's already accomplished, who's to tell her she can't do more?"

"That's easy, Phil. The Hawk."

*   *   *

The Hawk jabbed a finger at the intercom buzzing on his desk. Spano, Richey, and he were in the middle of discussing the Suriname operation. An easel stood alongside his desk with a map of Suriname on it. Arrows pointed in the direction of troop movements, and dots showed points of attack with jagged lines representing supposed Surinamese resistance.

"Yes, Gate," said The Hawk into the intercom.

"Got a woman here says you're expecting her."

The Hawk looked at the men below him on the sofa. Richey shrugged. Spano shook his head.

The Hawk turned back to the intercom. "Who is she?"

"Says she's Jackie Mustard, and that you want to hire her to fly for you."

Richey sat up. "Jackie Mustard! I thought she was dead."

"Just a moment, Gate." The Hawk flipped off the intercom. "Who is she, Richey?"

"She flies pot into California, or at least she did."

"Did?"

"She dropped out of sight a couple of years ago when the Feds busted her operation. They caught most of the gang, including her boyfriend, Ned Clanton, but Mustard slipped away. Walked away with nothing but the clothes on her back. Clanton was caught trying to go cross-country in a Land Rover."

"Maybe she's the one who set up the boyfriend," suggested Spano.

"What do you think?" The Hawk asked Spano. "This has to be our swimming pool pot dropper."

Spano held up two fingers. "One: run her off. If she returns, kill her."

"Shit," muttered Richey.

"And your other idea?" asked The Hawk.

"Let her in. I'll find out what her game is."

"What you talking about?" asked Richey, turning on Spano. "This is a pro, not some whore. She's flown in tons of grass and never spent a day in jail. She's one smart cookie."

"I thought they used boats out there," said The Hawk.

"They do, but Mustard used a plane with floats. Flew pot anywhere you wanted as long as there was water to land on. If we need pilots to fly the raw material into Suriname, then the finished product into the States, I'd think twice about turning Mustard over to Spano's goons."

"Goons, my ass—"

"But you've never seen her in action?" said The Hawk, cutting him off.

"Never. Just heard stories."

"Ever met her?"

"Once. At a beach party near San Diego."

"That figures," said Spano with a sneer.

"If she's so good, why's she looking for a job?"

"What are Spano and me doing here? Or Carlos? Or anyone else for that matter? None of us would be able to come up with this Surinamese deal and organize all the details. Mustard wouldn't be able to either. She's just a woman."

"I don't like it," Spano said. "Dropping bales of hay in swimming pools is screwy, and I don't like having weirdos inside the compound."

"Now look who's talking—you and your lost boys."

"Look here, beach boy—"

"Gentlemen. Please!"

Both men looked straight ahead, not at The Hawk but at the base of his elevated desk.

The Hawk jabbed the intercom again. "Is Mustard carrying?"

A laugh came over the intercom. "Yeah, and you've got to see it to believe it. She's wearing this red jumpsuit and strapped under her arm is a .44 Magnum. The gun's bigger than her tits."

"Mustard always wore red," Richey said, "and she always carried a Magnum."

"Bet she can't hit shit," Spano said.

"Why don't you try her?"

The Hawk interrupted their bickering with, "If Mustard gives up her piece, bring her up to the house."

The man at the gate laughed. "Yeah. I'll get the piece from the piece."

"Frisk her," ordered Spano from the couch.

133

"What was that?" asked the man at the gate.
"Frisk her," repeated The Hawk.
"Gladly," said the man with another laugh.

*　　*　　*

Tina didn't like the way Carlos looked when he returned from his meeting with The Hawk. She shivered as the doors of the warehouse closed behind the Cadillac, actually a double set of doors with a chamber in between that could be filled with poisonous gas in thirty-two seconds—one of Spano's ideas. Tina didn't like that man and she had been happy to learn he didn't like women.

The warehouse containing the money was half the size of a football field, but The Hawk didn't use the entire building. At one end an evangelical missionary service went about their business of printing religious tracts to be distributed in rest rooms and phone booths. The other end of the building held a supply house that shipped supplies to mom-and-pop janitorial services throughout the state. No interstate commerce was involved, and interference from the federal government was nonexistent. Each business had been chosen for its political beliefs, which suited The Hawk just fine. In the middle of the building, between the two businesses, was where the trucks were unloaded.

The people at each end of the huge building thought the middle of the warehouse was storage for their counterpart at the other end, and ignored the comings and goings of unmarked vans and trucks. The employees of these two legitimate businesses had no idea they worked in one of the securest areas in Miami. And as companies went out of business in the surrounding blocks, The Hawk's real estate service found people willing to reopen those buildings who were as paranoid as The Hawk.

Buttressing all this was a state-of-the-art, computer-driven security system using cameras not only to scan the interior and exterior of the warehouse, but also to spy on the neighborhood from various windows or the tops of buildings that The Hawk owned. Occasionally some small-time dealer would set up operations in the neighborhood or some fool would try to mug an employee. Each of those, including the squeegee people, were encouraged to leave by Spano's roving guards, who deterred all soliciting, loitering, or merely strolling through the neighborhood.

Once a truck entered the warehouse, the driver was informed through a PA system that he and his shotgun would be exiting at the other side of the warehouse, that he and his companion should dismount and make themselves comfortable. Their vehicle would be waiting for them on the other side. Any grousing was stemmed by an offer of hot coffee and fresh donuts on the other side of the building.

Once dismounted, the driver and his companions were told to follow the arrows leading from the chamber and down a hallway. Once the room was emptied and the door to the hallway sealed, a machine sprayed poisonous gas into the chamber, and the vehicle was left to sit for several minutes. After the gas was pumped out, a group of gas-masked, armed men entered the room. Two checked the cab while others threw open the back doors of the vehicle. Seeing nothing but cargo, the security detail went through the rear of the truck with German Shepherds trained to detect bombs.

A couple of times gunmen had been found inside—dead—and once a bomb was discovered. In the case of the dead men, they were left inside and the building put on alert, meaning there was no hot coffee and do-nuts for this particular driver and the guy riding shot-gun. In the odd case of the bomb, the device was dis-armed and another installed by Spano, who person-ally detonated it while the truck was crossing a lightly traveled bridge. The bridge was slightly damaged, but the truck was practically vaporized, as was an old black man who fished from that bridge every day.

Following a thorough search, a metal cable was hooked to the vehicle's bumper to tow it across the floor and onto a metal rack similar to those used by car mechanics who don't own a lift. With the rear of the vehicle open while it moved up an incline, the boxes, barrels, and coffee cans filled with money slid onto the floor, where they were pulled and poked at by a small army of women using sticks. Wearing light blue smocks, the women busted up each container, scattering the money across a conveyer belt that ran under the ve-hicle and pushing the busted containers off the mov-ing belt. The belt positioned the money under a set of tubes where it was sucked to the second floor and dropped into trays in front of Tina and other women. These women, who wore pink smocks, dumped the money on a belt that carried the cash to boxes at each end of the line, where it was sealed and weighed.

That's where the rub began. There was no way to dispose of that amount of currency, so much of it stayed in boxes marked "machine parts" or was returned to Colombia or was hand-carried to the Caymans. And despite the speed with which the money kept leaving the building, the cash still piled up, exhausting all available room. It filled a series of cabinets built along the walls where the vans and trucks were pulled up the metal ramp. Carlos's office was piled high with it, and even the rest rooms had stacks of cardboard boxes reaching the ceiling.

Piqued at a lack of freedom of movement in his own office, Carlos appropriated an eighteen-wheeler, filled it with cartons, and parked it inside the warehouse. When a delivery was made, the eighteen-wheeler was driven out of the warehouse for a short time. All the arriving driver and his companion saw was another truck leaving the building, presumably as empty as theirs.

Few thefts occurred. The women working the lines were paid fifty thousand dollars a year, then another five hundred a week under the table. The security detail was paid upwards of a half million dollars, depending on seniority. When security did catch someone stealing, the thief was killed in front of the other women. First, she was horribly mutilated, and the mutilations appeared to affect the women more than the executions. Then the body was dropped through a hole in the floor that emptied into a canal flowing under the warehouse.

Woman Against Herself

Tina had never been tempted to steal, because she had fallen in love with Carlos shortly after arriving. She had seen him return to the warehouse more than once with a concerned look on his face. Carlos fumbled with the door of the Cadillac as he climbed out, and Tina had to close it for him. She ignored the guards searching the Cadillac and helped her patron over to the elevator leading to the second floor.

Tina was only eighteen, had been on the streets since age fourteen, and had gravitated toward Carlos because he made no demands on her. Tina's vagina had been ripped to hell by a stepfather who had raped her so often that she ran away from home. She'd knocked around until she had been found outside the warehouse, where she had also been gang-raped by the security detail.

Tina sensed that Carlos cared about her. After all, wasn't he the one who had taken her to the emergency room? No man had ever done anything like that—without expecting something in return. Tina had paid for more than one trip to a hospital. Only after being employed to work in the warehouse did she fully understand why Carlos had flashed a false ID and hadn't hung around the ER. During the time it took her to plan how to steal a bunch of that money, Tina fell in love with someone she felt absolutely safe with. She even suffered his lack of attention, and finally Carlos's consuming interest became hers: protecting the money from all comers. With that, Carlos finally noticed her, became more attentive, and occasionally let her pick out the new smocks for the women working the line.

Now, as she helped her patron onto the elevator, she realized he was in a state of shock. Face white, unable to stand alone, Carlos had been shaken, as if the thing closest to him had been threatened. It had been—by the proposed invasion of Suriname.

*　　*　　*

"What you got for me, Julius?"

The black man took a seat across the desk from Taylor. "We came up empty, Wes."

"I don't want to hear that."

"What you want to hear? Some bullshit about how the investigation is proceeding normally? I'm here to tell you the woman's not in town."

"She has to be."

Julius shook his head. "No, she doesn't."

"What about the firing ranges?"

"They have her picture and they know she's a psycho. They'll call first time she sets foot inside their door."

"And the hotels?"

"And the motels and the flophouses. It took me and Mark and that private cop of yours longer than I care to remember, but we worked them like we did the firing ranges."

Julius didn't add that he thought his boss had gone wacko over this Beck woman. However, he would tell Taylor if he was pressed on the subject.

Taylor leaned back and tapped his fingers on the armrest. Julius watched those fingers. The man had definitely lost his cool over this woman.

"She has to be here. I know she's here. I can feel it."

"Wes, you're taking this way too serious. No way some woman's going to slip in here and blow our investigation. Last time we weren't expecting her, but this time we have our bases covered. Mark's locked down all the computers. Even the cops are looking for her."

"I don't know . . . ."

"What is it with this woman? I know she's good-looking, but—"

Taylor sat up. The tapping stopped. "Damn it, Julius! Looks have nothing to do with it. She broke into our computer. Her boss at IINTELL told me the woman can make a computer sit up and dance. And don't forget, Beck's the one who got close enough to kill The Hawk."

Taylor leaned back in his chair. "I have this new squeal, and he doesn't need any undue attention now that he's thinking of crossing over. Remember when the DEA was after that guy doing business with one of The Hawk's fronts? Spano got jittery and made everyone take a lie detector test and my predecessor lost the guy. I don't want Spano any more alert than he is, and that's just what Beck could do: alarm Spano." Taylor's fingers started tapping again. "I keep wondering what we don't know about her that could hurt us."

The two men sat in the spartan office, Julius not having a clue as to what Taylor meant.

After a few minutes of listening to his boss tapping away, Julius said, "I'll tell you what I *did* learn while on the street."

"What's that?" asked Taylor absentmindedly.

"Beck's not the only person the cops have an APB

out on. They have one for Ned Clanton, too."

The fingers stopped. "Clanton's on the East Coast?"

The black man nodded. "Clanton said he'd get you if he broke out. If Clanton's in Miami, he's here to kill you."

"Then I'll watch my backside."

"We will, too."

"Just tell the police to keep an eye on all the cowboy bars. That's where I found him, not racing across the desert in a Land Rover. Clanton loves that shit-kicking music."

Julius nodded but knew he'd watch Taylor's backside whether his boss liked it or not. The politics of drug busting were getting thicker and thicker, so you'd better keep your résumé clean. If your boss was assassinated, that wouldn't look good on anyone's résumé.

"Do the airport and car rental companies have Beck's picture?" asked Taylor.

"I was operating on the theory Beck was already in town."

"First thing tomorrow send that PI out to see them with Beck's picture."

"I'll do it." Julius stood up. "Now, can I get back to work?"

"Beck *is* our work."

"Yeah. You keep telling me that, Wes, and maybe, sooner or later, I'll believe you."

Eleven

On the second floor of The Hawk's mansion, Sallie stared at herself in the huge mirror over the lavatory. A series of lights surrounded the mirror. Below it, the ceramic bowl was a swirl of colors contrasting with the golden handles and spigots.

She shook her head at the sight. If anyone had told her she'd be dressing like a floozy this close to forty, she wouldn't have believed them: bleached blond hair, rich tan, and a red bikini.

What a horrible color. However, Jackie Mustard knows what catches a man's eye, and it caught The Hawk's eye. I'd prefer beige. Not so loud, and it would go with the tan. But I'm not here as a fashion critic. Hell, I'm not even here as myself.

Pushing back her shoulder-length hair, Sallie examined the roots for any hint of black, and found it.

I'll have to fix that. Can't take a chance on The Hawk remembering me from the community center. No prob-

lem so far with the color of my eyes, but damn these contacts for irritating them!

She'd wanted everything to be perfect, nothing left to chance. Sallie brushed through her eyebrows, examining their roots, and nodded to herself.

I've got to do something about my hair. That is, if The Hawk doesn't have a run planned for the weekend. And the sooner, the better . . . the drug run, that is, not the rinsing of my hair.

She pulled out her bikini bottoms and examined her pubic hair. They didn't seem to grow as fast down there. Sallie let the bottoms slap back against a flat belly.

And why would you care about those hairs? You're not planning to let The Hawk see that part of you, are you?

Are you?

She'd been expecting a pass ever since moving into this place, but the pass hadn't come. Is that why you spend so much time in front of the mirror? Are you wondering if there's something wrong with you, and in that case, it's not your disguise you're worried about, is it, Sallie Beck?

There had also been something wrong with her preconceived opinions about The Hawk. She expected orgies with dopers and whores running around in various stages of undress, loud music, and shooting up, but found only peace and quiet. And The Hawk reading the Great Books and listening to classical music! And he doesn't take drugs. Doesn't even allow them in the house.

But he makes millions off their sale. And kills people.

Woman Against Herself

Kills children. Kills little boys. Don't forget why you're here, Sallie Beck. Don't become enamored with this man and an atmosphere where you are waited on hand and foot.

She frowned at her image in the mirror. You know, you talk to yourself too much. Now why do you do that? Is it because you don't have anyone to talk to? Anyone to discuss your plan with? Or did you go crazy when you entered this surrealistic world? Or did you lose your mind when you lost your son?

Timmie.

Timmie and IINTELL.

Another world so far away. If Timmie hadn't been killed, about this time of day, he would've been—

Get off it! Leave it alone!

Sallie closed her eyes, and when she opened them she turned one way, then the other, checking herself in the mirror. Not bad for a woman close to forty. Of course, all you have to do is starve yourself to death and do a hundred sit-ups every morning, whether it's your day to work in The Hawk's warehouse or not.

A warehouse full of money. Where does all that money come from? No wonder people become so corrupt. There's so much money, it's not even counted, only weighed.

She tested the muscles in her arms: larger and sorer from long hours working in the warehouse. "Going to make a man out of you yet, we are," she said out loud.

Sallie jerked around, looking for the hidden microphones and cameras. Then she remembered where she was. No cameras or microphones in the bathroom. I made sure of that. I made Spano take them out. But the bastards are everywhere else. Looking, listening—dammit, I'll bet The Hawk doesn't have any of that shit in his bathroom.

Damn paranoid sons of bitches. Especially Spano. She shivered. Spano didn't believe she was Jackie Mustard. She could see it by the way he looked at her. He'd like nothing better than to get her alone and beat the shit, and truth, out of her.

God! Would you just listen to me? And my language. What was it Wes Taylor said? There are no ladies in the drug trade. You were right about that, Taylor, but wrong about me being able to infiltrate The Hawk's organization. She smiled at the image in the mirror.

I did it! I did it!

Sallie stood tall, and only had to suck in her stomach just a little. I did it, and now I'm going to bring down this whole damn operation. All I need is one little trip and I've got them. One little drug run and I've got them all, from The Hawk all the way down to that kid Tina who works in the warehouse. Me. I did it. And all for Timmie.

But I couldn't have done it without a sanctuary, a place where I can remember why I'm here. And I had to fight for my privacy from the very first day I moved in.

Spano had walked into her bedroom and found Sallie kneeling in front of her dresser, running a hand under the piece of furniture.

"What the hell you doing, Mustard?"

"Looking for microphones and cameras. I know how your dirty little mind works."

Spano grabbed her arm, jerking Sallie to her feet. "Where they are—if they're here—is no business of yours."

It felt as if her arm had been jerked out of its socket. Sallie teared up but didn't dare wipe the tears away. Not in front of this man.

She shook off his hand. "Well, you sure as hell aren't going to have them in my room, and every time I find one, I'm going to pry it out of the wall, bring it down-stairs and dump it into whatever The Hawk is having for breakfast." She rubbed her shoulder as she glanced at the door. "What the hell are you doing here anyway? I didn't invite you in my room."

"I go anywhere I damn well please. I take my job very seriously."

"I'll bet you do, and the ladies' rooms get top prior-ity, don't they?"

Spano's mouth became a tight line across his face. He glared at her.

"You'll search my room when I'm not here. Got that?"

"No one tells me how to do my job."

Sallie fixed him with a look, and then walked over to the bed where she sat down and punched up some numbers on the telephone.

"Now what you doing?" asked Spano, following her to the bed. "Calling The Hawk to take up for you?"

"Nope. I'm calling a cab to get the hell out of here. You can play your sick little games with other women." Into the phone she said, "Give me an outside line. I want to call a cab."

The security chief snatched the phone away and returned it to its cradle. He glared down at her and Sallie glared right back up. Spano opened his mouth to say something, but instead he turned on his heel and headed for the door.

"What about the microphones and cameras?"

"I'll have them taken out of the bathroom. But they stay in the bedroom. Got that, Mustard?"

"Yes, and I think you got it, too."

Spano slammed the door on his way out, and Sallie collapsed on her bed until she remembered the cameras and hidden microphones. She got up and went into the bathroom where she gave the tub and shower a thorough search. Finding nothing there, she pulled the curtain and sat inside the tub until one of Spano's men arrived to take out the camera and microphone in her bathroom. By the time the man arrived, Sallie was in tears and wondering what the hell she had gotten herself into.

She glanced at her hands. They trembled. She looked in the mirror. Her hands trembled there, too. Oh, God, and I took two little white pills before breakfast. I had to. Jackie Mustard might've been comfortable eating breakfast with a major drug dealer, maybe even flirted with him, but me . . . I'm a damn computer programmer.

What am I doing here? And do I have what it takes to put that man away, even with the help of my little white pills?

Sallie opened a drawer, took out a tampon, and separated the paper at one end, then dropped out the cylinder. When she pushed up from the bottom, a white pill popped out of the tube and dropped into her hand. Another fell out before she had time to retract the pusher.

She stared at them. *I can't take more than one. I haven't got many left and I need every single one.*

Holding her breath in hopes of calming her nerves, Sallie dropped one of the pills inside the tube, slid the tube inside the paper, and moistened the ends—which were becoming frayed—then stuck them together before dropping the tampon in the drawer.

She popped the pill in her mouth and leaned over, taking water straight from the tap. After throwing her head back, she made a face. *They taste horrible, but I can't make it without them, or their little yellow sisters that help me sleep at night.*

Ah, sleep. My hiding place.

But was it? At the very thought of sleep Sallie heard the tape play inside her head.

"Who are you?" Sallie heard herself ask.

"Jackie Mustard," her voice replied.

"Where do you come from?" she asked herself.

"San Diego. I'm a Padres fan," she heard herself say.

"What do you do for a living?"

"I smuggle grass, and I'm damn good at it."

"How do you get it into the country?"

"By plane. I can deliver it anywhere you want."

"How long have you been doing this?"

"Seven years, and I'll keep on doing it for the right deal."

The tone of her voice changed, becoming more strident. "What's that, Mustard?"

Steve Brown

"The kind of deal where they don't hassle you with polygraphs."

"Who you working for, Mustard?"

"Me."

"I repeat, who are you working for?" her voice asked with more intensity and a trace of impatience.

"Me, myself, and I."

"I asked what government agency you're working for? I want to know, and you're going to tell me."

Sallie shook her head as she had trained herself to do when they persisted in this line of questioning. And Spano *had* persisted in *this* line of questioning during the polygraph. Had she shaken her head while being tutored by the tape back home? Even shaken her head in her sleep? Sallie didn't know, and didn't think she wanted to know.

"I don't work for anyone, asshole. I do everything for me and mine."

Sallie smiled into the oversized mirror with the lights surrounding it. The tape played automatically in her head. She couldn't stop it if she wanted to. She'd heard the recording too many times, over and over again, in the middle of the night, with all those pills in her.

Would she continue hearing it after she concluded her business with The Hawk? After she put The Hawk away and someone asked who she was, what would she answer? Sallie Beck or Jackie Mustard?

Who was she now?

One thing for sure. She sure as hell wasn't the person she'd been a few weeks ago, in more ways than she cared to imagine.

149

Sallie looked at her hands. They'd stopped shaking before the pill had even had a chance to take effect.

Hmmm. Have to remember that. Use autosuggestion when you run out of pills. Think of the tape. Make it play in your head; because, eventually, you *are* going to run out of pills.

God, but this was crazy. She had to get this over with and get out of here. Maybe then she'd go back to school and learn something other than how a computer worked. Maybe she'd study how the mind worked. If she had any mind left to study.

Sallie left her room, taking along a beach towel. She went along the carpeted hallway, down the winding stairs with the chandelier-dominated foyer, and through The Hawk's study, heading for the pool.

The drug smuggler was working at his desk. He looked up from his computer. "Going for a swim?"

She nodded. "Been working in the warehouse too long. I'm losing my tan." *God am I losing it! In more ways than one.*

The Hawk smiled at her.

My Lord, but he did have a charming smile. And not at all bad-looking. Narrow face, narrow waist and hips. She'd overheard someone say The Hawk was a marvelous dancer. *At what else was he marvelous?*

"They being too rough on you down there?" he asked.

"They try. Some kind of initiation." She cleared her throat and brought the towel up between them. "Hawk, when am I going to get the chance to show these assholes what I really do for a living?"

"In a few days."

"Good—because I didn't come all this way to become a fucking warehouseman." She looked around the study with its book-lined shelves, heavy oak furniture and thick cushions, curtains pulled back to expose white sheers, and a sofa you could sink up to your neck in. "I feel like I'm wasting my time. I could be running in a few loads."

"Then why aren't you?"

There it is, thought Sallie. Another test. Another challenge. "I want to do it big time, and I want to do it steady, and I don't have the contacts after being out of the business for so long. I'd only waste time reestablishing contact and maybe get picked up for my trouble. It's better to bring my reputation and let you put me to work for a smaller but more consistent cut, even if there is a lot of downtime in an operation this size."

The Hawk regarded her. "You certainly know how the money's made, don't you?"

Sallie wanted to tell this man how closely his organization paralleled what she'd learned working at IINTELL. "I ought to. I've been around long enough."

"Well, you'll get your chance. We have one of our few grass shipments coming in a few days."

"Good. Er—Hawk, I noticed you don't sell much grass."

The smuggler leaned back in his chair. "Used to when the market demanded it. Used to sell so much I didn't sell it by the bale but by the houseful."

"The houseful?"

He nodded. "I'd rent houses, along the canals and rivers, cover the floors with plastic, and off-load into the house. I'd have houses—rather, I'd have addresses worth so much money. Give me the cash and pick up a fifty-thousand-dollar load at one house or a hundred-thousand-dollar load at another. Maybe there would be a load for a quarter mil, but that was rare. Not because of the size, but because I couldn't find many houses that'd hold that much grass and butted up to the water. Houses that large are well back from the water and with deep lawns. Better to leave the load aboard ship and throw in the boat free.

"But grass isn't the thing. I can't make money on it. Worthwhile money for the risk, that is. The market demands cocaine and will pretty much take all I can supply, so why fool around with all that bulk when smaller shipments will make several times the money."

"But you still bring in grass from time to time?"

"Just keeping my options open." He smiled again. *The man did have a gorgeous smile.* "Baby boomers who used grass have families now. Crack cocaine scares the hell out of them. The boomers keep the grass market alive. They think it's groovy to mellow out, and with seventy-six million boomers, or a third of the population, if only ten percent use grass . . . see what I mean?"

Sallie couldn't help but nod. The man was a treasure trove of information. Hard not to be awed by his operation. Or the man himself. Very hard.

A different kind of smile crossed the drug smuggler's face. "From where I'm sitting you don't need to work on your tan. It looks just fine to me, to the other men, too."

Sallie's stomach went hollow. This was the pass she'd

been expecting, and now that it'd come, she wasn't ready for it.

Been staring at that smile too much, haven't you? When you should have been thinking about Timmie.

She gripped her towel to keep her hands from trembling. I can handle this. I'm Jackie Mustard and I'm tough enough to handle this. I'm tough enough to handle him. "Thanks for the compliment, but the kind of guys you employ would gawk at their own grandmothers."

"That may be, but you're still one good-looking woman." He looked her over from head to toe and took his time doing it.

Sallie wanted to wrap herself in the towel. She felt positively naked standing there in her bikini. She wanted to run upstairs and hide. Hide in her bathroom. Maybe take another pill. Maybe gobble down a whole handful. She couldn't do this. The least little thing set her nerves spinning out of control.

"Something wrong?" No smiles now, simply concern.

"I was thinking next time I go into town I'll buy a new cover-up."

The Hawk laughed. "You do work at being a lady, don't you?"

"In this business you'd better act like one or the men will think you're just another whore."

"Surprised I haven't put a move on you?"

Sallie nodded. "Yes, and living in your house, too."

"I'm waiting on you."

"You're . . . waiting on me?"

"It's up to you to realize I'm building a billion-dollar business. It's up to you to realize what that'll mean to the people around me, especially the woman in my life. If you can't appreciate that, I doubt I'd have much interest in you, either."

"Then you can appreciate how I feel about the men not knowing I'm a top-notch pilot but thinking I'm just another whore." She left the room, crossed the patio, and walked to the pool with The Hawk's laughter ringing in her ears.

But how long could clever comebacks keep her out of this man's bed? Better question: how long before her admiration for him would draw her there? The bastard was a crook and a killer, but with his business acumen, he could replace anyone at IINTELL, not to mention several CEOs Sallie had met. Wes Taylor was crazy if he thought he could bring down this man. And it might be impossible even for a person inside this man's organization.

At the pool she took the first chair she came to. She had to. She had to lie down. This push-pull feeling she had for The Hawk was driving her nuts. There had been no man in her life for years. People said she should get out more, that she should date some guys they wanted to fix her up with. All she wanted was to be Timmie's mother. But she couldn't be and something was happening to her, and with the wrong man.

The Hawk was a smuggler and a killer. He might've been the one who killed Timmie. Or he might not have been.

People took drugs on their own. No one forced them.

Only Timmie had been murdered! And by this man in this huge house with all his servants around.

One of those servants was by her side. "Drink, Miss?"

Sallie looked up, shading her eyes. No way, Jose. I have too many pills in me and they don't mix with liquor. They might loosen my tongue. Something I learned the first night I dined with The Hawk. The long table had been set for two, and a handful of servants to wait on them. The Hawk had dominated the conversation, attempting to impress her with how large his business would soon be.

"There are three industries in Florida," he had told her that evening. "Tourism, farming, and drugs; each grossing a billion dollars. In a few years, there's going to be another. Mine."

Now, lying on this lounge chair, Sallie realized she'd bought into his line of bull, and it concerned her. "No," she said to the inquiring servant. "Nothing now, but if you would put a bottle of water in the freezer and bring it out in, say, a half hour."

"Yes, Miss."

When the servant moved away, Sallie saw The Hawk and Spano staring at her from the patio. It caused her to chill under the midday sun.

Three or four more days of this and I'm out of here. Only three or four more days . . . . I can hold out that long, can't I?

"You still don't believe her, do you?" The Hawk asked his security chief.

"You've got that right."

"She's too high-spirited for you."

"She's a fucking bitch."

"That's what I mean."

The two men watched as Sallie loosened the string holding up the top of her bikini. As they watched, she let the ends drop away, and then fitted the top snug over her breasts before settling in.

"I'm open to anything you dig up on her. Just like I'm open to anything on Richey or Carlos."

"Good, because Carlos has a new girlfriend, and I have a man in California digging into Mustard."

"Carlos . . . with a woman?"

"Oh, I don't think he's fucking her, but he's up to something."

"If not fucking her—what?"

"I don't know, and that's why I'm keeping an eye on them. Remember, he doesn't like the Suriname operation."

"Carlos has always gone along with us in the past."

"Maybe because he knows I'll fucking kill him if he doesn't."

"Then what's the problem? Mustard passed the polygraph, and Richey thinks she's who she says she is."

"That fucking beach boy . . . ."

"And you found the Wal-Mart where she worked while lying low. Your man in California showed her picture around, and her fellow employees and neighbors say the person we have living with us is Jackie Mustard, that she's the same woman who disappeared from that area a few months ago. Under a different name. It's not likely that someone in the government's witness relocation program would give up that information voluntarily. Not to mention there's nothing you can't ask her about the grass business she doesn't know. Some of it's out of date, but she does know how it works."

"That's just it. Her story's too neat. There are no loose ends. I've been giving that test since 'Nam and nobody has a story that tight. I don't like it. If I only had some prints to match . . . ."

"Admit it, Spano. You simply don't like the woman."

"You're fucking right about that."

"Do you know the number of people I have working for me that I don't enjoy being with, but they get the job done? And you see the time I lavish on Carlos so we don't have to count all that damn money."

Spano's eyes narrowed. "Then Mustard's just another pilot to you?"

"No, she's a good-looking pilot to me."

Spano glanced at the floor. "It looks like more, Hawk. You've never had a woman in here you weren't fucking."

"Oh, Mustard will sleep with me all right. It's just a matter of time before she realizes she belongs in my bed instead of the one down the hall."

Twelve

"**J**ust tell me that you've got something going on down there, Wes. South Florida's the most competitive part of the country for drug enforcement agencies, and I have congressmen asking me why your operation shouldn't be turned over to the DEA."

Taylor hunched over his desk, knowing he was in for a long siege. "The DEA doesn't want any part of The Hawk, Director. There's no chance of a quick collar. The DEA just wants D-Wars out of Florida before we embarrass them like we did in Texas and California."

"Just answer the question, Wes. You know how these congressmen think. They're charting their own course separate from the White House and they don't want to end up with egg on their collective faces."

"I've got a new contact inside his organization, sir."

"And what's he telling you?"

"Just what you've seen in my weekly reports."

"There's been only one since you brought this new

squeal on board and I didn't see anything in that report."

"Sir, I'll have something more concrete by the end of the month. My contact, Porter the Painter, says The Hawk has something big coming up."

"Is that all he told you?" asked Frazier.

"That's all he knows—so far."

"Then this Porter the Painter—where the hell they get these silly-ass names is beyond me—isn't much of a contact. Your problem is, Nelson's organization's always on a war footing. Spano has thrown up a wall between them and the outside world. They don't use telephones to transact business, even cellular ones; they have their own radio network with codes and frequencies, probably changed daily, along with scrambling capability. They have cutouts on their cutouts and have so compartmentalized their operation, one hand doesn't know what the other's doing. They'd rather take a loss than to hastily launder their money. I can imagine Carlos locked up in some warehouse, surrounded by all that money, and wondering what he's going to do with it. No one but someone who has access to the whole organization has any idea what's going on."

Taylor could imagine Director Frazier sucking away on his pipe in Washington, sucking away in frustration in his sparsely furnished office. Being tight with money was something that started at the home office for D-Wars.

"I'm getting a bad feeling about this one. If Spano or Richey, or even Carlos, squealed, you'd have something."

Woman Against Herself

No sense in waiting for the other shoe to drop. "You thinking of closing us down, sir?"

"I don't know. But what I do know is I have congressmen demanding a breakthrough on a case we've been working on for over two years."

"The Hawk will take longer, sir, but we'll get him."

"Sometimes you have to close down one line of investigation to protect the more productive ones."

"I'm going to make this one pay off, sir."

"Spoken from the heart instead of the head. Don't forget, I'm the one who sent you down there to salvage the mess left behind by your predecessor. You would've, if you hadn't lost your first snitch. You know as well as I do that you don't get many chances to smash a drug ring. Snitches are hard to come by, and the ones that really know something usually disappear—and awfully quickly. Personally, I always thought you were too lucky with your last assignment. It's not often you have two snitches in one gang. Maybe the law of averages is catching up with you."

Taylor didn't know what to say to that, so he said nothing. A pen lay in front of him and he began pushing it around the top of the desk . . . until the pen fell off—over The Drawer. Taylor stared at The Drawer while the director went about the business of tightening the noose around his neck.

"I hate to do this to you, son, but I'm putting you on formal notice; a memo will follow. By the end of the month, you'd better have something I can take to my oversight committee, and it'd better be more than smoke or I'm going to have to shift the few dollars they begrudgingly give me to more promising investigations. In that regard I'm no different than the DEA. I have to produce indictments."

Taylor didn't comment. He had opened The Drawer and was staring at a picture of his ex-wife and children. The children he was forbidden to see as long as he stayed in this damn business.

Not hearing anything on the other end of the line, the director went on to add, "I guess you've heard, Ned Clanton's on the loose."

"I'm not worried about him, sir." Taylor didn't think it would matter if he ran into Clanton again. Maybe he was looking forward to running into old Ned.

"That surprises me, you being so detail-oriented. I would've thought Ned Clanton was someone else you were keeping an eye on."

"I've got someone watching my backside."

"Julius?"

"Yes, sir."

"Clanton would just as soon shoot him as you. Julius was in on the bust, too."

"We didn't put him away. Jackie Mustard did."

"But we can't tell him that, can we? We let Shorty take that fall. Mustard just filled in some of the blanks."

Taylor didn't comment. He was staring at the photograph of his family.

A sigh came from the end of the line in Washington, then, "I don't think I can pull you out of this territorial squabble between us and the DEA without some dirt rubbing off on you. Agents will talk. There's nothing I can do, any more than I can do something about my mandatory retirement coming up next year, and the fact that you won't be my replacement. D-Wars has never failed to secure indictments against anyone we've targeted."

"Until The Hawk."

"Yes, and that's what the committee will look at when selecting my successor: whether you were successful or not. Well, good luck. You'll deserve my job if you pull this off."

Taylor had little chance to brood over the loss of his family or his future because Julius burst into his office and pointed at the telephone. "Beck's on line three and Mark's got a trace on it. Stall her!" He ran out the door and picked up Liliana's phone.

Taylor slammed The Drawer shut before picking up the phone. "Where are you, Sallie?"

"At a honky-tonk on the four-lane on the west side of the city. But that's not important. I'm using their phone because it's in an alcove to the ladies' room, and I can see the door. I think I'm being followed."

"Followed? Who'd be following you?" Phil Rainey was right. Beck was nuts. And Taylor wished he had a man doing just that: following her.

"The Hawk's men. Spano doesn't trust me."

"The Hawk's men! Spano? Do they know you're in town?"

"Of course. I'm working for him."

"You're what!" Beck was definitely loony-toons. They should throw a net over her, if they could catch her.

"Don't you remember? I told you I'd be back, and I'm going to get him like you told me to."

"Like I told you to?" Taylor looked to Julius, but he was no help. The black man stood at the door with his mouth hanging open.

"What—what did I tell you . . . ?"

"Come on, Taylor, don't you remember that day in the taxi? About how the conspiracy law works? That's how I'm going to do it."

Good God, this woman had to be saved from herself. "Where are you, Sallie? You and I need to talk."

"It's called the Ponderosa Playground, but we can't be seen together. It'd blow my cover."

Taylor put his hand over the mouthpiece. "Get someone out there and fast!"

Julius nodded and punched up another line.

Sallie was talking. ". . . close enough to shoot the man, then earn a job working for him, I think I know what the hell I'm doing." She paused. "Sorry about the language, but you were right. There aren't any ladies in the drug trade."

What had Rainey told him? Beck had a ton of drugs with her. In her. He had to keep the woman on the line until the police arrived. Once she was apprehended, Rainey would have her committed for observation. Shit! What was there to observe? The woman was certifiable.

"Er—Sallie, you say you're working for The Hawk?"

"That's why I called. Tomorrow night we're going to bring in a load of marijuana. I wanted you to know I'm coming in afterwards, and I wanted to double-check that it only takes one crime to put everyone in the organization away. That's correct, isn't it?"

"Er—yes. That would do it."

Taylor looked at Julius, hunched over and talking softly into Liliana's phone. Taylor's secretary was staring at Julius like he was nuts. Taylor could understand her concern. Liliana had been told that D-Wars fought a paperwork war, that all the security was window dressing.

"Er—how do I make contact with you after the run's over?" Taylor reached for something to write on. If the cops didn't get there in time he wanted to know where he could find Ms. Sallie Beck.

"I'll contact you. They watch me pretty close."

"But I don't understand. How did you get inside?" That ought to be good for a few laughs, and stall her, too.

"I'm not just inside. I'm living in his house. On the Pointe."

"You're what?"

"I'm living with The Hawk. He's shown me around his whole operation. He's quite proud of it, and he has every right to be. It's huge. Much larger than I ever imagined."

Taylor glanced at Julius being handed a piece of paper by an out-of-breath Mark, who had just rushed upstairs from the computer room. Julius glanced at the paper, then looked at his boss and pulled his hands apart, a motion that meant Taylor was to draw out the conversation.

Taylor didn't know what to say, so he said the first thing that came to mind. "So you learned women in the drug trade make their living on their backs."

Steve Brown

"Don't be silly, Taylor. You warned me about that. You said I'd be no good to D-Wars if I was whoring around. No. I set it up so I'd come in as someone they'd have to respect. That way I didn't have to work as a whore."

Christ! The woman had a snappy comeback for every question. "But why'd The Hawk let you near him? Didn't he recognize you from the dedication at the community center?"

"No way. I got an ID out of your—uh-oh, someone's coming. I'll be in touch."

The line went dead.

"Hello? Hello, Sallie?" Taylor looked from the silent receiver to Julius and Mark as they walked into his office.

"Don't worry, Wes," said the pimply-faced young man, "the cops'll catch her. That pay phone is on that four-lane she mentioned."

"Yeah," said Julius with a nod, "and the cops had a squad car in the vicinity. I gave them her description. Beck won't get away this time."

Thirteen

Sallie walked out of the rest room and right into the arms of Ned Clanton. In the dimly lit nightclub, Ned Clanton thought Sallie Beck *was* Jackie Mustard. He wanted Sallie to be Jackie.

"You bitch!" He grabbed her shoulders and got in her face. "I've waited a long time for this. I couldn't believe my luck when you walked in here. Now I'm going to take care of you *and* that bastard Taylor."

Sallie almost didn't recognize the drug smuggler Jackie Mustard had once loved, then come to despise, and finally set up and sent to prison. His hair was shorter and Clanton had lost a good bit of weight.

She tried to pull away. "No, no! Let go of me!"

"No way, Jackie. You and I've got a lot of catching up to do."

Trying to pry his hands off, she said, "I'm not who you think I am!"

"Your bullshit doesn't work on this old boy. I got

166

over you in the joint. Tomorrow they'll find you face down in one of those canals. I've been planning what I was going to do to your pretty little ass for almost two years."

Ned started across the smoke-filled room, pulling Sallie behind him. Passing the stage where a band played nightly, Sallie grabbed a table, dragging it into one where two couples sat, having a drink.

"Hey!" shouted one of the men, coming to his feet. "Watch what you're doing!"

"Help me! Please!"

Clanton jerked Sallie away. "Don't bother these people. Nobody runs around on me. When I get you home you won't be able to sit down for a week." And he spanked Sallie across the bottom before pulling her toward the door.

Those sitting at the table only laughed.

"No! Help me! He's kidnapping me."

That brought more laughter from other patrons and not a few catcalls. Men shouted at Clanton to show the little woman who was boss; their women flushed and smiled.

Going out the door, Sallie got a hand on the metal detector, a large rectangular unit inside the door, and pulled the rectangular frame into the door. This forced Clanton to stop. A downward whack across her arm caused Sallie to yelp and let go. The door-sized security device tipped over and crashed to the floor. The bartender screamed at both of them as Ned dragged Sallie away.

In the parking lot, Clanton pulled Sallie between a

row of Harley-Davidsons and alongside a pickup where a young couple was making out, the girl's blouse open and her boyfriend's hands all over her. Sallie banged on the window, but the couple never came out of their clinch. In a nondescript sedan, Fuentes and Payne sat up at the sound of the screams, then saw Sallie being dragged across the parking lot.

Payne opened the door, but Fuentes called him back. "Remember what the boss said. She's not to know we're here."

Payne closed the door. "I was doing it for The Hawk."

"Sure you were." The man behind the wheel smiled. "You'd like a little of that yourself, wouldn't you?"

Payne watched Sallie being dragged across the parking lot. Despite the red minidress Sallie wore that almost came up over her thighs, he said, "A little old for me."

"Sure she is," Fuentes said with a laugh. "Anyway, I don't think Spano cares if Mustard returns or not."

As they watched, the woman broke loose and ran for her life.

"Son of a bitch if she didn't get away!"

Sallie ran down a row of cars, then skirted the rear of a pickup with its tailgate down, trying to put the vehicle between her and Clanton. Clanton leaped into the bed and threw himself across it, landing on the side of the bed but where he could reach out and catch the woman's hair as she ran by. Sallie screamed as she was held up and jerked back. Neither one saw the flashing blue light coming down the four-lane.

"Shit! Cops!" Fuentes scanned the interior of the sedan. "Is it clean?"

"Do you have to ask? The Hawk would have our ass."

"Play possum, but keep an eye on the girl."

Fuentes pulled a bottle of bourbon from under his seat, took a hasty drink, and passed the bottle to his companion. Payne did the same, then tossed the bottle out of the window. Both men scooted down and watched as the patrol car slid into the parking lot, spraying gravel as it came to a stop. The flashing blue light was left on as the uniformed patrolmen ran inside the honky-tonk.

Behind the pickup Clanton twisted Sallie's arm up behind her back. "Keep your fucking mouth shut or I'll rip your arm off."

Sallie whimpered her agreement. Tears rolled down her cheeks. No amount of little white pills could ever make this go away.

A minute later one of the policemen came out of the bar and looked up and down the four-lane. Cars and trucks whipped by, and with approaching nightfall, most of the vehicles had their lights on. Not seeing what he wanted, the policeman took a flashlight and began working it around the gravel parking lot. He walked over to the pickup and rapped on the window until the couple came out of their clinch. The boy gulped and sat up, his hands going down to his sides. The girl pulled her blouse together. The policeman asked them a few questions while running his light over them, then moved on to Fuentes and Payne.

The cop tapped on the roof of the bodyguards' car with his light. "Hey, buddy, sit up and talk to me."

Fuentes sat up and rubbed his eyes. He saw the cop and rolled down the window. "What is it, Officer? I must've fallen asleep."

"Yeah. Sure." The policeman stooped down and checked Fuentes with his light, then Payne on the other side of the car. "Your buddy passed out?"

"I guess so."

"Well, I guess that's better than scraping you off the highway. By any chance did you see a slender middle-aged woman with long black hair come out of that bar? She'd be close to forty and have some gray in her hair."

The bodyguard glanced at the pickup where Mustard and the man who had grabbed her now hid. "No, but I don't think I had my eyes open."

"I guess you didn't." The light moved over to Payne again. "I guess your buddy didn't either. Or the kids in the pickup." The policeman stood up and tapped the roof again. "Well, buddy, keep it between the lines."

"Yeah, I will." Fuentes cranked his engine. "Say, this woman, what's she wanted for?"

"She's a nut. A real psycho."

"Shit, I don't need that." Fuentes put his car into gear. "I've got one of those at home."

The cop laughed. "Don't we all, don't we all."

As Fuentes drove away, the policeman walked to the four-lane and looked up and down the highway. There was no dark-haired woman to be seen, and the only woman in the parking lot was a blonde making out with her boyfriend against a pickup. And the way they were going at it, he doubted they'd seen anything either. He was about to approach the couple when his partner came out of the bar, making his way through the row of motorcycles.

"Any luck?"

"I don't think she was here. Nobody remembers seeing her, and she would've stood out. The place is full of regulars. Even the bikers are locals, but if you want more paperwork, there's several in there smoking dope."

"No, thank you," said his partner, climbing into the cruiser. "Let's ride up and down the highway and see if we get lucky. If she *is* nuts *and* carrying a pistol we'd best cover our ass."

After the patrol car left, two bikers pulled into the parking lot on their Harleys, and Ned Clanton came out of his clinch with Sallie.

"That's all I need," he said, his breath coming hard and fast, "to be run through some fucking computer."

Tears streaked Sallie's face. Her shoulder ached from where her arm had been thrust up behind her back. "That's what I am . . . Mr. Clanton . . . a computer programmer, not Jackie Mustard."

"All that shit's wasted on me. Maybe your tongue's the reason you didn't go to jail." He grinned wickedly. "It still tasted good after all this time, and I hope you remember how to use it because you're going to give my dick a real workout before I cut your tongue out. That's what I learned in the joint: cut a snitch's tongue out. It cures them of squealing."

"Please . . . please let me go. I'm not Jackie Mustard, really, I'm not. Please let me go." Sallie's shoulders sagged. "I'll go home and leave you alone. I'll go home and leave all of you alone. Just let me go."

"God, but it's good to hear you beg. Maybe I won't kill you right away." He scanned the parking lot, including the area where the two bikers were parking their Harleys. "Got your little red Z-car around here somewhere?"

"Please, Mr. Clanton," said Sallie, clutching Ned's shirt, "let me go."

Clanton grabbed her by the hair, jerking her head back. Sallie tried to scream but couldn't find the breath.

"When I ask you a question, bitch, I expect an answer. Is your car around here?"

"Yes—yes!"

"Where?"

"On the other side . . . ." Sallie's voice failed her and she had to collect herself to finish. "On the other side of the building."

"All right. Let's go."

Two bikers watched the couple disappear around the corner. They looked at each other before following Sallie and Ned to the other side of the building. The bikers wore jeans, T-shirts, and boots. Both had dark faces, scruffy beards, and long greasy hair. The only difference between the two was a leather vest one wore.

Clanton had Sallie up against the side of the car, fishing the keys out of her jumpsuit. He goosed her between the legs before unlocking the door, and Sallie moaned. More tears ran down her cheeks. Clanton let go of her long enough to open the door, but Sallie didn't run. The thought never occurred to her.

But when Clanton tried to force her into the passenger seat, Sallie came to life, fighting to get free. Clanton stopped this with a slap across the top of the head, then shoved her toward the front seat of the sports car.

"Get down there, bitch! I'm in a hurry."

Steve Brown

Sallie's legs gave way and she went to her knees in the gravel.

Slapping her across the top of the head, Clanton yelled, "Get up! Get up!"

The bikers walked up behind him. "Hey, cowboy, having trouble with your woman?"

Clanton didn't have to turn around to tell whoever the hell it was this was none of their fucking business. Besides, he had his hands full shoving Jackie into the car. She'd gone limp, becoming a dead weight.

He slapped her head again. "Get in there, bitch!"

"Maybe she doesn't want to go with you," said a voice from behind him.

Clanton let go of the woman and turned around. There were two of them, both about six feet tall and weighing close to three hundred pounds each, and not all of it pot gut. "It's none of your damn business what I'm doing."

One of the bikers snorted. The other asked, "You want to go with the cowboy, little mama?"

Sallie shook her head violently. "No! No! No! He's making me."

"She's my woman," said Clanton, standing as tall and impressive as he could. With the biker's height and weight it was a lost cause.

"I'm not his woman! I've never seen this man before! He was trying to make me suck his dick!"

Clanton whirled around and slapped Sallie across the top of the head again. "Shut up, bitch!"

"Help me!" cried Sallie, bursting into tears. "Oh, God, please help me!"

One of the bikers caught Clanton's arm as he swung again. "Hey, cowboy, don't you know it's more fun if they pretend to like it."

The other biker laughed. "Maybe the cowboy's more than a mouthful, Bruce."

"We could help with that." Bruce rubbed the holster on his belt holding a pocketknife. "Maybe cut him down to size."

From the ground, Sallie said, "He said he'd buy me dinner."

"Bitch!" muttered Clanton, glaring at her.

One of the bikers gave Clanton a sly smile. "Well, you old dog, you."

The one named Bruce jerked a thumb over his shoulder. "You're out of here, cowboy."

Clanton opened his mouth to protest, but the bikers spread their feet and folded their arms across their chests. Ned snorted at this show of machismo but said nothing as he pushed his way through the two men. At the corner of the building he turned around. "I'm not through with you, bitch."

The bikers ignored him and pulled Sallie to her feet. "You okay, little mama?"

She nodded and wiped the tears away. "Yes, yes. Thank you."

"You don't look so good."

"No, no, I'm . . . okay."

The bikers let her stand, then caught her as Sallie's legs gave way.

"Yeah, you're real okay," said Bruce. "Come on. We'll take you home."

The other biker found Sallie's keys and locked up her car. He joined Sallie and Bruce at the bikes.

Sallie was staring at the huge machines. She'd never ridden a motorcycle before. "I don't know—"

"You can come back for your Z in the morning," Bruce said. "Hey, this place where we're taking you isn't where that asshole lives, is it? If it is, I might not let you go home."

"Absolutely not. I ran into him inside. He thought he knew me."

The bikers glanced at each other, one saying, "I've used that line myself."

Sallie's shoulders sagged. "I just want to go home."

Bruce threw a leg over his machine, saddled up, and cranked the engine. "Put her up behind me, Jack."

Sallie was lifted up behind the biker to sit on a long and narrow back seat. She looked around for something to hold onto but found only the man in front of her. She wrapped her arms around Bruce's huge waist and held on tight as they rode out of the parking lot.

But the bikers didn't take her home like Sallie asked. They returned her to The Hawk's. Trailing them was Fuentes and Payne, and bringing up the rear, in a truck he'd hot-wired from the parking lot, came Ned Clanton.

*   *   *

On the other side of the country, in a much smaller town and a completely different time zone, a blonde walked into a bank in the Pacific Northwest and stepped up to the next available window. The teller was a fat woman wearing a sack dress to disguise her weight. Her jowls bounced as she joked with the customers at her window.

She smiled at the blonde. "And how are you, today, Mrs. Daley?"

"Er—just fine. I—I didn't know you knew my name."

The fat woman continued to smile. "I make a practice of knowing all the new people in town. I've known Mr. Daley for years. How is he?"

"Okay, but he has to work six days."

"Yes, but it's good to have the logging business back. Heard you were pregnant."

The blonde nodded and glanced at her abdomen.

"How far along?"

"Three months." Daley ran her hand over her stomach. "Does it show?"

"No, dearie, but you'll be glad when it does, at least with the first. This is your first, isn't it?"

It was a moment before the blonde said, "It makes me sick in the mornings."

The teller nodded and her jowls shook again. "Happened to me, too, dearie, and I've had four of them. Men don't know what we women go through. But you'll be fine. What can I do for you today?"

"I'd like twenty dollars in change. Mostly quarters. All in coin." The blonde shoved a twenty-dollar bill across the counter.

The teller took the twenty and counted out the change. "Like an envelope to put it in?"

"I've got something."

The blonde tugged at a cloth hung up on something

inside her purse. When she finally pulled the sack free, she scraped the coins from the counter into it. Several of the coins hit the lip of the cloth sack and slipped off, but the young woman was quick enough to snatch them out of the air or step on them before they could run across the floor.

She looked up from jamming the sack into her purse. "Thanks."

"Anytime. Anything else we can do for you today?"

The blonde glanced toward the rear of the bank. "I might have to come back and get something out of my safe deposit box."

"Just see Ellie. She'll let you in. And don't forget your key."

"I've got it right here." The blonde patted her purse. "It stays here all the time."

The teller watched the pregnant woman push her way through the heavy double doors at the front of the bank. What a woman who worked at a convenience store whose husband was a lumberjack needed with a safe deposit box was beyond her. Oh, well, that's what safe deposit boxes were for, to make people feel important.

The young woman in the adjoining cage said, "She was in yesterday while you were on break."

"She was?"

"Yeah, and wanting twenty dollars in change just like she asked for today."

The fat woman glanced at the door. "Probably wants to call mama about her morning sickness without hubby knowing. Daley's known for being tight with his money."

Woman Against Herself

Outside the bank the blonde stopped in the middle of the sidewalk to shift around the contents of her purse. With the heavy sack of coins, her purse was too heavy at one end. The blonde pushed a .44 Magnum into one corner, the sack into the other, and then continued down the street looking for a pay phone. An out-of-the-way pay phone.

✳   ✳   ✳

Tina took the stairs to the second floor in The Hawk's warehouse where the money was sorted and weighed. It was also where her benefactor had a small office. There was finally room to move around, and Tina had spent a good bit of time straightening up the area. Her mentor didn't seem to notice or appreciate what she'd done. He sat, slouched in his chair, arms limp on the armrests, eyes closed.

Tina had seen Carlos like this—before he rented the three tractor trailers that sat outside the warehouse and held over ten million dollars. Each. As a security precaution, the wheels had been removed from each trailer. For a few days, Carlos had visibly brightened, noticing the work she had done in his office. Now those days were behind them.

The teenager spoke from the door. "Carlos?"

The accountant's eyes opened. He said nothing, only stared at her, so Tina stepped inside the office and took a seat on the edge of a chair.

"Are you all right?"

"You know I'm not. I'm about to lose everything."

"I'm sure that won't happen. The Hawk wouldn't let it happen."

"The Hawk is making all this happen."

Tina held her breath. Was this the opening she'd been waiting for? Tina wanted to tell this dumpy, middle-aged man that they had so much in common. Both were searching for the same thing: security. Tina because she'd never had a home, or a safe one, Carlos because he didn't know where he belonged.

After fleeing their island homeland, Carlos's family had resisted assimilation into American culture. As a boy, his parents vowed they would return to Cuba once that devil Castro was driven out. Now his parents were both gone, Castro having outlived them, and their children had grown up being told they belonged in Cuba, not America.

The fallout had been intense. Not only had Carlos's parents refused to learn English or secure anything more than the most menial of jobs, but, one by one, their six children had been shown the door. They had been corrupted by the easy money to be made in America, said the parents. The children had evidently been corrupted by something. One of the six had committed suicide, three became alcoholics and attended regular counseling. All found it impossible to resolve the conflict between the land of milk and honey and the Spartan habits preached at home. Carlos was the only one to escape this purgatory. Learning from his siblings' pleasure seeking, he created an environment where those Spartan values thrived.

Woman Against Herself

He picked up a piece of paper and glanced at it, then let the paper fall to the desktop. "Twenty million dollars for aircraft and parts, a hundred and fifty thousand for maintenance, another quarter of a million for uniforms, a half million for food and related items, six hundred thousand for miscellaneous supplies including a Red Cross team and battlefield surgeon, almost a million for new electronic gear, four million dollars for armaments, and this is the absolute worst: two million dollars for a landing strip in Guyana. How much of this is going for bribes I don't know."

"Guyana? I thought we were going to Suriname."

"The Hawk says he must have a backup in case anything goes wrong when we lift off from here."

"Such as?"

"Such as trouble on the ground."

"Like a tropical storm?"

"Like if the Surinamese don't like the idea of us seizing their country," Carlos said sarcastically. "I have supported this man for the last six years and this is the way he treats me." A hand flicked at the paper on the desk. "What waste. I understand the necessity for backups and backups on your backups, but two million dollars for a landing strip we may never use? Then there is the landing strip north of Miami where the planes and the commandos will rendezvous. Richey is having it reconditioned at the cost of over two hundred thousand dollars. I argued long and hard against this invasion but got nowhere. The Hawk doesn't listen to me anymore.

"Me! One of his trusted advisors, and I can say nothing that will stop this madness. God knows why he has to do this thing, but I have never seen him so set on anything." The accountant shook his head. "And moving ahead full speed. I have never seen that either. In the past he was always so careful, weighing his options, looking for pitfalls. But now, I don't know . . . ."

"What are you going to do?" asked the teenager in a low voice. The room became quiet, so much so, Tina could hear the security detail downstairs, kicking back and enjoying the fact that the last truck for the day had been unloaded and was gone.

"There is nothing I can do." Carlos rolled his head across the back of the chair so he could see the counting room. "Soon all this will be gone. And me with it. To some South American paradise I've never even heard of. Growing up as a child, I dreaded the thought of returning to Cuba. I love this country."

"Why don't we run away?"

"Where would we go? Where could I carry on my work? Who will have me?"

"Will you be able to work in South America?"

Carlos nodded. "In some fashion . . . but those people will steal us blind. They have nothing, least of all a sense of honor. Here we at least have honor among thieves. Or once did."

"Who put this idea in The Hawk's head?"

"The Americans' invasion of Haiti. The Hawk dreams of being bigger than General Motors. Bigger than the Mafia." The accountant's voice drifted off and he looked into the next room, then farther off into the distance.

"What should we do?"

"Go with him, I suppose. What else is there to do?" He smiled. "What would you have me do, girl? You're the one who's always nagging me about exercise and eating my vegetables. How should I handle my future?"

"Do what my friend did!" blurted out the girl.

"And what did your friend do, my dear?"

"She went into the witness relocation program."

Carlos sat up and looked out the door. "Watch what you say. The walls have ears. Eyes, too." He stood up and went to the door.

Carlos looked around the counting room. No one there. The women had gone home hours ago, and the security detail was on the lower level. Once Carlos could identify them all by voice, he returned to his chair but only after turning on a radio on an overhead shelf.

"Talk like that could get you killed."

The girl scooted back in her chair and tried to appear calm. If she was going to get this man to take her advice, she must appear confident and relaxed. "I'm only telling you what she did. I didn't say we had to do what she did."

"How would you know if she was in . . . the program?"

"She was talking about it before she left town."

"She might be dead for all you know. Who did she fink on?"

"A bank robber the FBI was looking for. She was working the street, and, after fucking her, he gave her a big tip and told her there was more where that came from. She hung around—to steal some of that money—and found out where all that money came from. She realized the robber could be her ticket off the streets. And she's not dead. She called me from where she's living. She kept my number."

"And people probably tapped your phone and traced the call and now your friend *is* dead."

Tina leaned forward. "We wouldn't have to call anyone. We would have each other."

Carlos studied the girl. "You would go away with me?"

"You take care of me. I take care of you."

"But I'm old enough to be your father."

"Be whatever you want. I just want out of here, and I can't do it alone. If I leave on my own, I end up on the street working for some pimp." The girl glanced at the counting room. "I'm scared to be around all this . . . poison gas and machine guns. The men have shown me everything. They want to fuck me, but I won't. Anyway, one day something will happen, and I don't want to be here when it does."

"You can leave anytime you wish. I made you that promise the night you returned."

"Carlos, are you not listening? I'm not leaving without you. You're the only reason I've stayed. You don't abuse me. You don't try to get me high. You never sold me to another man. If you won't leave, then I'll stay and take my chances. It's better than the street. I know. I've been there."

"You could've stolen some money and left long ago. Everyone who works here thinks they know of ways to steal from The Hawk."

The girl nodded. "I know of three."

Carlos smiled. "Sorry, my dear, but I wouldn't know

any more about how to sneak away than your fanciful ways of stealing could possibly work. I'm watched all the time."

"You're only watched when you're around the money. Other times . . . ." She looked at the floor. "Hawk and Spano don't respect you. They don't think you have the nerve to leave."

"I may not."

The teenager stood up and came around the desk. "Then I'll give you the nerve."

Carlos smiled as he swiveled to face her. "I thought you didn't like to do that."

"I hate doing it. It hurts. But if it will get you to leave I will." She smiled. "Besides, maybe there's something I can do that you'd also enjoy." She knelt in front of him and reached for his zipper.

Fourteen

Sallie circled the Colombian freighter until the last of The Hawk's boats arrived, then went into her final approach a mile from the boat's running lights. It was a quiet, starlit night over the Gulf, very little breeze, and no swells. Still, the tanned young man next to her gripped his armrests.

"Oh, shit! I'm not going to like this."

He was in his early twenties, wore long hair, faded jeans, and an Oakland Raiders T-shirt. His well-developed muscles caused the T-shirt to stretch tightly across his torso and upper arms. Strapped across his chest was not only his seat belt but also an oversized pistol with a very short barrel. His name was Danny and he was a member of Spano's security detail from the warehouse.

Sallie turned on her lights and lit up the Florida Straits seventy-five to a hundred feet ahead of them. She flew a Canadir 215 with twin Pratt-Whitney engines that had a cruising range of over a thousand miles.

"That's more like it," said Danny, settling back in his seat. "All the way down I've been wondering how you were going to see to land."

"The headlights were on when we took off in Miami."

"They were?" The young man did not take his eyes off the lighted tunnel that bore through the darkness ahead of them. "I never noticed. Back there we had a bunch of landing lights across the water."

The first waves broke ahead of them, showing their tips in the light.

"The water!" He turned to her. "Do you see it?"

Sallie nodded, kept her eyes on the surface, and leveled out, slightly bringing up the nose. For the ocean, the water was smooth as glass. Even so, Danny's eyes grew larger and he leaned forward into his seat belt as they closed with the surface. The pontoon plane thumped and bumped through the waves before skidding to a halt. Sallie reversed the engine and the plane came to a stop about a hundred feet from the freighter and several other smaller crafts.

Sallie glanced at Danny and saw the young man's eyes were closed. When he opened them, he let out a deep sigh.

"We made it, thank God! We made it!"

"Yes. Thank God."

She brought the plane around and headed for the freighter lit up by the spotlights on The Hawk's boats and the freighter's onboard lighting system. Lit up like a Christmas tree and only a few miles outside the territorial waters of the United States, thought Sallie. Only The Hawk would have the gall to bring a grass-filled freighter this close to shore. Sallie realized there was more to this smuggling business than just the money.

"I'll tell you something, Jackie, if you won't tell the other men."

"What's that?"

Sallie maneuvered through boats on this side of the freighter. None of them moved out of her way. Men armed with rifles, shotguns, and automatic weapons stood on deck and ignored the spray kicked up by the propeller. A couple of the smugglers spit in the ocean as the plane passed by.

"Nobody else would fly down with you. I was the only one who'd do it. They said they didn't want to go on any operation with a woman, that you'd jinx it, but that wasn't it. They didn't have the guts."

Unsaid was the lack of seniority Danny might have, or that he might've pissed off Spano who figured he would get rid of both problems in one night. For that reason, Sallie had crawled all over her plane, searching for anything suspicious. The mechanics at the airport merely shook their heads and returned to other work in the hangars.

Danny saw his fellow smugglers staring at the plane and saluted them with a middle finger. "How low did you say we were flying?"

Sallie was following the movement of two orange Lucite wands motioning her alongside the freighter. "Less than two hundred feet."

The young man's head whipped around. "Two hundred feet! Are you kidding? I couldn't tell. There's no moon out. How'd you know how high we were?"

Cutting her engines and letting the plane drift toward the ship, Sallie said, "I guessed."

"Shit! Don't tell me that." Danny scanned the gauges. "You have to have something on this panel that tells you how high you are from the ground, I mean from the water."

Sallie chuckled but didn't point out the altimeter. "Don't worry, Danny. It's my ass, too."

The young man's face brightened. "That's what I like about you, Jackie. You're just one of the guys. I mean, and don't take this wrong because you're a good-looking woman, but you don't get bent out of shape over how we act."

"Allowances have to be made for animals."

She looked up a wall, which was the side of the freighter, then scanned the heavily armed smugglers on the decks of their small boats. What the hell was she doing here? She should be home, in bed, getting a good night's sleep for the next day's work at IINTELL. But here she was, in the middle of the ocean, about to smuggle drugs into her own country. More drugs to kill more children. Kill more Timmies. And that's why she was here. For Timmie. She was doing this for Timmie and she'd best not forget it.

But flying down, whenever she thought about what she was about to do, she became rattled. Could she really pull this off? Did she have the nerve? Wes Taylor hadn't thought so, and Sallie was beginning to have her doubts. To distract herself, she checked and rechecked the instruments, avoided looking at Danny and his ugly pistol, and forced herself to remember happier times when her father taught her how to fly. Times when she'd been younger, flying at night, landing on the water near the places her parents rented for the summer, and scaring the bejesus out of any boy alongside her in the cockpit. Sallie shivered. Now it was her turn to have the bejesus scared out of her.

Danny was saying something.

"What'd you say?"

"You're more fun than most girls. Calling the men animals, teasing them. That's why we don't mind showing you around. You're interested in what we're doing. Most women don't give a shit. The Hawk's a lucky man."

"I don't sleep with him, Danny. I don't have to, and I don't give a damn what those assholes think."

The young man nodded and for a long time. "Neither do I. I'm with you on that, Jackie."

Danny gazed at the freighter, its side towering over their plane, and as he did, Sallie slipped her trembling hands off the stick.

Sallie pulled out a little white pill and popped it into her mouth, then washed it down with some warm beer from a holder between her and Danny.

"Hey, you want a cold one?" The young man pointed at the cooler between his feet.

"No," Sallie tried to say and beer ran up her nose. She gagged and coughed and couldn't get her breath. The beer stung, especially her nose.

Danny pounded her on the back. "You okay?"

She coughed and nodded, then wiped her face on

the sleeve of her jacket. "I'm okay. Shouldn't be drinking and talking at the same time." She pointed at the other smugglers. "There'll be plenty of time to knock down a few cold ones after we've shown these bastards what we can do—right?"

Danny glanced at his friends. "Yeah! Right! We'll show those bastards."

Yeah, right, if I don't lose my nerve. Why don't the little white pills help? That's the third one I've taken, and I'm still shaking. Dear Lord, just let me get out of this alive and I'll go home and stick to my own business. I'll never try to—

A voice barked over the radio. "Mother Goose! Mother Goose! This is Godfather. Come in!"

"Hey!" said Danny. "That's us, isn't it?"

"Yes. Yes, it is." Sallie fumbled with the handset. "Mother Goose here."

"They want you to load first—to see if you can do it. If you can't, back off and get the hell out of the way."

"I—I can do it!"

"Good, and don't forget, we'll be off-loading on both sides of the ship."

"Roger that. I have this side." She glanced at the compass. "The south side."

"Roger and out." Godfather went on to give instructions to the boat on the north side.

Sallie maneuvered alongside the freighter while Danny climbed into the cargo bay and opened the hatch. Once done, he shoved a wooden raft, or pallet, bolstered with Styrofoam, pushing it toward the door.

"Don't forget to turn on the lights."

"Gotcha."

Danny flicked on the strobes at each corner of the raft and kicked the wooden structure out the hatch. The raft plunged into the water, surfaced, and floated about twenty feet before stopping at the end of ropes Danny was fastening to the hatch. Once the raft ran out of line, it jerked to a stop and drifted back toward the plane.

"Use the pole to keep it away from the plane, Danny. Always protect the wings. We can't leave without them."

The young man laughed. "It's my ass, too." He patted his snub-nose machine pistol. "They fuck with us and I'll give them a few rounds of this up their ass."

The first bale started down, swinging over the side of the freighter, then lowered away, toward the raft. Danny leaned out and watched the marijuana come down. Sallie stared through the Plexiglas at her wing. Imagine getting stuck out here without any wings. She didn't think any of the other boats would give them a ride home.

"It's your show, Mother Goose," said the voice over the radio. "Don't get the product wet."

Sallie's hand moved toward the radio to wilco the transmission, then pulled back. *No, sirree, two can play that game.*

The bale settled on the raft and bits and pieces of the marijuana tumbled into the ocean. The ropes from the ship's hoist went limp, but by then the bale sat squarely among the strobe lights.

"Got it!"

Danny tugged on the ropes and the raft floated over

to where he could put a hook into the bale, then wrestle it inside the hatch. He shoved the bale across the plastic-covered deck, against the far bulkhead.

He grinned as he turned around. "Just like you said, Jackie. You must've done this before."

"What? Oh, yeah." Sallie was observing Jackie Mustard's system of smuggling pot into Southern California, in awe of how easy it was. "You wouldn't believe the number of times I've done this."

Danny kicked the raft away. "We can go places boats can never go, and faster, too."

"If you don't mind flying two hundred feet above the water."

The young man laughed, leaned out, and looked up the towering side of the freighter. "Okay, you bastards, get your asses in gear." He wiped his forehead with a red bandanna and then tied it around his head. When the next bale arrived he wrestled it into the plane.

Sallie shook her head. I can't believe I'm doing this. I'm smuggling drugs into my country. The same drugs that killed my son. I can't believe I'm really doing this.

From where he sat on his haunches, Danny glanced at Sallie and flashed a big smile.

How can you do this, Danny? Don't you know drugs hurt people? They killed my little boy, and I'm sorry, but you're going to prison. All I wanted was The Hawk, but the rest of you fell into my hands.

As Sallie glanced at her instruments she noticed three green dots appear on her radarscope. They were coming from the south and coming fast. Who could they be?

Glancing to the south, she saw nothing but darkness. They can't be the Coast Guard. We're too far out and they're coming from the wrong direction. More smugglers? Could be. No reason to think The Hawk has an exclusive on AWACS flights scheduled over the Straits. Anyone could buy an airman if they had enough money. And The Hawk had the money.

Sallie picked up her microphone as Danny loaded another bale. "Mother Goose to Godfather. Mother Goose to Godfather."

"What's your problem, Mother Goose? You know the rules about radio silence. You already loaded?"

"Not yet. Give me a few more minutes. Got anything on your scope?"

There was a pause before Godfather returned to the air. "Nothing, but you've got a stronger scope. What do you see?"

"Three dots moving on line and coming in fast from the south."

One of the speedboats cranked up its motor and roared off to the south. Other captains saw nothing on their scopes and said so.

"Shut up and clear the net!" ordered Godfather.

The net went silent.

"If they were coming from the north," Godfather said, "I'd know who they were."

"What do we do?" asked Sallie.

"You get off the net. This is a job for security. Roger Dodger, did you copy Mother Goose?"

"Roger Dodger," a Southern accent drawled over the roar of his engine. "But I don't see nothing."

"Give him a bearing, Mother Goose."

Sallie did.

"Give me a sit rep soon as possible. I want to know what's going on."

"Roger Dodger here. How far out, Mother Goose?"

"Ten to fifteen miles and closing fast."

"I'm gone," Roger Dodger said. "Be in touch."

Sallie opened the mike to reply but closed it without saying a word.

"Okay, children," Godfather said, "spread out. If this is who we think it is, we'd best be ready. Switch to orange running lights so we'll know friend from foe. You got orange lights on your plane, Mother Goose?"

Sallie checked the cargo hold. Danny was loading another bale. "No, but I'm out of here with one more bale."

"Okay. Whoremaster, you're up next. Remember, if it's pirates, take no prisoners. They won't."

Sallie shivered in the hot night air. Nobody'd mentioned pirates during the briefing. What was going on? She was supposed to fly down, pick up a load, and fly to Alabama, not fight pirates. She fingered the Magnum under her arm; still couldn't hit shit with it.

"Danny, we need to get out of here."

"No sweat." He leaned out the hold and looked up. "Last one's coming down."

Sallie glanced behind her. Whoremaster had pulled up behind her, engine running, actually never turned off. If the green dots *were* pirates, the boats doing the loading would be the most vulnerable. She glanced at the scope. Roger Dodger was racing toward the moving dots. Roger Dodger didn't run grass but ran interference for the other boats. He bragged that his go-fast boat was the quickest in the fleet, but as Sallie studied the dots moving in from the south, she saw them moving toward Roger Dodger faster than Roger Dodger was moving toward them. What kind of boat could be faster than Roger Dodger's?

"I've still got nothing on my scope," shouted Roger Dodger over the roar of his engine. "Am I closing on them or are they veering off?"

Sallie snatched up the mike. "They should be right on top of you in the next minute."

Sallie heard Roger Dodger throw his boat into idle and shout to his men: something about getting the machine gun pointed south, then the mike closed. She continued to watch the scope as the dots not only closed with Roger Dodger but also passed him.

"They're moving past you!"

"What?" Roger Dodger killed his engine. "Are you sure? There's nothing here, and I've got the starlight working. I can hear boats in the distance, but they're nothing to worry about."

"That's impossible! One of them passed within a hundred yards of you."

"And I'm telling you there's nothing out here. Do you know how to read that fucking scope, woman?"

Sallie opened her mike but stopped again. Behind her Danny finished loading the last bale of grass.

"You sure you got those dots on your scope, Mother Goose?" asked Godfather. "I don't see them and they'd be in range by now."

"Three dots," Sallie repeated in a calmer voice. "Less than four miles out. They never broke formation."

"And I'm telling you there's nothing out here!"

A nervous voice came over the net. "Let's load up and get the hell out of here!"

"I'm for that," said another captain. "I've got a hot woman and a cold beer waiting and both are changing temperature."

Hoots of laughter carried across the water, and Sallie's neck warmed in the cool night air.

"I'm coming back," drawled Roger Dodger.

"All loaded." Danny cut the raft free, leaving it and its flashing lights behind.

"Mother Goose loaded!" screamed Sallie into the microphone.

"Then get the hell out of there!"

"Yes, sir!"

Behind her the hatch slammed shut. Sallie glanced at the scope again. Roger Dodger was following the dots. The dots were less than two miles out and coming fast, whatever the hell they were. Sallie cursed and slapped at the radio, hanging up the handset and accidentally turning it off; then her attention was focused on getting them out of there.

Danny came forward and climbed into his seat. He wiped his face with the bandanna. "Whew! Quick, but tough work." He strapped on his pistol and seat belt. As he did, Danny saw the tunnel of light growing ahead of them. "Oh, shit! I'd forgotten about this."

Sallie snorted, then glanced at him. The young man's T-shirt was wet from loading the marijuana and pieces of grass stuck to the front of the fabric. The eye-patched mascot of the Oakland Raiders appeared to be smoking a joint.

"What was that on the radio?" he asked.

"Don't know. No one knows." She opened up the engine and the plane picked up speed.

"What's this?" asked Danny, seeing the dots on the scope for the first time.

Sallie glanced at where the young man was pointing, and without thinking, said, "That's to alert you that there are other planes in the area." Her head jerked back to the radar. Roger Dodger was falling farther and farther behind.

"They're planes! They're fucking planes! That's what they are! No wonder Roger Dodger couldn't see them." She shook her head. "Talk about making a complete fool out of yourself."

"What'd you say?"

"Oh, nothing. I was talking to the plane. It's a pilot thing. We think of planes as people."

"That's weird," said Danny in a cautious voice as he watched the tunnel of light boring through the darkness.

When Sallie opened up her engines the plane picked up speed, and she and Danny were slowly pushed into their seats. They rushed through the tunnel.

"Oh, shit! I don't want to do this!"

Moments later, Danny realized the plane hadn't lifted off. "What's wrong? Why won't she take off?"

Sallie gestured toward the cargo bay. "We've picked up some extra weight."

Danny grabbed the back of her seat, twisted around, and stared at the grass. "Should I throw some out?"

"If you don't mind how those Alabama boys are going to feel once they find out they've been short-loaded."

"Fuck them! I just want her to take off."

Slowly, the plane lifted off and began to rise. Danny's head did, too, as if willing the aircraft into the air. Sallie cut the lights and they soared off into the darkness.

"Why'd you do that?"

"Take it easy, Danny. We flew down here without them, didn't we?"

"Yeah." He looked into the darkness. "I guess we did."

Sallie swung the plane around and, after a long sweeping turn taking almost five minutes, she brought her aircraft back over the freighter. Small fires burning on the surface of the water lighted up the ship.

"What's that?" asked Danny.

"Don't know."

Sallie realized the radio was off and flipped it back on. Screams of "Mayday" filled the net until there were so many they distorted the net.

"My God, they're on fire down there!"

"*What?*" Danny pressed his face against the Plexiglas and tried to see. "But how? What happened?"

"I don't know."

Roaring out of the darkness and across their bow came an aircraft with no running lights. In the light from below, Sallie thought she saw four engines but couldn't be sure. She was too busy jerking back on the stick. Hard.

"What the hell was that?" Danny tried to look behind them as the unidentified plane flew by.

Sallie glanced at the scope. The three green dots were below her, not very far away and circling the freighter. "Pirate aircraft! That's why Roger Dodger couldn't see them. They were in the air."

"They bombed us!" Danny stared open-mouthed at the fires on the water behind them.

"And did a damn good job, too."

Danny unbuckled his belt and climbed out of his seat. "I'll dump the grass so we can get out of here!"

Sallie grabbed him as he went by. "No! That doesn't make sense."

Danny fought free and climbed into the hold. "I've done it before. The Hawk'll understand."

Sallie didn't dare look at him. She didn't know when one of those dots, one of those aircraft, would race across her bow again. "Danny, you open the hatch and we'll end up in the water right after the grass. Maybe before."

Danny stopped fumbling with the hatch. "What are you talking about?"

Sallie kept her eye on the scope. The rest of the world could go jump, but she had to concentrate on keeping her plane away from the larger aircraft, had to concentrate on the dots swarming around her like angry hornets. Why weren't the assholes using running lights? If one of those wings clipped hers . . . .

"Our plane's out of balance as it is," she explained. "You can't open one side and expect us to stay in the air. I won't be able to keep her stabilized. Keep it level," she added. "Just come up here and sit down."

The young man's hand was still on the hatch. "Are you shitting me?"

"Have I ever before?"

"No, but this is hairy stuff." Danny relocked the hatch, came forward, and sat down. After rebuckling himself in his seat he looked around. "What do we do?"

Sallie tapped the scope. "Keep an eye on them and head for home."

Danny peered at the scope with its three dots. One of those fucking dots seemed awful close. "Where are we on this, Jackie?"

"We're not."

"We're not?" He looked at her. "Why not?"

"We're the center of the scope."

"Oh," Danny's voice was low, not understanding.

They flew on with Danny's attention glued to the scope. In a minute he said, "I think one of them's following us."

Sallie glanced at the scope. One of the dots had broken out of formation and was headed in their direction. "He'll be here any moment because he has more horsepower."

Danny gripped his holstered pistol and tried to look behind them. "What do we do?"

Sallie killed her running lights and dimmed the ones on the control panel. "Play hide and seek and hope we win."

Fifteen

While Sallie was flying for her life, an agent of the Drug Enforcement Agency found his boss at home, schmoozing with the "right people." His boss's wife wasn't so sure. She was the one who had to put on all these parties and take phone messages for her busy mate. Still, this was one agent her husband would want to talk to. This agent was working on something really big. Something big enough to get them out of Miami.

For the first time in a long time she handed the phone to her husband with a smile, then returned to the living room for another session of brown-nosing. No wonder people ran for public office: the attraction of having a person as important as her husband falling all over himself to please folks such as themselves was too much of a temptation to pass up.

"Sorry to bother you at home, sir," the agent said over the sound of traffic in the background, "but I had a call from our contact inside The Hawk's organization and you said to give her top priority."

"What I said was: you better give top priority to running D-Wars out of South Florida. They're after your job. Now, what do you have for me?"

"She says we have to bust The Hawk, and we have to do it within the week."

"That is simply not going to happen. The first order of business is the collapse of D-Wars. Tell your contact to stay in place. We'll tell her when she's to come out."

"Yes, sir, but this time she really sounded scared."

"She'll always be scared. It's the price you pay for leading a double life."

The sound of traffic was all that was heard on the other end of the line, then the voice of the agent again. "She says The Hawk has something really big coming up and Carlos is beside himself with worry."

"And did our young friend happen to tell you what this something 'really big' was?"

"No, sir, she didn't."

The senior man chuckled. "All snitches are the same." He glanced through the serving window of the kitchen. His wife was doing her job, keeping the pols happy. "Be firm with her. Make her understand who's boss. She's only a kid. Tell her we're sticking to our original deal. She puts The Hawk away and we put her into the witness relocation program—with Carlos. Why she even thinks that wimp will come with her is beyond me. But whatever we do, we do it by our timetable, not hers."

"Yes, sir," said the agent with little enthusiasm.

"Your problem is your snitch is about to betray her

friends and can't sleep at night. Even when she does, she wonders if she talks in her sleep and if Spano has her room bugged. In her present condition everything's a crisis. It's her nerves talking. I've been through all this before."

"Well, you know what's best, but I've never heard her talk this way. She became hysterical and abusive. By the end of the conversation, she was shouting about how we'd be responsible for whatever happened because we had the power to stop The Hawk."

"If she won't tell us what we have to stop, how can we judge the danger?" He paused. "If she's really worried, she'll call back, and you'll be able to get it out of her."

"I told her she had to be more specific, but she says only four or five people know what's going down and that's too small a number for Spano to concentrate on. She says we'll have to bust The Hawk without knowing what he has planned."

"Ridiculous. D-Wars is on its last legs in South Florida. Pressure's being applied in Washington. In a few weeks they'll be old news; then nobody will tell me what cases to back off of. I'll go after anyone I want, even if another agency's trying to bust him. Then, after D-Wars has been forced out, *I'll* indict The Hawk myself and D-Wars won't dare return to South Florida. We'll never have to cooperate with them again. Anywhere. Tell your snitch I don't care if The Hawk's planning to assassinate the president, she's to stay in place until *we* say she can come out." The senior man glanced at his watch. "Aren't they in the middle of that big grass shipment right about now?"

"Yes, sir, and if everything's going according to plan, the pirates should be attacking The Hawk's ships at this very moment."

The senior man harrumphed, then glanced through the serving window. His wife was showing their guests into the dining room. Time to suck up and move up—because Washington picked its leaders based on how well you got along with the local pols. And results from the field. Well, he had the results, and he was about to have a lot less competition.

"You can never count on anything going according to plan," he said, wrapping up the conversation with his field agent. "But after this attack, you *can* count on Spano warming up his trusty lie detector and cross-examining everyone but The Hawk's inner circle. That'll flush out any D-Wars agent. Might even scare your snitch enough to tell us what The Hawk's up to."

The RD hung up, and as soon as he did, another call came in. "Mr. Cortina?" asked a male voice.

"Yes?"

"About this party—how many hot dogs did you want?"

"Only one."

"Then it's on its way, and with mustard."

*　　*　　*

Twenty minutes into the game of hide and seek, and after several near misses, the larger plane caught up with the smaller one. The pirates had a man at the open door of the cargo hatch, a machine pistol in his hands, and a harness across his chest. He leaned out and sprayed the smaller plane with bullets. Danny threw up his hands and screamed.

Sallie choked back a scream of her own. *Oh, my God! This can't be happening!*

But this is for real, and you can't change channels. These people are trying to kill you. They could kill you! They will kill you!

Sallie pulled back on the stick and the plane lifted its nose, veering off into the wake of the larger aircraft. A whistling noise came from a hole in the Plexiglas.

Oh, God! We've been hit! "Danny!"

The young man didn't answer.

"Danny! Talk to me!"

Still no reply.

"Don't play games with me. Say something!"

Still no answer.

Sallie reached over and touched the young man's chest, then jerked back, her fingers coming away sticky wet.

Danny's been shot!

"Oh, dear God, no!"

Sallie's body convulsed and her stomach rebelled. Bile rose in her throat. The plane went into a dive. Sallie sat up, swallowed back the foul taste, and pulled the plane out of its dive. She shook the young man's shoulder. "Danny, wake up! Please!"

Still the young man didn't move, and Sallie forced herself to feel his chest again. There was no heartbeat, only a gooey place where the blood puddled up as the young man slumped in his seat. Sallie let go of the stick, doubled up, and puked into the bulkhead, the power of the act catching her by surprise.

She gagged, coughed, and then wiped her mouth and her forehead, which was cold and damp. Her breath came in gasps. Finally she remembered to level out. She wiped her hands across her jeans, gripped the stick, and told herself to calm down.

This was no time to panic. Danny might be dead, but she—she was still alive. So far. And she had to find a way of staying alive. The other plane would return. It would return to kill her. She had to find a way of contacting them and telling them why she was out here, that she was only out here to put these smugglers in prison because they'd killed her Timmie.

Good God! What was she thinking?

What an idiot she was! No wonder Taylor didn't think she could do this job. She glanced at her radio. It wouldn't do any good to contact them. Not only do you not know their frequency, but they don't care why you're here. Or give a damn that your son is dead or care how many Timmies die. They're *in* the business of killing people, whether it be with guns or drugs.

Enough of this whining. Where were they now?

She looked at the scope. Nothing there. The green dot was gone. The plane was gone! The pirates had disappeared. They were off the scope.

Impossible! You couldn't simply wish them away . . . .

Sallie glanced at the darkness surrounding her; saw nothing, heard nothing but the sound of her engine. Where the hell had the other plane gone?

Double-checking her scope, she saw no green dot.

Could it be possible the pirates were really gone? That they'd disappeared. Or crashed? That she was actually safe? What the hell had she done to lose them?

Sallie was staring at the scope when the green dot began to reappear . . . in the center of the scope. Right on top of her.

"Oh, God! They're right on top of me!"

Sallie pushed down on the stick and her plane lost altitude. Now she could see the green dot once again.

But now the green dot could see her, too. They hadn't been able to find her when she was underneath them.

What better place to hide?

The green dot reappeared near the middle of the scope, and Sallie maneuvered to make the dot disappear.

That's what she'd do! She'd hide underneath them until they went away or she figured how to get out of this. The Canadir could cruise at over a hundred and eighty miles an hour. Maybe she could do this. Maybe.

For the first time she noticed the back of her blouse was wet, her forehead, also. Her hair had to be flat as a pancake. She regripped the stick, let the sweat run, and kept an eye on the scope, watching for the green dot to reappear.

Thirty minutes later she was over the freighter—where she saw the ship being unloaded by another set of smugglers. Small fires continued to burn on the water—but there were no other dots on the scope. She was by herself with the last pirate aircraft. How long should she wait before making a run for the coastline?

Woman Against Herself

The pirates made up her mind for her. After cruising over the freighter, they gained altitude, leveled out, and turned up the power to their engines.

Sallie pressed forward but couldn't keep up; she was already at max speed. The green dot reappeared and moved away . . . and there was nothing she could do about it. No more than she could bring Danny back to life. Eventually the pirates would notice her, and then they would play their game of hide and seek once again—until her plane was shot out of the sky. Or, if she was lucky, she ran out of fuel.

Well, they wouldn't find her waiting around. If they wanted her, they'd have to work for it. Sallie dove for the Gulf and prayed the larger plane was already on automatic pilot and its crew relaxing after winning their one-sided dogfight.

✳   ✳   ✳

"Where the hell you been, Taylor?" demanded the voice on the phone. "I've been trying to reach you all day."

Taylor recognized that voice from long ago. "I still have to work for a living, Jackie. I'm not retired like you."

"Knock off the shitty jokes. Listen to me. I just got word from California that 'Jackie Mustard's' back on the street, in the drug smuggling business again."

On the other side of the country, Taylor sat up in his chair. "How do you know—wait a minute! Are you telling me after all we did to relocate you, you were foolish enough to stay in touch with friends in California? That could get you killed. Ned Clanton's on the loose."

"I'm not worried about Ned as much as I am about this ringer using my name. Where'd she come from? Have you stuck my name on some bitch to draw Clanton out of his hole?"

And something clicked in Taylor's head.

"I never agreed to that," came the voice from somewhere near Portland, Oregon. "I want Jackie Mustard forgotten, never to be heard of again."

Taylor didn't reply. He was putting two and two together . . . about Sallie Beck . . . and Jackie Mustard. Something Phil Rainey had said about Beck having grown her hair longer and lost weight. *Certainly she could access the D-Wars computer, but could Beck actually fly a plane? Could she off-load grass like Jackie Mustard had done in the past?*

"Taylor, are you still there?" screamed Mustard from the Pacific Northwest. "You sure as hell better not've hung up on me if you know what's good for you."

"I don't know what you're talking about," said Taylor, now focusing on what this woman was telling him. "It's not from my end. I can assure you of that. Sounds like Clanton's trying to flush *you* out. Where'd you hear this impersonator's operating?"

"That's why I called you, dumbass! She's in Miami."

Now Taylor was sure. There was only one more thing to check out. But to Jackie, he said, "Impossible. She's not here. I know all the major players in this town."

"Bullshit! How many have you put away?"

"That's none of your business."

"You haven't done diddly-shit. You never would've busted Clanton if it wasn't for me. I don't know why I even called. You can't keep up with what's going on in your own backyard."

From outside Portland, Jackie stood at an out-of-the-way pay phone, rubbing her abdomen. Had she felt the baby move? No way. At three months that was much too soon. This baby represented a new life, in many ways, and now some asshole was trying to fuck that up, too. She wouldn't let it happen.

Wes Taylor was saying something, but it didn't matter what that asshole said. He was the dumbest cop known to man. Could only make busts if a snitch held his hand. Well, she'd done his dirty work before and might have to do it again.

Jackie cut him off. "I'm not going to let you ruin what I've got going here. If you can't get that phony bitch off the streets, I'll come down there and do it for you."

*　　*　　*

"Redwing, this is Mother Goose. I'm ready for the lights. Show me the way home."

"You've got them, Mother Goose."

Sallie peered into the darkness of the Alabama river, saw no lights, and told Redwing so.

"We can hear you, Mother Goose. You're south of us. I'd say maybe five miles. No more."

Sallie flew on, scanning the river. There was a glow

up ahead, beyond the tree line. Around the bend of the river, at the bottom of a backward S, was the landing zone: two parallel rows of lights the length of a football field. Cutting back on her power, she began her descent.

Moments later, she was skimming across the surface, pontoons scraping against the water. The river was smooth as glass, and much more inviting than the ocean had been. In more ways than one. The plane slid to a stop beyond the lights, and Sallie let out a sigh of relief. Wheeling the pontoon plane around she saw nothing. The landing lights had destroyed her night vision.

"That was great, Mother Goose," came the voice over the radio. "What a way to get grass. The cops can stake out all the landing strips, but they can't cover all the rivers."

Sallie shook her head and grinned. These damn smugglers, they were all the same. They loved this slipping and sliding around. And no wonder. It was so easy to beat the cops.

Danny sat still in the seat next to her.

But not so easy for you, was it, my boy? You've got to be lucky, and your luck ran out. Me? I'm on a roll. Not only did I get close enough to kill The Hawk, but I'm within hours of busting his whole operation. What would Timmie think of his mom now?

One by one the lights went off as forms in boats moved up the parallel lines toward her. She unbuckled her seat belt, stood up, and stretched, then pulled off her pistol, dropping it into the seat behind her. She climbed into the cargo hold, and before opening the hatch, wiped some crusted vomit off her arm. Sometimes the shit you have to go through to get a job done . . . but there was a nice breeze blowing across the river.

The shallow boat took only a minute to arrive and cut its engine, gliding toward her position. A dark figure waved from the bow. "Yo, Mother Goose! Got something for me?"

"Got a bunch of something if you've got the package."

The dark figure held up a briefcase. "I think this is what you're looking for."

The smuggler tossed the briefcase to Sallie, then grabbed the side of the plane, stopping the boat at the hatch. After tying up, he scrambled aboard.

Sallie popped open the briefcase and rifled through the contents. The Hawk had warned her that smugglers occasionally tried to pad the currency. After closing the briefcase, she tossed it in the seat on top of her pistol, and then switched on a dome light in the cargo bay.

Redwing whistled at the sight of the marijuana stacked in the cargo hold. "Looking good, Mother Goose, looking good!"

He saw the dead Danny strapped in his seat and slumped against the window. A brownish-red smear ran down the Plexiglas window. "Sweet Jesus! What happened to him?"

"He didn't make it."

"I can see that." Redwing looked around. "So there's only you?"

"Yeah," said Sallie, leaning against her seat. "But that doesn't mean I'm going to help unload this shit."

The drug smuggler gave her the once-over. "No sweat, Mother Goose. I've got Joe with me."

Another boat clunked into the pontoon and a second man climbed inside. He was a carbon copy of the first smuggler, wearing the same camouflage clothing and combat boots. If Sallie hadn't known better, she'd have thought she was selling her grass to members of the United States Army. Hell, maybe she was. A military base was upriver.

"Joe, this here's Mother Goose." Redwing pointed at Sallie, then the dead Danny. "The other guy didn't make it, so Mother Goose is here all alone."

"Oh, I'm not that alone." Sallie pulled out her Magnum. She pointed it at the two men, bracing the pistol with her left hand and spreading her feet. "I've got this good buddy with me."

Redwing stepped back into Joe, who stood slack-jawed behind him. "Hey, Mother Goose! Cool it!"

"You're damn right I'm going to cool it and right back to Miami. So you'd better get your ass in gear if you don't want all the product thrown in the river. I'll give you thirty minutes to get it unloaded." She grinned. "But before you do, how about that fill-up I was promised."

Almost forty-eight hours later, Sallie strode into The Hawk's study and tossed the briefcase on top of his desk. Paperwork went flying, but The Hawk made no move to stop it. He only stared at Sallie.

Richey came off the sofa. "Jackie! We thought you were dead!"

Spano crossed the room, shoving the hippie down on the couch. "I'd like to know why she's not. We lost a lot of good men out there. Why weren't you one of them?"

Sallie put her hands on her hips. "For probably just that reason: I'm not a man."

"Where the hell have you been?" demanded Spano.

She pointed at the briefcase on the corner of The Hawk's desk. "Where the hell you think? Bringing home the bacon. And there it is."

The Hawk only stared at her. He said nothing.

"You bitch!" shouted Spano. "You think we don't know you're working for someone? How the hell those pirates know where to hit us?"

"Anyone could've hit us with the security we have around this place."

Sallie glanced at The Hawk to see if he got the point. She didn't see the hand heading in her direction. Spano clubbed her upside the head and everything went black before Sallie hit the floor.

Sixteen

Julius laid the photograph of Jackie Mustard on Taylor's desk. "With this I got different results." He sat down across from his boss and propped up his feet on Taylor's desk. "I found the firing range Beck used before moving in with The Hawk and where she rents her planes, some with pontoons on them. But it's her first flight you'll find most interesting."

"What'd she do?" asked Taylor, looking at Julius's feet on his desk.

"Not what she did, what her plane did. It lost power over the Pointe."

Taylor looked at him. "Over the Pointe?"

"Out where the rich folks live, man. Where The Hawk lives. Plane went right off the scope. Scared the hell out of the boys in the tower. They still talk about her. They grounded the plane and had a mechanic check it the next day."

"What did he say?" asked Taylor, looking at the feet.

"Nothing wrong with the engine. Plane shouldn't have stalled out."

"Do they still rent planes to her?"

"They don't know what I know, and besides, they like the way she fills out that red jumpsuit." Julius noticed the look and pulled his feet off the desk. "The same day she rented that plane, she flew north of the city and bought a bale of hay from a farmer. Landed on a lake he has on his property, picked up the hay, and returned to Miami where she, and get this, Wes, dropped the bale in The Hawk's swimming pool. That little bit of information courtesy of The Hawk's neighbors. Neighbors who aren't all that excited about having a drug dealer living in their neighborhood."

Taylor nodded. "I'll bet The Hawk about creamed in his jeans thinking how exciting it would be having someone like Jackie Mustard around. He's never met a woman like her. All he's ever known were whores."

"But where'd she learn to fly? I know she's using Mustard's certificates, but Beck can actually *fly*. And she never takes up the same plane twice."

"Her father was a pilot for Northwest Airlines."

Julius slumped in his chair. "Aw shit, Wes, why didn't Rainey tell us?"

"He thought, like you and I, that Beck would show up with another gun and take a shot at the bastard."

"But to be this proficient . . . ."

"Beck was flying before she could drive, an only child with a father who wanted a son."

"But pontoon planes?"

"Not much different from regular landing gear, from

216

what I've been told. Just seems that way to you and me. Her father is one of those back-to-nature nuts. He had a month's vacation every year and took it on one of those thousand islands in Minnesota. Dragged the whole family up there. They flew in by plane, too."

"By pontoon plane, I would imagine."

Taylor nodded. "No phone, no electricity, no contact with the outside world. A teenage girl can't stand that for a whole month. She has to be in touch with civilization, especially where the boys are. Beck used to fly in and out of wherever they were staying, and according to Rainey that was the attraction for the former Mr. Beck, just as it is now for The Hawk. After Beck's mother died, her father retired to one of those ten thousand islands. Lives there now with his own pontoon plane."

"You always said it was what we didn't know about that woman that could hurt us."

"And if we'd known she could fly, or that she was taking refresher courses, we would've caught her renting her first plane. That doesn't take anything away from Beck. She's still one hell of a woman, since she evidently found a way to pass Spano's lie detector test."

"Come on, Wes, you know she didn't take the test. She must've conned The Hawk into not having to take it, probably by sleeping with him."

"Julius, she's not that kind of person."

Instead of arguing the point, Julius asked, "How are we going to get her out of there? Any moment they could find out she's not who she says she is, knock her over the head, and drop her in the Waterway."

"Damned if I know. Anything we do runs the risk of

Spano giving everyone another lie detector test. I can't have that. It might blow Porter the Painter."

Liliana's voice came over the intercom. "I have Lieutenant Suarez on the phone from Metro Dade."

Wes picked up the phone. "Taylor here."

"I'd like to go home," said a tired voice, "but I've got paperwork to do and you're holding me up."

"What you got, Leo?"

"A body we pulled out of the river. Want to come down and take a look? I think it's someone you know."

A chill ran through Taylor. "Where are you?"

Suarez told him. "And let Julius drive. You'll get here faster, I'll finish my paperwork sooner, and be home, hopefully, before the sun comes up."

Twenty minutes later, after a fast ride down to the harbor, they stood in the fog off the river and stared at a body on the dock. A plain white sheet covered the lump under the sheet. Orange light from an ambulance reflected off the fog, and the two drug enforcement agents, a solitary policeman, and a couple of paramedics. An empty body bag was held by one of the paramedics. They were ready to finish with this job and move on to the next drug-related death.

"Mind if I take a look before you put him away?"

"That's why I called you," said the dark-skinned detective. Suarez wore a poorly matched suit that looked as if he had slept in it. "It ain't pretty, Wes. Couple of fishermen found it. One of them said he's gonna give up fishing forever. Can't say I blame him."

Taylor knelt alongside the body and swallowed hard

before pulling back the sheet. He held his breath. Underneath the sheet was a young man with a dark beard, long hair, and a bloated face. The face was bloated not only from too much time in the water but from a cord wrapped around the neck.

Wes gulped. Julius turned away.

"Porter the Painter," Suarez said. "Strangled to death by the cord, *then* dropped in the water. And I don't have to see an autopsy report to know that."

The dead man wore a small machine tucked under one arm. Suarez gestured at it with his foot. "You know what this is no matter how damn small the Japs make them."

Julius turned back to the body as Taylor stood up. "A polygraph."

"The sign of The Hawk, or should I say his main man, Spano. And I can't touch them while you're putting your case together. Should I ask how your investigation is coming along?"

Taylor didn't answer. He was staring over the river, trying to control the rage and helplessness sweeping over him. There would be no end-of-the-month report from Porter the Painter, his last contact inside The Hawk's organization. The director might as well roll up the investigation today. Even tonight.

"He was our man," Taylor heard Julius say.

"Sorry 'bout that," Suarez said, "but you know how we feel, being straitjacketed by Uncle Sam. They oughta let us bust that organization, then we could stop some of these killings."

Julius opened his mouth to explain that jailing The

Hawk would only fractionalize his organization, creating more headaches, but Taylor was heading for the car.

"Thanks for the call," Taylor threw over his shoulder. "I'll return the favor."

"If D-Wars is still around for you to do it."

Taylor didn't answer.

"You *do* have more going for you than Porter the Painter, don't you?"

It was Julius who turned back to the police detective. "You don't think we'd have only one man inside an organization the size of The Hawk's, do you?"

*   *   *

The EMS vehicle was alerted to the location of the girl and picked up her trail when she turned onto a less-traveled street. Two blocks down this street most of the storefronts were boarded up. The men following the girl thought she was a fool for taking this street, but she had gotten away with more than they expected in the last few days, so they would stay on their toes. The girl did know the street.

A voice from the rear of the vehicle said, "I'll get out here. Take her when she passes that old five and dime."

The driver nodded, stopped, and waited until the rear doors opened and closed. There were few cars along the curb, and in the next block, a group of black teenagers hung out, smoking cigarettes. The girl had to skirt three bums inside the recessed storefront of an old pharmacy. She glanced at the bums and gripped her pocketbook.

"Might be a pistol in that purse," said the man riding shotgun.

"Uh-huh," said the driver.

The driver passed the girl and stopped at the corner. His companion opened the door, stepped down, then up on the sidewalk. He wore the uniform of an EMS tech. The girl slowed as he approached her.

"You know where 1748 is on this street, Miss?"

The teenager shook her head, gripped her purse, and looking at the sidewalk, pushed on.

The man dressed as an EMS technician grabbed her arm as she went by. "Hey! All I asked was . . . ."

The girl jerked away and, seeing the driver coming around the front of the vehicle, turned and ran back in the direction of the thoroughfare . . . where she came face-to-face with the man who had climbed out of the rear. The man from the EMS vehicle smiled that awful smile the girl hated to see. It meant something terrible was going to happen.

"Hello, Tina," said Spano. "We were just on our way to pick up Carlos. Why don't you let us give you a lift?"

*　　*　　*

Sallie rolled her head over so she could see the door. The Hawk drifted in and took a seat on the side of the bed. He brushed back some of the loose strands of hair, and Sallie wished he would touch more than her hair. He did by cupping the side of her face.

"How do you feel?" he asked.

Sallie snuggled into that hand. It was a strong hand.

A solid hand. The kind of hand that belonged to a man who could take care of you. "Kind of lazy," Sallie said. "Like a sleepy Sunday morning."

The Hawk ran his hand down her face, caressing Sallie's neck, then her shoulder, which was covered by a silk dressing gown. He pulled down the bedcovers, and, before that hand reached her breasts, her nipples were anxious for his touch. The Hawk cupped one breast, then the other. The nipples became erect.

The hand ran across her stomach, and the moment it left her breasts, Sallie wanted that hand back where it had been, but now, where that hand was heading was even more exciting. Down there, the need even more urgent. The hand stopped at Sallie's panties.

No, no, don't stop! Please don't.

She had never been so totally aroused. The effect this man had on her . . . . And what kind of effect did she have on him? Here she was, lying here, reveling in his touch, wanting him to do even more, but how did he feel? For some reason it was important to know. Did he find her desirable? Was she still pretty?

The Hawk loosened the ties holding her gown together and pulled back the sides, exposing Sallie from the waist up. Sallie felt her breasts cool, but that did nothing for her ardor. She was on fire, and this man was the only one who could put out that fire.

His hand ran down her stomach, and Sallie spread her legs, inviting him to touch her there, to love her there. He caressed the most important point of her pubic triangle and Sallie moaned, shuddered, and almost came. Her need was so overpowering that she almost cried out in pain when he abandoned that place to stroke the inside of her thigh. How long had it been since she'd slept with a man? How many lonely nights had there been because men were turned off by her growing strength and independence?

It had been months.

It had been years.

Years and years of empty beds and damp pillows. But that was all behind her. Now she could drift away under the magic fingers of a man who could not only take care of himself but her, too. A man who wasn't threatened by Sallie Beck and what she'd become. Sallie trembled as The Hawk started another exciting journey to where her legs came together. She was wet and ready. She wanted him inside her, taking her, but most of all—

The bedroom door was thrown back, Sallie's eyes popped open, and The Hawk's hand slipped away. Wes Taylor rushed into the room, gun in hand. He wasn't the only one. Spano stepped out of the bathroom.

Good God! Spano had been there all along. Watching. Seeing everything. In the security chief's hands was a sawed-off shotgun, but before he could use it, Taylor put a bullet through the large man's forehead.

A small hole appeared above Spano's eyebrows and blood began to leak out. Spano stood there, arms at his sides, blood dripping from his head, then rushing out the hole, spilling on the carpet. Blood ran everywhere!

The Hawk stood up and faced Taylor. There was no fear in his eyes. Instead he seemed to be daring Taylor

223

to take his best shot. The government agent did, slapping the drug dealer across the face—with his pistol!

The Hawk's head never moved. Taylor hadn't fazed him. Taylor hit him again and The Hawk just laughed. Again Taylor hit him, failing to make a dent in her lover's face. But when Taylor stuck his pistol at The Hawk's forehead, Sallie leaped between them.

"No! Don't!"

Taylor turned on her. "What the hell are you talking about? It's the only way we're getting out of here."

"Please don't hurt him."

"Why not?"

"Because . . . I need him." She became aware that Taylor had noticed her being naked but for a pair of panties. As he checked out her breasts Sallie made no move to conceal them. She was pretty and she knew it.

"I can't believe this! I've jeopardized my whole operation for some whore." Taylor slapped her across the face and Sallie fell back on the bed.

"Jackie, are you all right?" The Hawk reached for her, but not even The Hawk could make the pain in her face go away, or the pain in her heart.

Again she heard, "Jackie, are you all right?"

Sallie opened her eyes. Richey, not The Hawk, was standing over her. She was in bed and her face ached where Taylor had struck her.

Impossible. Taylor couldn't get inside The Hawk's compound. Taylor wasn't in the room. Neither was The Hawk or a dead Spano. And there was no river of blood.

"Are you better? I couldn't leave well enough alone. I had to come up and check on you."

Sallie ran her hands under the bedclothes. Her clothes from the drug run to Alabama were still on, and a wet cloth lay beside her where ice had melted and soaked into the mattress.

"Jackie, you don't have to be scared. Spano was called away on a security matter."

"What happened?" She touched her face and winced. "My head . . . it hurts."

"Spano hit you."

She raised up on her elbows. "I'll kill the bastard!"

The hippie took a seat on the side of the bed and pushed her down. "I understand how you feel. That's why I'm here. You have to leave. It's not going to work, and it's not worth getting killed over. Spano won't stop coming."

"That asshole's not running me off!"

"Well, it's your ass, but this isn't California. This is the big time, and I'm here for the same reason you are. We want to hitch our wagon to a star, and The Hawk's a supernova, but it's not going to happen for you."

"The hell it won't!"

"Well then, consider this: We've got something big coming up next week and The Hawk won't want his security chief distracted."

Sallie studied the young man, the only person in the whole organization to show the least bit of empathy. "This deal—is it bigger than the snafu in the Straits?"

"The Hawk hasn't told you?"

Sallie shook her head.

"Still another reason to move on."

"Maybe if I slept with him."

Richey chuckled. "I don't think you really want to do that, and The Hawk knows it. You two need time to grow on each other, but Spano won't give you that time. Since the fiasco in the Straits everyone's had to take another lie detector test. Spano found a couple of weak links and eliminated them. You have a test scheduled for tomorrow. There's lots of questions he could ask. Like what happened to Danny. How could one come back and not the other?"

Sallie shivered and wondered if Richey had noticed. She couldn't take another lie detector test. There wasn't enough time to reprogram herself. If it could even be done. No. She had to get out. Like Richey said.

He was talking. Maybe she should be listening. Like her life depended on it. "What'd you say?"

"I asked what happened to Danny?"

Sallie told him. "On the return flight I threw him out over the Gulf."

The hippie shook his head. "Sheesh! Everything I've heard about you is true. You are one tough broad. But where were you? You were gone another twenty-four hours."

"I had to clean up the plane before turning it in. There was lots of blood. The people renting it might wink at a few holes in the fuselage, once I slipped them a few bucks, but not a lot of blood. Spano can check it out, including where I bought the Plexiglas to replace the piece that took a bullet."

Richey squeezed her shoulder. "You've got to tell The Hawk all this."

"I don't think whining's going to make Spano back off."

Steve Brown

"Well, handle this any way you want," said Richey, letting go of her shoulder, "but I wouldn't think twice about leaving if I no longer had The Hawk's support. There are just too many ways Spano could make me disappear."

Seventeen

As the fat sheriff took a seat on the bunk opposite his prisoner, metal springs groaned under his weight, and he had to shift around to get comfortable. These damn low bunks were too much for a middle-aged man. Maybe when he'd been in the army, but now, old age was getting to him. Hard to breathe, sitting with his stomach jammed into his chest. He leaned back against the wall to get comfortable.

To the woman, he said, "You've got a lot of nerve calling me back to the cell block to make a deal on a murder charge. We caught you in the room with your john and the knife still in your hand. Maybe if you two hadn't made such a ruckus . . . ."

Sitting on the opposite bunk bed, Jasmine smoked a cigarette. Wearing drab prisoner garb, she looked nothing like the expensive hooker he had booked last night. Gone was the sparkling jewelry, the flashy, tight-fitting dress, and both high heels. All that was left was her fancy hairdo, and that needed some work. It was flat on one side from Jasmine's sleeping on it.

The hooker let out a smoke-filled breath. "I called you back here, Lloyd, 'cause you and me, we go back a ways."

"I've got no pull when it comes to murder. And you killed the wrong john. An important man in this town. You're gonna pay in full. His wife will see to that. You and her husband embarrassed her to death, and you're the only one she's got to take it out on. It's out of my hands."

"We went through high school together, Lloyd. I was your first piece of ass."

"You were a lot of boys' first piece of ass."

"You've busted me more than once for solicitation."

"Just doing my job, you know that."

"And you've busted me when I've been running a string of girls."

The sheriff sighed. In truth he wished there was something he could do for this woman. He'd never liked the man she'd killed. He was the kind of man who whores around on Saturday night, then shows up at church the following morning as one of the deacons. A deacon who'd come from money, married more, and had everything going his way until this woman stuck a butcher knife in his chest. Nothing at all like how Jasmine had grown up: molested by her stepfather, and when her mother died, forced to take her mother's place in her stepfather's bed.

And she was right about being his first piece of ass. But the sheriff had stopped fucking all whores after becoming a cop. Not because someone might think there was a conflict of interest, but because he'd learned whores didn't like men. There was something about climbing in bed with a woman who didn't like men that made him a little nervous.

He studied the woman, but she didn't seem worried. Did she really think she could beat this rap?

"Jasmine, has this conversation got a point to it?"

"I was running a string of girls last month, too."

"Why don't you just spell it out for me?"

She took a drag off her cigarette and let out another smoke-filled breath. "A guy flew my girls down to the lower part of the state."

"For a party, I would imagine."

"Yeah, but not like any party you've ever been to."

"I would hope not."

Jasmine was putting the cigarette to her mouth for another drag when she stopped and eyed him. "This party was for over one hundred and fifty horny niggers."

"What?" The sheriff sat up on the bunk bed.

The whore took the drag and let it out, this time slowly. "Had to nurse one of my girls back to health, and she weren't much good to me for several weeks. It would've been easier on everybody if we'd had more girls, but I couldn't find but nine girls who wanted the business. And the money was damn good. You know, Lloyd, there's still a good bit of racism in this state. Whores just don't want to fuck niggers."

"Jasmine, what in the world are you talking about? You're not making sense, and you're surely not making me envious."

She shook her cigarette at him. "I'll tell you what I'm talking about, Lloyd. They paid each of my gals five thousand dollars, and me, ten—all for a one-night stand."

"Well, put it in your memoirs," said the fat man, trying to stand and having to use a bunk post to do it. "Sounds like some kind of record." When he got to his feet, he released the post. "I'm sorry about what's going to happen, but I've got to get back to work."

"Okay, Lloyd, treat me like shit, but if I were you I'd get somebody down here from the FBI or one of them secret agent men."

"Why for God's sake?"

"Because all those niggers did a lot of bragging. They didn't think we could understand what they said, but Missy could. I wasn't supposed to bring Missy along because she could make out that Dutch talk, but I was in a bind. I could only find nine girls and they wanted at least twenty." The whore took another drag off the cigarette and let it out. "Missy's going to be my ticket out of here. I ain't never going to jail for killing that sorry bastard 'cause somebody's gonna make it right."

"Jasmine, you can say anything you want, make up all kind of stories, but there's nothing that's going to stop you from going to prison and for an awfully long time. You may not get the chair 'cause they don't usually give it to women, but you're surely going to prison."

"Don't you worry about me none. You just get someone down here and I'll make my own deal. I'll give you until six tonight."

"For what?"

"To get someone down here who can cut a deal."

The look on the woman's face stopped the sheriff from reminding her that he was the one in charge and she the prisoner.

"Lloyd, if I have to make that call myself you're gonna have to listen to your wife tell you, for the rest of your married life, that you should've listened to your old girlfriend. They might reelect fat sheriffs in this county, but they ain't never reelected a dumb one."

※　　※　　※

"Where the hell you think you're going?" demanded Spano when he saw Sallie coming down the circular stairs.

"I'm getting the hell out of here."

"On whose authority?"

Sallie pulled the Magnum from behind the leg of one of her jeans. Her top was red and her blond hair was pulled back in a ponytail. "On this authority."

Sallie leveled the pistol at the security chief as she finished the stairs. Spano stepped back toward the door and reached for the weapon inside his jacket.

She crossed the foyer and pointed the Magnum at him. "Do it, fool! They need a new security chief around here. Your work sucks!"

Spano's hand stayed near his jacket but didn't go underneath it. "You don't have the guts." It came out as a snarl.

Sallie tilted her head in the direction of the bruise on her face, both hands never leaving the Magnum and

232

her attention never leaving Spano. "But I do have the proper motivation."

Slowly but surely, Spano's hand came away from the jacket. Behind him Richey came through the front door.

"Jackie, I found your car at . . . ." His face lost its smile. "What are you doing?"

"Getting out of this place."

The hippie held up his hands. "Not this way. Don't do it, Jackie."

Sallie still stared at Spano. "Is there any other way, Mr. Security Chief?"

Spano's eyes narrowed. "Not for you there's not." To Richey, he said, "Mustard's afraid of taking the lie detector test. That's why she's clearing out. She knows we'll find out who she's working for." He looked at Sallie again. "But I'll find you, Mustard, no matter where you hide. Downtown, out of state, back in California. I'll find you—then your ass is mine."

"Not a very pleasant thought considering your interest in young boys."

Spano stepped toward her. "You bitch—"

Sallie stuck the pistol in his face. "Shut the fuck up, asshole!" Without looking at Richey, she said, "Take Spano's piece out of his jacket and slide it down the hall."

The hippie glanced at the security chief.

"Stay away from me, wimp!"

Richey looked at Sallie.

She pointed her gun at Spano's groin. "If you want to continue having fun with little boys, you'll let him take your piece."

"Come on, Spano," pleaded Richey. "The Hawk needs you a lot more than he needs another pilot."

The security chief continued to glare at Sallie. Slowly, his hand rose to his jacket again.

Sallie pulled back the hammer on the Magnum. "Anytime, asshole. Anytime."

"Think about what you're doing, Spano," pleaded Richey. "We aren't going to pull off Operation Cut-Out without you."

The security chief gritted his teeth and allowed Richey to take his weapon out of the holster and slide it down the hall.

"I'm not through with you, bitch."

"Oh, I think you are. Richey, toss your piece down the hall." The hippie did as he was told, and Sallie motioned him through the front door. "Now, we go."

"What?" asked Richey.

"You're my ticket out of here."

"You'll need more than that," spit out Spano. "I'm personally going to punch your ticket."

"If you can catch me."

Outside the compound and down the street, Sallie dropped Richey off.

The hippie leaned down to the window. "Don't do this, Jackie."

She grinned at him. "Looks like I already have."

Sallie raced off, and as Richey watched, another car, a big Ford, pulled out behind her. Ned Clanton let Sallie make it as far as the road leading to the county airport before he pulled up alongside her. When Sallie saw who was driving the other car, she pressed her accelerator to the floor. Before she could slip away, Clanton wrenched the Ford over, forcing Sallie off the road, across the sand shoulder, and into a shallow but wide concrete drainage ditch. As her car sped down the ditch, Sallie fought to free it, but the Z-car was trapped between the Ford and the other side of the ditch, a squared-off curb against an adjoining berm. Beyond the berm lay small trees and the brackish backwater of a swamp.

Clanton continued down the road, slamming into the Z repeatedly, trying to force it over the low hill and into the trees. Each blow shook Sallie's hands off the wheel, but the curb kept the car from being pushed up on the berm. The Z-car was built too low to the ground to be shoved out of the ditch. Sparks flew as metal to metal and concrete to metal bit into each other. Sallie looked over and saw Clanton scream in frustration at not being able to shove the smaller car over the berm.

A few yards ahead of them the squared-off gutter poured down from the road and across a concrete apron. For a moment the ditch had a downward slope to both sides, and there, Clanton finally pushed Sallie up on the berm. Another good shove and the Z would go over the hill, into the swamp.

Sallie jammed on her accelerator but couldn't get away. Clanton laughed as he swung his car into hers. As he did, however, his right front wheel hit the next gutter, which had no concrete apron and was nothing more than a hole with rocks jutting out of it. The right front of the Ford dropped into the hole, a tire blew, and

Clanton lost his grip on the wheel. He was thrown into the steering column as his car spun around and kicked Sallie's car in the rear, knocking it off the berm and down into the ditch again.

Sallie was thrown against the seat and the steering wheel jerked out of her hands. For the moment the ditch steered the car. Then Sallie regained control and, at the next apron, maneuvered onto the road. The taste of blood in her mouth told her she'd bitten her tongue.

Clanton rubbed his chest as he watched Mustard disappear. "At least I know where to find you. And you'd better never come out of that fucking compound again, if you know what's good for you."

*   *   *

Fifty miles north of Miami, Wes Taylor paced back and forth in front of the weather-beaten landing tower. Only one story taller than the airstrip, both the tower and the airstrip had been abandoned years before. Windows had been knocked out by vandals, weeds grew through the broken tarmac, and an exhausted windsock hung, tailless, from a pole a short distance from where Taylor paced. Many holes in the tarmac had been recently filled in and leveled with asphalt. He would have to put this strip on the Watch List. On the other side of the old runway stood two warehouses along with a smaller shack.

How appropriate to meet Beck here. Since their last meeting she'd become a drug smuggler herself, then called and bragged about it—and told him to meet her here. Didn't ask him to come. It definitely sounded more like a command than a request. The woman Taylor was about to meet didn't sound anything like the tormented soul he'd sent packing a few short weeks before. Now she sounded cocky and quite sure of herself. Certainly not a change for the better.

From the west, a light aircraft appeared. Less than twenty minutes later, the plane was on the ground and taxiing to where Taylor stood. The hatch opened and a blond-headed pilot climbed out.

Taylor could not believe what he was seeing. The only difference between Sallie Beck and Jackie Mustard, as he remembered her, was about two inches in height. Beck was the taller of the two but both were blond and slender. They even wore the same clothes, jeans with a red top. Maybe Beck looked older.

"Good to see you again, Taylor." The woman extended a hand.

Mechanically Taylor shook it.

"What's the matter? Something wrong?"

"Er—no, I was just . . . I was just looking at—what happened to your face?"

"Spano hit me."

"He what!"

She told him what happened after returning from the drug run to Alabama.

"The man's a sadist. I'm glad you're out of there."

"I'm going back."

"You're what?"

"The Hawk has something big coming up. Something called Operation Cut-Out." She touched the side of her face. "Maybe if he had taught Spano to be more gracious to his houseguests . . . ."

Taylor grabbed her arm. "Come out now! You have all you need. You could get hurt."

Sallie threw off the hand. "If I'd taken your advice when I first came to Miami, I wouldn't be ready to take The Hawk to court. Neither would you. Porter the Painter is dead."

"You know about that?"

"I know everything that goes on in there." Sallie pulled a pack of cigarettes from her jeans and lit one. She let out a smoke-filled breath. "Those people are just as you said. They don't take women seriously. I hear things I'm not supposed to hear and tonight I'm going to be told what Operation Cut-Out is. Only then will I come out."

"But what happened to Porter the Painter, doesn't that frighten you?"

Sallie frowned. "Why should it?"

"For starters, Spano slapped you around."

"And I put him down, in front of Richey. That's the way things work in there. Tit for tat."

Taylor was aghast. "My God! What did you do?"

Sallie told him how she'd escaped from the compound a couple of hours earlier.

"That's crazy. Now I'm sure you have to come out."

"Hell, all this is crazy. What I'm doing, what you do for a living, what The Hawk can get away with . . . it's all nuts. But it keeps the adrenaline flowing. I used to take pills, but I've finally adjusted."

"You've been lucky. Real lucky."

She nodded. "I'm on a roll, and in a few days I'm going to roll up The Hawk." She told him about the attack on the freighter and how she'd outsmarted the pirates by flying underneath their plane. "Pretty nifty—eh?"

Taylor could only stare at her. After finding his voice, he said, "I'm scared for you, even if you're not."

"Why?"

"There're only two reactions people could possibly have who've done what you've done: they either turn tail and run or become pumped up and want to do more. You're pumped up. That in itself could get you killed."

She smiled. "You wouldn't be jealous of what I've accomplished, would you?"

"What are you talking about?"

Smoke poured from her nose before she said, "Just what I said."

"Absolutely not. I'll support anything you do. You're my agent in place."

"Maybe that's what's bothering you."

"That you're my man in there?"

Sallie nodded.

"I'd make a pact with the devil to bring down The Hawk. Where you and I differ is I know when to quit. I'm tempted to hit you over the head and drag you back to Miami."

"I'd go to prison before I'd cooperate, and before I was brought to trial I'd be dead. I'm going to do this my way or I'm not going to do it at all."

"I'd already figured that out."

She dropped her cigarette onto the ground and snubbed it out. "Look for me in the next few days." Sallie tapped her head. "I have your number and everything else to bust The Hawk locked away in here." She started for the plane but stopped. "There is one thing you could do."

"What's that?"

"Get Ned Clanton off the streets. I don't need him breathing down my neck. He could give me away."

Taylor stepped toward her. "You've seen him?"

Sallie told him about running into Clanton, but not about the bikers having to rescue her. "I'd try the Ponderosa Playground. If Ned finds a place where he likes the music, he can't stay away."

Taylor could only stare. Beck sounded more like Mustard than the genuine article. When the woman continued toward her plane, it broke the spell cast over him. "For crissake, Sallie, come out. You could get killed."

Before climbing inside the plane, she said, "Taylor, be honest about this. You're not worried about losing me, you're worried about losing your case against The Hawk."

"You're wrong, Sallie. It's more than that."

"I don't think so. What else could it be?"

*　　*　　*

Sallie leaned against her dented car and watched the guard search it. From a wooden perch overlooking the gate, a red-tailed hawk regarded her, canting its head one way and then the other. The red-tailed hawk had been drawn to the stone column by a member of the security detail who always tied a piece of fishing line to a hind leg of a hamster he put on the top of the stone post when he came on duty.

Taking a final drag off her cigarette, Sallie flicked it into the bushes. "Find what you're looking for?"

"No." The guard pulled his large torso out of the back. It had been a tight fit. He glanced at where Clanton's Ford had rubbed up against the Z. "Looks like you ran into a little trouble yourself."

"Nothing I couldn't handle. Can I have my gun back?"

"Not tonight, Jackie."

Sallie stared at him.

"Spano's orders."

"And what if I just got in my car and drove away?"

"I've got orders how to handle that, too."

She pushed her way past him and slid into her car. "Then open the damn gate! I'm going in there and find out who's running this goddamn organization."

Inside the study Spano placed both of his huge hands on The Hawk's desk and leaned across it. "You're crazy if you let that woman back in here. She could kill you. She could kill any of us."

"I'm not afraid of her," said Richey from the sofa. Spano ignored him and watched his boss tap the ash off his cigar. The Hawk didn't like it when his men stood in front of his desk. There, they were always taller.

"What's it about Mustard that bothers you?"

"Why's she coming back? That doesn't make sense."

241

"To make money, you idiot," said Richey from behind him. "The same reason you're here."

Spano turned on him. "Shut up, beach boy! Security's no concern of yours. If it was, we would've had our throats slit in the middle of the night long ago."

"Hawk," Richey said to the man behind the desk, "Spano doesn't want Jackie here because she embarrassed him."

"Fuck you, Richey! I'm not afraid of any woman."

The young man smiled. "I'm glad you cleared that up. I've always wondered about that."

"You little shit," said Spano, stepping toward the sofa. "I'll—"

"Did she pass the polygraph test?" asked The Hawk from behind him.

"Yes," said Spano, turning around, "but she needs to take another one."

"Agreed, but when you administered the first test, didn't you run through a laundry list of government agencies and other groups Mustard could've been working for?"

"Yes, but—"

"And her California background checked out, and she brought back the money from Alabama, didn't she?"

Spano nodded.

"And she's come back now despite the fact you might cold-cock her again—right?"

They all looked toward the front of the house at the sound of a car door slamming.

"Then all I can conclude," said The Hawk, returning his attention to his security chief, "is that the woman is determined to be part of my team. Mustard's returning even though Richey advised her to get out."

The hippie looked at the floor.

"So I suggest to you that Mustard was making a point: that she wasn't going to be pushed around. I might add, I don't think she likes being left out of Operation Cut-Out. An operation she's certainly qualified to participate in."

"Agreed," Richey said firmly.

Spano didn't look at the man on the couch.

The Hawk leaned back. "I remember breaking into this business. For my trouble I was shot twice, had my money stolen more than once, and I'd be too embarrassed to tell you how many times people didn't pay and I had to eat the deal. That's why I hooked up with you, and if it was tough for me, it's got to be tougher for a woman. From what I've read, women have to become more like men to make it in the business world. So if that's all that's bothering you, you'd better get over it. At the moment you have no reason to ride her, and you know as well as I that there's nothing worse to have around than a woman with a sour disposition."

The Hawk paused as the front door opened and slammed shut. Heels clicked down the hall. "I recommend instead of working so hard, that you back off and give Mustard the rope she needs to hang herself. So the bottom line is: the woman stays and you stay alert. However, don't let your mind wander. Concentrate on the task at hand. We're going into Suriname in less than forty-eight hours and I don't want anything lousing that up."

"But what Carlos was doing—doesn't that bother you?"

"From the sound of the confessions, I'm not sure he was doing anything. It was all the girl."

"And this is another girl."

"And you stay alert—understand?"

Sallie opened the door and walked in. Her arms were full of packages that had been searched by the gate guard. She walked over to the desk and gave The Hawk a peck on the cheek. "Miss me?"

The smuggler smiled. "Now that you mention it."

She glanced at the other two men. "Can I have a drink?"

"Certainly, my dear."

The Hawk pressed the intercom and ordered drinks for the two of them. He leaned back in his chair as Sallie put her packages on the sofa near Richey. He didn't see the smile she flashed the hippie.

"Where've you been?" asked The Hawk.

Turning around, she tossed her hair. "I got my hair fixed. How do you like it?"

"Very nice. Is that all?"

"I've been spending some of my cut from the grass run. Bought some new culottes." Sallie pulled the skirt-like shorts out of a box and held them up against herself, modeling them. They were red, as were the pair she wore, along with a white blouse. "How do you like them?"

"You've been flying, too," Spano said. "Don't forget to tell him about that."

"Sure, I've been flying. It helps me forget how you got my partner killed."

Spano's hands became huge balls at his side. "Where have you really been, Mustard?"

She took a seat on the corner of The Hawk's desk. "You mean, where did I go that your piss-poor pilot couldn't follow."

"You bitch, I'll beat the—"

Sallie turned her back on him. "You want me out of here, Hawk, just say the word and I'm gone. I don't need the hassle."

"Well, Spano?" asked The Hawk.

"I'm not responsible for logistics. I'm responsible for security, and that's why I don't want you here." The security chief left the room, closing the door behind him.

Richey got up from the couch. "Don't mind him, Jackie. Spano's just jumpy. We leave in less than forty-eight hours and it's gotten on his nerves."

"For where?"

"That's for The Hawk to tell you."

After Richey left, The Hawk ran his hand up and down the inside of Sallie's thigh. "Wearing these for me?"

She looked down. Her culottes had been pushed up into her crotch. "I wear them for you and I become your girl. I become your girl and you'll want to take care of me. If you haven't noticed, I'm not that kind of gal."

The Hawk continued to run his hand up and down the inside of Sallie's thigh. It made Sallie tingle all over. What was wrong with her? Why was this man affecting her in this way? Perhaps, because after meeting with

Woman Against Herself

Wes Taylor, she had finally seen the drug enforcement agent for what he was: a dreary little policeman, with no more to his life than what his opponents gave him. The action was on this side of the fence. That's where you got the rush.

"Well," said The Hawk, "we'll have to take our relationship one step at a time."

Sallie took the hand off her leg and put it on the desk. "Fine, and the first step is telling me where we're going in less than forty-eight hours. If you don't trust me enough to tell me, then you're just another guy who wants to fuck me."

The Hawk smiled. "You're all business, aren't you?"

"Friends may come and go, but money is always money. How much am I in for?"

"How does a million sound to you?"

"A million bucks?"

"Right."

Visions of what she could do with a million dollars danced through Sallie's head and she wondered if she should bust The Hawk *after* getting her hands on the money. She could think of at least a million reasons why.

Eighteen

Ned Clanton stood in front of one of the urinals in the men's room of the Ponderosa Playground. He was feeling good. This afternoon he'd scoped in the fucking hunting rifle intended for Wes Taylor, now to be used on Jackie Mustard.

The bitch!

There was a great deal of activity around the fucking compound owned by some guy known in the trade as The Hawk. Lots of comings and goings, and Ned had been in the drug trade long enough to know another deal was coming down. It also meant the bitch would be coming out of her hole, and this time old Ned would be waiting for her—with his newly scoped rifle. He didn't have to be within a thousand yards of the fucking woman to drop her. How would this fellow The Hawk like that? Maybe he'd wait until the shot was just right—and splatter Jackie's brains all over her new boyfriend.

Ned knew what he'd done wrong. He'd tried to do it

face-to-face. He'd wanted Jackie to know it was old Ned doing the killing, and he'd wanted to know if Jackie had been the one who'd sent him to prison. He was willing to cut that information out of her.

It had to be her. Anyone with half a brain would've left in the getaway car. That was the only thing that made sense. But Mustard had refused to go along. If the cops were coming, she had said, the only way out was down the stairs to the beach.

There might be cops there, too, he'd argued. Maybe there were, and they had taken her into custody and spirited her away so Jackie could fink on him.

Oh, sure, Shorty had been the one taking the witness stand, but someone was behind all the moves the prosecution was making. Had to be. Shorty was some scared half-wit Taylor had reached through his mother. Shorty's mother had cancer, and Taylor told him he was going to prison and he would never see his mother again. Taylor had used the oldest line in the world and cracked that fool wide open. Cops had been using that line ever since there'd been cops. And robbers. Didn't matter. Shorty's momma would outlive her boy. Right after he did Mustard and Taylor, he was going to look up Shorty, and an old woman being treated for cancer would be easy to find—even in witness protection.

But first Jackie. Thought she could squeal and let Shorty take the heat? That'd be the day. She couldn't outsmart old Ned. He'd show her. Jackie was about to have her brains—what little there was of them—splattered over ten yards of anything. Including this fellow The Hawk, if he got in the way. Sorry about that, good buddy. Nothing personal, but a man's gotta keep his reputation. Nobody fucks with Ned Clanton and gets away with it.

He grinned at the wall, and not because of the graffiti. No, you couldn't fuck with old Ned, especially since he had a guardian angel. But who was this angel and how did he know Ned? What he really wanted to know was: Who in the hell had enough pull to spring him from the joint? Spring him from the joint, move him across country, and point him in Wes Taylor's direction? Who wanted Taylor dead as much as he did?

His guardian angel must've known Jackie Mustard was in Miami. It had to be part of the plan—whatever that was. The plan suited Ned just fine. Even if he had to figure it out on the fly. He was going to fix Mustard good. She'd never have another baby. Shit! Probably hitting on The Hawk to have one right now.

Have a baby. Damn! That's all a man needs.

Ned chuckled, moved away from the urinal, and zipped up his fly. This fellow, The Hawk, better watch out or Jackie would have him changing diapers before he knew it. She'd tried that on old Ned, but he'd made her have the abortion. Jackie hadn't liked it, but Ned had gone with her to make sure it was done.

Clanton left the rest room to return to the bar. He had made some new friends in Miami and he planned to do some serious drinking with them. Tomorrow he'd do Mustard.

Wes Taylor came out of the darkness and grabbed Ned's hand in a come-along grip. Ned tried to resist, but only for a moment. Then it felt like his fingers were about to be snapped off.

"Let go of me! You're breaking my fucking hand!"

"And I will if you don't walk out of here." The drug enforcement agent pushed Clanton toward the door by putting a shoulder into him.

Several patrons at the bar stared at the two men as they walked by. One of the patrons was Ned's new drinking buddy who shared Ned's love of country music and knew Ned as Ted. A beefy man with a pot gut and thick beard, the drinking buddy put down his beer, slid off his stool, and intercepted the two men.

"Hey, Ted, where you going? You promised to buy the next round."

"Back off, friend," ordered Taylor. "I'm a—"

"He's going to break my arm!" screamed Ned. "Just 'cause I owe him some money."

"Shut up, Clanton!" said Taylor.

"Help me, Norris!" screamed Ned. "I can't pay! My old lady left with all my cash."

The beefy man grabbed Taylor, and because the drug enforcement agent insisted on holding onto his prisoner, was able to get him in a headlock.

"Run for it, Ted!" shouted Norris.

Clanton shook out of Taylor's grasp and ran through the broken metal detector and out the door.

"Let go of me! I'm a government agent!"

His protests were muffled under the arm of the larger man. Taylor tried to force the arm off his neck, and when that didn't work, rabbit punched Norris in the kidneys. The arm loosened, and Taylor slipped out of the grasp and followed Clanton out the door.

Outside, in the evening dusk, nothing moved. No

one ran down the highway in either direction. The parking lot was practically empty, but behind the building, on the other side of a line of bushes, something splashed into one of the canals lacing the city. It was the only lead Taylor had and he took it.

But before he could, Norris came up from behind, wrapping his arms around him in a bear hug and locking Taylor's arms down along his sides.

"You're going nowhere, you son of a bitch!"

"You dumb bastard! Your friend's an escaped convict; may be responsible for several murders. And you're liable for aiding and abetting."

When that didn't reach the larger man, Taylor stomped down on the toes of one of the man's boots, then the other.

Norris let go. "You lousy bastard! I'll—"

As Taylor came around, he swung the flat side of his hand into Norris's throat. When Norris stumbled back, hands at his throat, trying to catch his breath, Taylor sprinted for the wood line.

The government agent crashed through the bushes . . . and ran into a fence hidden by undergrowth and plenty of morning glories. He flipped head over heels and landed flat on his back on the other side of the fence.

Taylor raised his head and looked around. It took a moment to get his breath; then he crawled in the direction of the canal. Along the way he made sure he hadn't lost his pistol. By the time he reached the water, the blackness had receded to the periphery of his vision and Clanton's feet were disappearing on the other side, where a pipe crossed the canal.

Woman Against Herself

"Hold up, Ned," croaked Taylor, "or I'll shoot."

Taylor pulled out his pistol and pointed the weapon at the bushes, which had as their backdrop a row of houses. Taylor thought better of it, holstered his pistol, and ran for the pipe. Ahead of him, the drug dealer was moving on all fours through the waist-high weeds. He could see where Ned was, but because of the residential area Taylor would have to be on high ground before he could take a shot at him. Clanton heard Taylor's feet scuffle on the pipe, leapt to his feet, and ran for the houses.

Taylor finished shuffling across the pipe and started through the weeds. Ahead of him, Clanton leapt a wire fence making up a side of a chicken coop, but as he went over, his foot caught on the top strand and he pitched into the yard, scattering chickens. Clanton sprang to his feet, raced through the birds, frightening them even more, and kicked open a gate. He ran across a backyard, then down the driveway. A black woman came out of the house, snatched up a broom, and shook it at him.

Taylor finished with the weeds, leapt the fence, and landed in the coop, rescattering the chickens. Several of the birds ran through the gate as the woman was trying to herd them back inside. The black woman hit Taylor across the shoulders with the broom as the drug enforcement agent ran down her driveway and out into the street.

The street was every law enforcement officer's worst nightmare: empty and quiet. Until a dog barked two doors down, then yelped in pain.

Clanton!

Taylor ran down the street and around the corner of the house . . . where he found a small boy comforting his dog and crying for his mother. Taylor's quarry was on top of a woodshed that had a stack of wood against it. The wood and the shed were the easiest route over a hurricane fence enclosing the adjoining neighbor's backyard.

"Stop, Ned!" Taylor pulled out his weapon. "I've got you covered!"

Clanton jumped into the adjoining yard, which was filled with cars up on blocks, auto parts, batteries, and other junk. Clanton came down on a bumper, almost turning his ankle, but the rounded piece lay on its face and rolled with him as he went down. Getting to his feet, he looked back to see Taylor climbing the side of the shed. Clanton ran between cars up on blocks and down a driveway alongside a new Cadillac. Ned never noticed the driver on the other side of the car. The black woman was bent over, taking sacks of groceries out of the backseat of her car.

Taylor ran up the stack of firewood as it unraveled underneath him and leapt to the top of the shed. "Stop, Ned! Or I'll shoot!"

From this height, Taylor felt safe and fired a warning shot, trying to take out one of the smuggler's legs, but only succeeded in kicking up some gravel alongside the Cadillac. Rocks slapped against Ned's legs, causing him to take cover behind the large car. That was okay. Sooner or later Taylor had to come down from that shed, and when he did, old Ned was going to run for it again. He peered around the Caddy.

Woman Against Herself

From the top of the shed, Taylor shouted, "Give it up, Ned! You can't get away!"

Clanton thought about taking a shot at him, then saw there was a better option. A middle-aged black woman stood between her car and her house, arms full of groceries.

"Oh, shit!" muttered Taylor, seeing the woman for the first time. "Hey, lady! Get away from there!"

The woman only stared at the man standing on the shed—until Clanton slipped up from behind and got an arm around her neck. She screamed, grabbed at his arm, and dropped her groceries.

"See you later, Taylor," said Clanton gleefully. "They just pulled up my car." When Ned took a shot at the drug enforcement agent, the woman screamed and tried to cover her ears.

Taylor leapt into the backyard, just missing a tire rim. He went to one knee behind a car on blocks and groaned as he planted his knee. He glanced at what he had landed on: a child's metal six-shooter. It lay next to a broken Barbie and several plastic soldiers. Broken washers and dryers, automobiles on blocks, refrigerators with doors missing, and boxes filled with auto parts surrounded Taylor.

A black man walked out of the garage, wiping his hands on an oily rag. "Hey, what you boys up to?"

Taylor motioned him inside the garage. "Get back! He's got a gun!"

The mechanic saw the white man with an arm around his wife's neck. "Hey, what you doing, mister? That's my wife you got there."

"Stand up where I can see you, Taylor!"

Taylor sighed and looked around. His gaze fell on the toy gun mashed into the ground beside him. The toy mocked him, symbolizing his impotence when it came to dealing with drug dealers. Hell, even Sallie Beck was doing a better job than he was.

The mechanic looked at Taylor. "Hey, mister, I don't know what you two boys are up to, but that's my wife down there. Stand up like the man says."

From down the driveway came, "I'll kill her if you don't."

The woman moaned and rolled back her eyes. She was having trouble staying on her feet.

The black man looked from his wife to Taylor. "Get up, mister. Please!"

Taylor stuffed his pistol into its holster, picked up the toy gun, and, after rubbing the dirt off, stood up.

"That's better," Clanton said. "Now lose your weapon."

"What kind of chance will that give me?"

The drug smuggler stuck his pistol in the woman's ear. "One hell of a lot better chance than she's got."

Taylor looked at the fake six-shooter and threw the toy into the next yard. Sunlight sparkled off the metal as the toy flew through the air.

"Now that snub-nose .38 in your ankle holster."

Taylor bent down, took the weapon out, and tossed it into the adjoining yard. "You can't get away, Ned. Every cop in Dade County will be looking for you. I'd be surprised if you got out of the neighborhood."

"Then maybe I should take along some insurance."

Woman Against Herself

The black woman closed her eyes and started praying.

Her husband started toward the car. "No, mister, don't be saying that. All you want is the car and you can have it." The pistol moved in his direction and the mechanic stopped. "Listen, mister, the keys has got to be in the car. She's always leaving keys in the car."

"No," said Ned, grinning. "A car's not all I want."

Taylor motioned the mechanic inside his garage. "Get in there. He means to shoot me."

The mechanic looked at Clanton, then to Taylor. "What about my wife?"

"I'm working on that. Now get back inside. I can't do anything with you out here." After the black man backed away, Taylor moved around the car up on blocks, where Clanton could see him. "You can't hit me while you're holding onto a hostage. Which one of us do you want the most, Ned?"

Clanton pushed the woman away, and she stumbled toward her house. "I want you, Taylor! I've always wanted you. That's what I came to Miami for!"

Taylor dove behind the car he had been standing beside. Clanton's first bullet blew out a taillight and sprayed glass across the drug enforcement agent's feet. The second shot hit the trunk as Taylor rolled behind a concrete block and pulled out his gun from its holster. From there, he could look under the car and see Clanton hurrying up the driveway as his former hostage crawled into her house. From the garage, her husband was encouraging his wife to hurry.

"Remember what I told you when you sent me away, Taylor. Nobody fucks with Ned Clanton."

256

From under the car Taylor rested the butt of his pistol on the ground, leaned the muzzle against the concrete block, and took aim. He squeezed off a careful shot, shattering one of Clanton's ankles.

Ned screamed as his leg gave way and he fell to the ground. "You bastard! I'm going to kill you for that." He dragged himself behind a concrete block of his own.

Clanton peered under the car, but all he saw was some dead grass, a few cardboard boxes, and several batteries. There were no feet for Ned to aim at. No ankles to be blown apart. Where'd Taylor gone?

There was a loud thump and Clanton looked up to see the drug enforcement agent come sliding over the top of the car, across the trunk, and into his face. Clanton brought up his weapon but not quick enough to stop the muzzle of Taylor's pistol from being jammed into his mouth, shattering several teeth in the process.

As Ned fell backwards, Taylor straddled him. "Now, drop your weapon, Ned, or I will surely blow out what little brains you have left."

Nineteen

The Hawk stared at the deserted airstrip below them. "Put her down near the smaller building, Jackie. That's my command center."

Sallie took her bearings on the old runway and brought the plane around in the twilight. Hadn't she been here before? Just a couple of days ago. With Wes Taylor. In minutes it would be dark, and before morning the invasion force would assemble. Did Taylor know that? If D-Wars wanted to stop The Hawk they had a window of opportunity of only about twelve hours—and all in the dark.

The Hawk planned everything to come together at the last moment, a concept he'd learned from how cars were built in Japan. In addition, there was less chance of a breach of security that way. She and The Hawk were landing at dusk; the men and equipment waited below, and the invasion force would leave under the cover of morning darkness.

When The Hawk had explained how he would seize Suriname, his plan had seemed too incredible to pull off. It was impossible to overthrow a foreign government and install one of your own. It sounded like a throwback to the swashbuckling days of the eighteenth century. But now, as his plan came together, Sallie's admiration grew. There was no end to what this man could do, and no way anyone, including Wes Taylor, could stop him.

After the plan was revealed to her, Spano had refused to let Sallie leave the compound, and The Hawk had deferred to his security chief. Was that the tradeoff for having her around? And if The Hawk wanted her around, did she really want to tell Taylor what this man was up to? The invasion of a foreign country by a Napoleon such as The Hawk was something she'd only read about in history books. Now there was an opportunity to participate, alongside The Hawk. Hell, he'd even swapped his usual pilot to ride in her plane.

"Hawk, I'm going to take your word that the strip down there won't ruin my landing gear."

Her companion chuckled, put his hand inside her leg, and began running it up and down her thigh. A tingle ran through her body. Again she was responding to this man and this time it was no dream.

"Richey had the potholes filled in last week." He smiled. "You do know what's important, don't you?"

Sallie ignored her traitorous body. "This plane can't lift off without its wheels."

The Hawk chuckled and stopped rubbing her thigh. Sallie wasn't sure whether she liked that or not. She was as pumped about the mission as he was. Did that mean something would happen between them tonight, down there in the smaller building where The Hawk had his command center? Or did The Hawk have some place special set aside? Wouldn't it be ironic if Wes Taylor broke in on them like he had in her dream?

The Hawk began stroking the inside of her leg again. "It's been fun having you around the last few days, Jackie. To tell the truth, I didn't think you'd return after Spano slapped you around."

"I figured that was as much a set-up as the attempted rape at the Ponderosa Playground." The Hawk's hand stopped its roving. "The only time I really considered leaving was when security broke down over the Straits and almost got me killed."

The hand started moving again. "If you want to make the really big money in any business you have to learn to get along with your associates."

"That, Hawk, is a two-way street."

The hand stopped moving. "If push came to shove, I'd choose Spano over anyone in my organization. I wouldn't be where I am today if I'd always had to watch my backside."

The smuggler's hand started moving again, his fingers brushing up against the lips between Sallie's legs. Her breath quickened and the nose of the plane came up.

"Hawk, would you be able to land a plane if I grabbed you between the legs?"

"Sorry," he said, pulling his hand away. "I didn't know I had that kind of effect on you."

"Actually, it's the money that turns me on."

The Hawk chuckled. "One thing about you, Jackie, you're more fun to have around than Spano."

"I would hope so and not because I'm a woman. The man's obsessed with security. Thank God for the invasion. It's kept him out of my hair the last few days."

"You passed the second lie detector test."

But I wouldn't have, thought Sallie, if I hadn't put my foot down and said I'd only answer questions about the fiasco over the Straits, that I was going to be treated like a member of the team or I was out of there. I'd done my job: making the run to Alabama and bringing back the money. In addition, I demanded Danny's cut as hazardous duty pay, because Spano, not me, was responsible for the breakdown in security.

The bluff had worked, though she hadn't received Danny's cut. That paled, however, in comparison to what The Hawk had promised her if the invasion was successful.

A million dollars. With that kind of money a person could live anywhere, not some two-bit country in South America where a bunch of Neanderthals would ogle her, and the only taste of culture and refinement came by way of satellite.

"Spano and I began as rivals but realized our talents complemented each other. I wouldn't even consider developing an offshore business if it weren't for what you call Spano's obsession with security. Instead of launching this invasion, which will increase my business tenfold, I'd still be off-loading the product along some damn river and wondering if I'd get all my money.

Having Spano around means never having to worry about getting my money. Or the country I want."

"You're kidding yourself. When this is over, I'm history. There are just too many accidents I could have flying around South America. It's best to take the money and run."

The Hawk began moving his hand up and down Sallie's leg again. "We'll see about that, Jackie. We'll just have to see about that."

*　　*　　*

Wes Taylor got out of his car and walked over to the airplane hangar. The building was closed so there was no way to tell what was happening inside. The hangar was located away from all others and was painted olive drab: the primary color of the United States Army. A tall man in a blue suit waited at a door. They shook hands but neither man smiled as planes took off and landed on the other side of the airfield.

"Nothing to be ashamed off, Wes. D-Wars not being able to collar The Hawk. We lucked into this. If Washington asks, however, I'll tell my boss it was legwork, pure and simple. That's what the director will want to hear."

Taylor didn't comment. There was nothing he could say that would dissuade this man's agency from busting The Hawk. That government agency, as all others, could see only as far as their end-of-the-year figures. In that, they were no different from the DEA. Or D-Wars. Wanting another damn bust. Even if putting a collar on The Hawk was like sending a gust of wind to put out a forest fire.

The FBI agent appeared compelled to add, "If that whore hadn't been caught red-handed killing her john, we'd never have known what The Hawk had planned. Both of us would've woken up tomorrow and learned there was a new government in Suriname, not knowing the invasion had been launched from here." He paused. "You got someone inside?"

"Yeah, Ben, I've got someone inside."

"Can you get him out before we go in?"

Taylor shook his head.

The two men were quiet for a moment. "Wes, there's nothing I can do. They're set to go in just before dawn. The decision came from the White House." The agent gestured at the door. "Want to talk to them? I got it okayed with their CO. You can tell them who to look out for."

Taylor tapped his jacket. "I've brought photographs. Who you sending in?"

"An all-white company of Airborne Rangers so they'll know friend from foe."

"Well, that ought to get the job done."

"In spades," said the agent with a laugh. When Taylor didn't return his smile, he quickly opened the door.

Inside the hangar, a captain was using an overhead projector to outline the Rangers' plan of attack. The strip The Hawk was using to launch his invasion was the same one where Taylor had met Sallie Beck. You know, thought Taylor, Jenny was right. I should've gotten out of this damn business a long time ago.

The Rangers sat in long rows of folding chairs, and very few heads turned as the government agents stepped through the door. That didn't surprise Taylor. Failure to listen during this class could cost you your life.

After the commanding officer finished describing his tactics, his first sergeant ran through a list of tasks he wanted accomplished before the men sacked out for the night, and the first sergeant wanted them sacked out early. Once the sergeant finished, the captain invited the D-Wars agent on stage. Along the way, Taylor asked the Rangers at the ends of the rows to pass out the photographs of Jackie Mustard.

Once on stage, Taylor nodded to the captain and first sergeant, then watched as the pictures moved down the aisles. Behind the tight group of chairs stood four Hueys and their accompanying gunships. From his tour in Vietnam, Taylor remembered those narrow-faced monsters and how they could drop out of the sky, machine guns blazing, rockets blasting, and ruin a perfectly good day for anyone on the ground.

And where would Sallie be when those monsters came out of the night and started spewing their deadly fire? Taylor muttered a curse and the army captain glanced in his direction. He *should've* knocked Beck over the head and dragged her back to Miami. Whatever happened to her was his fault, not hers. He was the man in charge, the one supposed to be able to read his agents, and he'd seen a cockiness in Beck that could get her killed. Damn! Would get her killed! In a matter of hours.

Taylor glanced at his watch before looking over the sea of faces. He couldn't ask these men to be too careful when going up against a band of revolutionaries, and in the dark to boot. Sallie would be killed and, dying with her, the case she'd so painstakingly put together against The Hawk. Once again the organization would survive and prosper under whoever was lucky enough not to be snared in the early morning raid. Taylor could think of more than one government agency that would be pleased with tomorrow's headlines heralding the demise of D-Wars in South Florida.

As the photographs were passed down the aisles, eyebrows rose and low whistles could be heard. Once the men quieted down—with a little help from their first sergeant—Taylor was introduced to the group.

"Like the looks of her?" he asked.

Heads bobbed up and down and there were quite a few "yeah, mans" and some out-and-out wolf whistles. The first sergeant shut them up again.

"She's an amateur, men."

A murmur ran through the Rangers and they glanced at each other, then back at Taylor. The first sergeant muttered something about sending fools on errands, and the FBI agent, who'd been leaning against the hangar, rolled off the wall and looked over a Ranger's shoulder at the pictures.

"This woman came forward after her son was killed by drugs. She insisted on going inside. She insisted on that when she knew she might not come out alive." Taylor paused to swallow, then went on. "And you're going to ruin everything she's put together, everything she's risked her life for." Taylor waved off their objections. "It's not your fault. We've all got jobs to do, and if I'd done mine better maybe you wouldn't be taking up my slack."

He glanced at the floor of the platform before going on. "I just want you to know this woman doesn't know you're on your way and there's no way I can warn her. She'll be as surprised to see you as the smugglers, and I'd appreciate any care you can take bringing her out alive, this side of getting yourself killed. Then, you'll learn, just as I have, that this is a very special woman."

Taylor walked off the stage and out of the hangar. The whole room was silent as the Rangers watched him go.

Twenty

Spano came through the door of the command center where The Hawk and Richey were double-checking last-minute details of the invasion. Both men expected to be up all night, so Sallie had taken a seat at another table, feet propped up. The security chief was dragging a blonde behind him. He threw the woman, who wore a red jumpsuit and empty shoulder holster, on the floor in front of the table.

Sallie's feet came off her table and she sat up. The blonde cursed as she pulled herself up from the floor, and Spano clubbed her over the shoulder with his fist. The woman went down on all fours, stunned. The three men stared at the blonde, then looked at Sallie at the other table.

Sallie came out of her seat and Spano was there to meet her. He grabbed her by the arm and slung her to the floor. Sallie caught her breath and looked up through hair that had fallen in her face. It was like looking in a mirror. The other blonde looked just like her.

Spano slapped an unloaded Magnum on the table and stood over them. "This other Jackie Mustard was snooping around in Miami. I had her brought here." He glanced at Sallie. "I knew there was something fishy about that bitch!"

Sallie tried to get to her feet. "Hawk—"

Spano cut her off with a blow, and Sallie cried out as she went down. Richey was on the other side of the table, half standing, half sitting, looking from one woman to the other.

The Hawk took out a cigar and lit it. When he had his cigar going, he asked, "Okay, Jackie, what's your story?"

Both women started talking at the same time.

Spano slapped Sallie across the back of the head. "Shut up, bitch! You've had your turn. Now it's hers."

Sallie rubbed her head and tried hard not to burst into tears.

The other blonde took too long explaining why she was the real Jackie Mustard and this other blonde the impostor. Spano slapped her across the head and she fell forward. She came off the floor cursing. The security chief backhanded her as she came up.

Jackie stumbled into the wall with a loud "Oh!" Her legs went out from under her and she slid to the floor. Blood ran out of the corner of her mouth.

"If you're smart, bitch, you'll stay there." He turned to The Hawk. "Okay, Al, you've heard pitches from both bitches. Now which one's the real McCoy?"

The Hawk leaned back in his chair and examined his cigar. Richey had sat down but couldn't stop looking from one woman to the other. He saw Sallie's eyes pleading with him. He turned away.

"Once again you've allowed yourself to become distracted by this woman," said The Hawk, "and there's no way of knowing how much that's jeopardized the mission."

The security chief opened his mouth, but The Hawk cut him off with a raised hand. "Finding this snooper was important, but which one is the real Jackie Mustard is irrelevant, unless your men were followed when they brought her out here."

"You know better than that."

"Well, since discovering that there's more than one Jackie Mustard, have you checked the perimeter? Doubled the guard? Monitored for additional radio traffic from the target area? Asked the men baby-sitting Lucas Tasman what our noble leader's been doing the last twenty-four hours? Or have you been too busy patting yourself on the back for simply"—The Hawk gestured at both women—"doing your job?"

"But I thought—"

The Hawk sat up, his voice snapping like a whip. "No! You didn't think! That's my point. My only point." He gestured at Sallie on her knees in front of the table. "This Jackie Mustard has been sequestered since learning of our invasion plans. She's no threat to you, but it seems I should've let you kill her days ago to keep *her* from distracting *you.*"

Spano looked at the two women. "Then I'll kill them

both. That way they'll never distract anyone again."

"And why would you do that?" asked The Hawk, relaxing in his chair again. "They're women, not men, and in that they can still be useful, and made to suffer more than you could ever imagine. Parade them in front of the freedom fighters. Promise those niggers they can have both women after, but only after, they've overthrown the government of Suriname."

"Hawk," said Sallie from the floor. "I thought you and I had something special."

The drug smuggler stared at her, his voice like ice. "I've never picked pussy over profits and I don't intend to start now."

"You can't do that to me!" Jackie said, supporting herself by the wall. "I'm three months pregnant."

Spano's smile stopped her. "You won't be tomorrow."

When the door to the storeroom in one of the empty warehouses was locked behind them, Sallie turned on Jackie. "You damn egocentric!" she said, trying to keep her voice down but finding that impossible. "You fucking smugglers are all the same. You actually thought you could walk in here and your reputation would mean something. It means shit."

"That's the pot calling the kettle black," said Jackie, getting in Sallie's face and making no attempt to lower her voice. "What the hell are you doing here? Are you working for Wes Taylor?"

"No! I work for me and mine!"

Jackie stared at her. "Now what the fuck's that supposed to mean?"

Sallie was taken aback. She'd automatically said what first came to mind—from the tape. She was losing her mind. Perhaps she had already lost it.

Jackie used the lull in the conversation to curse her, making numerous references to her good sense and ancestry, then went on to detail The Hawk's sexual practices, especially with animals. Interwoven throughout her tirade were plenty of who the hell do they think they ares? and didn't they know who the hell she wases?

Sallie could only stand there and stare at her mirror image. Was this what she'd become? A foul-mouthed shrew? What would Timmie think of his mother now?

"Have a good night, girls!" shouted Spano as he turned off the lights in the warehouse.

Mustard's distorted features were the last thing Sallie saw as the room went dark. That, however, didn't stop Jackie's mouth. "You assholes! I'll have your ass for this!"

"Shut the fuck . . . ." Sallie's voice trailed off. "Shut up, Mustard!"

Instead, Jackie turned her wrath on her double. Sallie backed up and felt her way to one of the long wooden shelves running along the wall. There she waited for Jackie to run down. It took a few minutes.

Then, out of the darkness came, "Well, what are we going to do?"

"Figure how to get out of here. Are you really pregnant?"

"Three months. No shit."

Sallie couldn't help but think of her own son. The Hawk had killed Timmie and now he was going to do the same to Jackie's unborn child. Poor Jackie. She couldn't catch a break, and now she was about to have a more serious abortion than the one forced on her in California by Ned Clanton.

"Did you ever consider if I'd been killed impersonating you, nobody would've ever come looking for Jackie Mustard?"

"Fuck you, too!"

Sallie sighed. "Is it possible to call a truce until we get out of here?"

"About that long, then I'm going to kick your ass all the way back to Miami for what you've done to my reputation. Those people don't think shit of me, all because of you."

Sallie wanted to ask if she was to blame for Jackie's being caught snooping around back at The Hawk's compound in Miami but didn't dare. There was work to be done, and the sooner they started, the better chance they had of escaping, however the hell that was going to be done.

Jackie seemed to sense she'd gone too far. In a more reasonable tone, she asked, "What's your plan?"

"First, we inventory this place and find out what we have to work with."

"I've got a lighter."

"So have I. Let's get started."

"Shit! Do you have everything I've got?"

"Yes, and believe me, Jackie, you've worked yourself up over losing nothing."

Mustard let go with another stream of invectives, which ended in a matter of seconds, and then the two women combed the small room with their lighters, smelling the scent of wooden boxes and oily wrapping paper. They found little to work with.

Jackie's lighter went out and she cursed and hurled it against the far wall, then joined Sallie, who'd taken a seat on one of the shelves. "I wish I was as well-built as this fucking place."

"Its weakness is the back wall. Some fool built the room right up against the back wall. They put a roof overhead so you couldn't get to the weapons, or whatever was stored in here, but you could rob them blind through that back wall."

"Sounds like you're describing our way out."

"I hope so. Let's get to work with some of those empty ammo lids."

They did. But in a matter of minutes, before the first board loosened, the lights came on both in the warehouse and the storeroom.

"Shit!" Jackie said.

The door opened and Spano stood there, a pistol in his hand. "You bitches better stow the noise or I'm going to come in there and lay this pistol upside your heads. That ought to keep you quiet until lift-off." He slammed the door and locked it again.

Jackie fussed for a moment but finally joined Sallie on one of the shelves. The overhead shelf poked them in the back of the head. And they sat there long after the light had been turned off.

"What's next, smart guy?"

"Spano came in alone, didn't he?"

"Yeah, but in case you didn't notice, we didn't leave

because he had a fucking pistol."

"Remember the twine we found and the nails left in the corners from building this room?"

"So?"

"I thought we might string the twine across the door, a few inches off the ground, and lure Spano back in. He might be mad enough to rush us." Sallie looked toward a door she couldn't see. "I think he's spoiling for a fight. Otherwise, why didn't he bring someone with him?"

Jackie leaped off the shelf. "Let's do it!"

"And there's always the chance we might knock loose one of those boards in the back wall."

Jackie slapped Sallie across the back, misjudging where she stood in the darkness and laying her forearm across Sallie's back. "You know, kid, you're all right. I might not kick your ass after all."

"If I get you out of here."

"Yeah, there's that. Say, what's your name anyway?"

"Unless I get you out of here, it really doesn't matter, does it?"

Later, with the string anchored in the jamb, they returned to work on the rear wall. In a few minutes, the light came on.

Sallie motioned Jackie to the rear of the small room. "Spano's not coming in unless he can see both of us."

In a moment a voice asked, "Jackie?" It was Richey and he didn't open the door.

The women looked at each other, then the door. In unison they said, "Yes?" and glanced at each other.

"I want to talk to the Jackie Mustard who was living with The Hawk."

Sallie stepped near the door. "Can you get us out of here?"

"No. But I can tell you the next time Spano has to come in here, he's going to kill you. Both of you. He got the go-ahead from The Hawk. There are to be no more distractions until the mission is completed."

Jackie rushed the door and slammed her fists against it. "What he's got planned for us is worse than death! I'd rather go down fighting!"

"It won't be much of a fight." Richey was quiet for a moment. "I've brought something you might want to use. The Hawk doesn't know anything about this."

Sallie's eyes lit up. "Is it a weapon?"

"I'm not that stupid. Just because you and Carlos won't be around to cash in on this deal doesn't mean I'm going to screw it up for myself. I warned you to clear out."

Richey pushed something shiny and flat through a slit in the door, then left them alone. Jackie bent over and picked up the razor blade, holding it up before the light went out.

"That asshole thinks we're going to slit our wrists."

"I guess he thinks us gals will consider the alternative and come to our senses. There's over a hundred Surinamese and they were all chosen because they want to prove something to the world."

"Shit! The worst kind of man. Well, I'm not killing myself. I'm taking some of them with me." She looked at the razor blade. "And this little item will help me do it."

Sallie glanced at the rear of the storeroom. "How are we coming with the wall?"

"Not even close. They don't give us enough time." Jackie held up the blade. "What about suckering Spano in here? When he comes I'll cut off his fucking balls."

"Uh-huh. Let's wait until just before lift-off. Spano will've been up all night and have a lot on his mind. During the briefing he told us the mission will be the most vulnerable when the freedom fighters fall back from the perimeter to load the planes. Spano should be edgy. Maybe steamed up enough to come in here and finish us off."

"And all we've got to worry about is whether he'll be coming alone."

Twenty-one

Before the first plane touched down, the light came on in the storeroom. The women sat up on their respective shelves, blinked, and looked across the room at each other.

"But we weren't making any noise," Jackie said.

"Yeah," said Sallie, slipping off her shelf. She stretched and brushed back her hair. "Looks like this is it." She glanced at the twine strung across the door-way. It had been run back and forth three or four times to reinforce its strength.

"But we haven't done anything to piss him off."

"Well," Sallie said with a smile, "I thought you might be able take care of that."

Jackie gripped the razor. "Fucking A!"

"Remember, if there's more than one, we can only be sure of taking the one who goes down. We'll have to hope the other guy doesn't want to risk shooting the man on the floor."

"Shit! What do we have to lose?"

What did they have to lose? Sallie was thinking of everything she'd given up for one roll of the dice: her job at IINTELL, her new promotion, and Phil Rainey, a man who cared about her more than Sallie wanted to consider.

"Yeah," she said, joining Jackie in the rear of the storeroom, "what do we have to lose?"

The locks were taken off, the door was opened, and Spano stood there. He was alone and holding a pair of hunting knives. "Seems like when we come for you, we'll find one of you smuggled a knife in here and there was one hell of a cat fight. You'll both be dead and I won't have to fuck with either of you again. Whoever the hell you are."

Jackie raged at him. Why did he need weapons for a pair of defenseless girls? What was he afraid of? And was it true, the only reason he was doing this was that he was into little boys?

The security chief laughed and eased into the room, watching them. When Sallie saw he wasn't going to trip over the string, she reached for an ammo lid lying on one of the shelves. Spano faced this threat and pulled his trailing foot into the twine. The toe of his boot caught on the string and caused him to hop into the room.

Spano glanced down to see what he'd tripped over and Jackie rushed him with the razor. She slashed the arm he threw up to protect himself, cutting the security chief to the bone. Before Spano could scream, blood poured out a seven-inch wound. He dropped one knife and went after her, as Mustard bounced away, up against the shelves.

When Spano turned, Sallie hit him squarely across the back with the flat part of the ammo lid. The security chief stumbled toward Jackie and the razor, then recovered by throwing himself on the ground. He rolled away, toward the rear of the storeroom, saving himself from another slice of the razor.

"You bitches!" he screamed, struggling to his feet. He dropped the last knife and pulled out his gun. "I'll kill both of you!"

"Too late for that!" Sallie was already swinging the top of the ammo box again.

She clubbed the security chief's hands up against his chest with the flat side of the lid. When Sallie pulled away, Jackie followed with another slashing blow. Spano roared in pain as the blade bit into his hand. He turned the gun on Mustard, and when he did, Sallie pasted him across the back of the head with the narrow edge of the ammo lid. Spano dropped his gun, went to his knees, and collapsed on the floor.

"You're dead, asshole." Mustard moved in for the kill.

"No!"

Jackie whirled around, arching her hand and the blade. "The bastard tried to kill me. And my baby."

Sallie backed off and Jackie turned her attention to Spano again. "He'll wish he'd never fucked with me. I'll cut off his balls, his tongue, then put out his eyes."

Sallie swung the flat side of the ammo lid against Jackie's hands. Mustard screamed and dropped the razor. She clutched her hand as blood oozed between her fingers.

"You asshole! We're on the same side."

"Not when you start killing people in cold blood." She glanced at the open door. "Let's just get out of here."

Jackie glared at her, then snatched up Spano's pistol and raced out the door. "It's every woman for herself!"

After locking Spano in the storeroom, Sallie caught up with Jackie at the entrance of the warehouse. Mustard was peering around the corner of the open doorway. She held up a bloody hand to stop Sallie. Helicopters were landing a couple of hundred yards away, and two C-47 transports idled on a lighted landing strip. Black men in camouflage uniforms moved out of the darkness and lined up at white x's chalked on the concrete slab.

A guard stood about twenty feet away, smoking a cigarette and watching the embarkation. Jackie slipped up behind him and clubbed the man over the head with the butt of Spano's pistol. The guard dropped his rifle and his legs buckled, but Jackie didn't wait for him to go down. She hit him again, and this time Sallie heard the bone crack.

Jackie turned to her as she loosened a bandanna from around the man's neck. "That's how it's done. Never give the bastards an even chance." She wrapped the cloth around her bleeding hand. "Now where's your plane?"

Sallie pointed it out. Unfortunately, between them and the plane, the invasion force was loading onto the C-47s.

"We'll have to go around that little building or they'll see us."

Jackie picked up the rifle and set off to skirt The Hawk's command center. After another glance at the unconscious guard, Sallie followed her.

On one side of the command center, the farthest one

from the airstrip, Fuentes leaned against The Hawk's Cadillac. He held an automatic rifle and was watching the exposed rear of the revolutionaries as they were loading.

"Shit!" muttered Jackie. "Can't go that way without making a lot of noise."

Without breaking stride she ran to the front of the building, dropped to her knees, and placed the rifle across her arms before crawling on her hands and knees under the windows overlooking the tarmac. Sallie followed her under the muted light from the windows.

From inside they heard The Hawk ask, "Seen Spano lately?"

The two women froze, holding their breath, listening. They heard Richey say, "He told me he'd be checking the perimeter while the Surinamese were loading."

"Good to hear he's thinking about security again. I was beginning to think he had lost his mind about that bitch as much as he thought I had."

Jackie Mustard looked over her shoulder at a blushing Sallie Beck. She didn't look long. An Airborne Ranger landed beside the building. He slapped at his harness, his parachute billowed away, and his rifle came up.

"Hey," said the Ranger, "they didn't tell us there'd be two of you."

Jackie brought up her rifle and fired.

The soldier grabbed his stomach and doubled up. "No! I'm here to help."

"What going on out there?" shouted The Hawk. "Are those niggers playing with their rifles again? Richey, get out there and stop them or we'll have the whole countryside down on us."

The door burst open and Richey ran around the corner where Jackie and Sallie had flattened themselves against the side of the building. More Rangers dropped out of the sky. Richey brought up his automatic pistol, killing one in the air, another as he landed.

"Shit, Hawk! It's the fucking army."

"That's right, bub," said a Ranger, approaching from behind and shooting Richey in the back. The hippie pitched forward, clawing at his back. The paratrooper motioned with his rifle at the two women. "Okay, ladies, over here and drop your weapons."

As Jackie came out of the shadows, she shot the Ranger in the face, blowing off most of it. From the other side of the command center, Fuentes screamed for The Hawk to get his ass out there. The bodyguard jumped behind the wheel of the Cadillac, cranked the engine, and shifted into gear. The Hawk rushed outside in time to see a descending paratrooper rip up the Cadillac and its driver with automatic weapons' fire. Bullets punched holes in the hood; the windshield spider-webbed.

The Hawk let off a burst with an M-16 and the Ranger was dead before hitting the ground. Fuentes's foot came off the brake and the Cadillac edged away. The Hawk ran for the car but was driven back when the engine burst into flames. He slipped into the shadows as the car rolled away. From the darkness, he saw helicopter gunships over the assembly point, spewing bullets and cutting down his troops.

Steve Brown

Artillery flares drifted down, illuminating the airstrip. More paratroopers landed and formed a cordon around the C-47s. A helicopter tried to lift off but got only a few yards before a gunship threw a rocket in its direction. The chopper exploded in a ball of flames and skidded across the airstrip before stopping on the far side.

The Surinamese saw this and threw down their weapons. They were being advised, over bullhorns and in Dutch, to surrender, that they were surrounded and their command center taken.

"Not yet," muttered The Hawk, stepping out of the darkness.

When Jackie rushed around the corner of the command center The Hawk shot her, knocking her into Sallie.

"Oh, my God! My baby!" Jackie dropped the rifle and clutched her abdomen.

The Hawk pointed his gun at Sallie. "You got a weapon, Mustard?"

Sallie shook her head. She was staring at the woman she held in her arms. Another child gone! How many more babies would have to die before this devil was stopped?

The Hawk didn't appear interested in the question. "Then get inside!"

Sallie, however, was mesmerized by the red spot growing larger on the woman's stomach. "But Jackie needs help."

"We all do, but the ones with weapons usually get the lion's share."

He grabbed Sallie by the arm and dragged her inside the command center. Mustard was unceremoniously dropped to the ground, where she whimpered in pain.

Inside the building, The Hawk threw Sallie across the room. "Stay here! Come outside and I'll kill you!"

Sallie nodded numbly and held onto a table for support. She couldn't get the image of Jackie Mustard out of her mind. She really was in over her head.

More gunfire erupted and Sallie flinched. A moment later, The Hawk returned, dragging a soldier through the door. It took him less than a minute to pull on the pants, blouse, and cap of the dead man. To complete the disguise, he smeared the soldier's camouflage paint across his cheeks, then stuck a pistol in the belt behind his back and picked up the dead man's M-16.

He took Sallie's arm and they headed for the door. "You're flying me out of here, Mustard, or whoever the hell you are. And if you do anything to give me away, I'll make you wish you were dead."

He pulled Sallie into the night and she got a last look at Jackie Mustard lying on the ground, dead. A paratrooper ran up and The Hawk shot him.

Sallie gasped. "Why would you do that now?"

"As serious as you are about smuggling and you have to ask that?"

The Hawk kicked the soldier's weapon away. He hustled Sallie in a flanking maneuver around the captured Surinamese invasion force and toward her plane, where a lone Ranger stood. Occasionally a searchlight from a helicopter ran over the aircraft, but the action was on the airstrip, and that's where everyone's attention was focused.

As they approached the plane, The Hawk whispered, "Play it cool and you might get out of this alive." He glanced over his shoulder at the invasion force being rounded up by the Airborne Rangers. "Whatever the hell *this* is. By the way, how'd you get loose?"

"Spano came to kill us. Instead, we killed him."

"That fool! I warned him one day his fixations would be the death of him."

"Halt! Who goes there?" demanded the soldier standing guard at Sallie's plane.

The Hawk glanced down at the name on the soldier's uniform he'd appropriated and continued toward the plane. "Wiggins," he answered over the noise of the helicopters. Even the gunships were being called in. "They want to keep this woman away from the action while we're mopping up. She's supposed to know something about this caper."

"You kill this man," whispered Sallie, "and I won't fly you out of here."

"That's because you'll be dead alongside him."

"Where will that leave you? You don't know how to fly. All that money and you never learned how to fly."

"But I do know how to delegate."

"And look where that got you."

"Okay, Wiggins," said the paratrooper, "but you should always use the password. Just because we're—"

The Hawk cut him off with a blow from the M-16. The soldier grunted, fell to the ground, and dropped his rifle.

"Satisfied, Mustard?"

Sallie was already climbing into the plane. The Hawk

followed her, closing the hatch behind them. He joined her in the cockpit where she was checking the instruments. Through the Plexiglas he saw two soldiers and a civilian approaching them from the firefight. The three men were less than a football field away.

"Get us out of here," he said, buckling his seatbelt.

"How much am I in for?" asked Sallie, turning over the engine.

"What the hell are you talking about?"

"It ought to be worth something to fly you out of here."

The Hawk stuck the pistol in her face. "Your life, if you're a good girl."

Sallie cut the engines. "Not enough—for this woman."

The Hawk glanced at the men. Fifty yards away and closing fast. "Hell, I don't know what your game is, Mustard, but I like your style. You always keep your eye on what's important: the money."

"What else is there?"

"Okay, the original deal. You get one mil for flying me out of the country." He gestured at the men. They were close enough for Sallie to make out the civilian as Wes Taylor. "You still have to get me out of here."

"Piece of cake."

Sallie restarted the engine and maneuvered the plane away from the men. They ran after her with Taylor shouting something Sallie couldn't hear. Probably more nonsense about what she couldn't do.

The plane made a tight turn at the far end of the airstrip, revved up its engines, and started forward. As Sallie built up speed, the soldiers accompanying Tay-

lor knelt down on opposite sides of the drug enforcement agent and began firing slow sure shots at the
plane. A couple of bullets hit the fuselage before Taylor
brought down his hands, forcing the shooters' barrels
to the ground. Sallie sped by, and as she did, got a
glimpse of the two soldiers trying to jerk their rifles out
of the hands of a stoned-faced Taylor.

The plane raced down the airstrip, staying on the
far side and avoiding contact with the blades of the
helicopters. Rangers saw her coming and ran on the
strip to flag her down. As she blew by and lifted off,
they leaped out of the way and opened up with their
rifles.

Flying at treetop level, Sallie pulled hard to the right
and sailed into the darkness. It was good she did. One
of the Cobra gunships lifted behind her and threw a
rocket in their direction. The rocket took off treetops
for twenty yards, exploding behind her. Sallie pulled
the plane into an even harder right, leveled out, and
was gone.

Moments later, The Hawk looked around. Except for
the stars and the lights of Miami the night was dark.
At the horizon he could see the approaching dawn.

"Damn good flying, Mustard."

"Worth a million dollars?"

"Can they catch us?"

"In the dark? Hell no! That's what I do best."

Sallie bore left, leaving the gunships behind. Flying
fifty feet off the ground where no radar could touch
her.

"Just who the hell are you anyway?"

"Just a gal who got tired of sitting behind a computer and stole Jackie Mustard's identity so she could come to work for you. It didn't work out."

The Hawk began running a hand up and down the inside of Sallie's thigh. "Give it time, Mustard. Give it time."

A half-hour later the sun was up, and The Hawk saw Miami below them. "What the hell are we doing here?"

Sallie picked up her radio and opened a channel. "Miami International, this is Jackie Mustard. I'm having trouble with my engine again. I'm coming in."

"What the hell are you talking about?" The Hawk scanned the control panel and listened to the engines. "There's nothing wrong with this plane."

"You don't think so?"

Sallie cut the power to the engines and the plane went into a dive. The Hawk screamed unintelligibly.

Air traffic control in Miami said, "You couldn't have picked a worse time, Mustard. We're just starting the morning rush hour."

Still, they gave her instructions on where to land as the ground rushed toward them. The Hawk didn't hear a word. He babbled something about turning the engines on and how much money did Sallie want to do it.

"Nothing more than you tossing that pistol out the slot in the hatch, Al."

It wasn't long before he did, and Sallie restarted the engines and slowly pulled out of the dive.

Again the voice from Miami. "Are you the same Jackie Mustard who lost power over the Pointe a few weeks ago?"

"Roger that, Miami."

"That's too bad. The FAA will be waiting for you when you land."

"That's just what I was counting on."

She jerked a rope lying alongside her seat, and a storage compartment in the rear of the plane fell open, spilling several pounds of marijuana across the floor.

About the Author

Though he is best known for his Myrtle Beach mysteries, Steve Brown has also written *Radio Secrets*, about a radio therapist with a secret past, *Fallen Stars*, featuring an antiwar reporter who is shot down and crash lands in Cambodia during the Vietnam War, and *Black Fire*, which asks the question: What would a modern-day Scarlett and Rhett be like? Steve lives in Greenville, South Carolina, and you can contact him through www.chicksprings.com.